My Secret Lover

My Secret Lover

Imogen Parker

W F HOWES LTD

This large print edition published in 2003 by
W F Howes Ltd
Units 6/7, Victoria Mills, Fowke Street
Rothley, Leicester LE7 7PJ

1 3 5 7 9 10 8 6 4 2

First published in 2003 by Black Swan

A CIP catalogue record for this book is available
from the British Library

ISBN 1 84197 6334

Typeset by Palimpsest Book Production Limited,
Polmont, Stirlingshire
Printed and bound in Great Britain
by Antony Rowe Ltd, Chippenham, Wilts.

For Connor – who always makes me happy

Acknowledgements

Thank you to everyone who helped me research and write this book particularly David Young, Martha Kearney, Ben Brown and Lucy Chippendale.

Thank you everyone at Transworld, especially Marina Vokos and Linda Evans, who look after me so well.

Thank you Nick Duggan and Becky Parker, my favourite teachers.

Beginning

CHAPTER 1

January

Am I happy?

Does everyone have thoughts like this when they're stuck in a traffic jam, or on a train, or any time really that's not quite one place or another? Especially if it's a special day, like a birthday, or the first day back to work after the Christmas holidays.

Another one is . . .

Is there something wrong with the temporary lights? You're first in the queue and you suddenly wonder why all the cars behind you are indicating and overtaking, and by the time you've worked out the lights have stuck, the traffic in the opposite direction has taken advantage, and if you go now there'll be a head-on collision.

. . . What sort of person am I supposed to be?

Is it better to be an aggressive driver or a patient one? It doesn't matter what time you get there as long as you get there, says my mother. But she hasn't got a job to go to. And she can't drive. I'm somewhere in between. I don't knowingly take risks, but I swear a lot.

★   ★   ★

. . . I know what sort of person I *am*. I am an ordinary person. If my life were a How Successful Are You? quiz in a women's magazine I would score mostly bs. I'm not an a (brilliant high-achiever with a slight tendency to be neurotic. Even if you've done a full twenty-eight-day detox, Pilates and home-made pesto, they're still wondering if you're leaving yourself enough Me Time). And I'm not quite a c (lazy slut whose idea of a dinner party is a bucket of KFC and please keep reading till the little ads for liposuction at the back). I'm definitely a b (Starts a detox once or twice a week and lasts until the drink after work, offers freshly made pasta from the chilled-food section for dinner, signs up and pays for the Pilates course, but only goes once because it's the same night as *Footballers' Wives*).

I am towards the high end of body-mass-ratio range but still within normal. I have a little terraced house, with a knocked-through downstairs room, which I bought before prices got silly, a car, a job I love and a boyfriend, whom I'm marrying this summer. For this, and many other reasons, which my mother would gladly list for you if you were interested, I am a very lucky girl who should be grateful.

I *am* grateful (I tell my mother in the grumpy voice of a sulky twelve year old which only seems to happen when she's around). Then, in the car on the way home, I start thinking, OK, I'm grateful, but is this *really* what happiness feels like?

I thought I would be more grown up by my age (36). I do always watch the News and *Newsnight*, and sometimes even *Despatch Box* (to be honest, only if I've dozed off on the sofa during *Newsnight*). I try to get a handle on the Middle East situation, but I find I'm sitting there wondering how the reporter keeps his shirt so nice and white amid all the dust and shooting and then he's saying '. . . for the Ten O'clock News, Jerusalem.'

Faced with a choice of stories on my home page, my mouse instinctively moves towards

Weird dreams, what do they mean?

and avoids anything that includes the word Zimbabwe. Before I know it, I'm in the middle of a

How Deep Are You? Quiz

(answer: b) and it's then time for bed.

I had the weirdest dream last night. I dreamt that the wedding dress I was trying on turned into a cake. A great white stiff wedding cake with lots of tiers and, frankly, it looked rather wonderful, like something by Hussein Chalayan, but was incredibly heavy and restrictive and as I started to sweat, the icing on the tier beneath my armpits started to melt, and I woke up to find a big wet patch next to my face where I had dribbled on my scatter cushion and three backbenchers talking about fox-hunting on the telly. I think it's a washable cover.

Everyone who lives in the suburbs knows that foxes have swapped countryside for town anyway. They can enjoy a better quality of life here, more fast-food drive-thrus with brimming rubbish bins, far less opportunity for vigorous aerobic exercise in the fresh air.

The car behind is beeping at me. The lights have changed.
When did that happen?
I stall, start the engine, stall again.
F off your F-ing self.
This is not an omen for the year ahead. Definitely not.

There's a pleasant smell of washing powder and new shoes as we all gather for assembly in the hall. A sudden shaft of sunlight strikes the windows as the headmaster is talking about being kind and helping each other. It spotlights a piece of tinsel from the Christmas Fayre that was stuck too high up for the caretaker to get down without a ladder. All eyes watch the silver fronds dancing in the warm air current above the only working radiator. For a moment, the Year Three whispering ceases. There's an almost celestial feeling as Miss Goodman thumps out the first few bars of 'Sing Hosannah!'

'Did anyone do anything they'd like to tell us about over the holidays?' The usual hands shoot into the air as if they're straining to reach something on the ceiling. If we sent them up the caretaker's ladder, the tinsel would be down in no time.

'I helped my brothers, Miss.'

'Very good, Dane. What did you help them doing?'

'Selling things,' he says darkly. 'And, by the way, my name's Dean.'

It's the 'by the way' which is chilling in a six year old.

I have taught both his brothers, Shane and Wayne. Shane was the Santino of the family. Wayne was the Fredo and Dean is going to be Michael Corleone. I have an idea what they were selling, and I don't think the class needs to know.

'Anyone make any New Year's Resolutions? Ethan?'

'I'm going to learn to fly.'

His resemblance to Harry Potter has had a marvellous effect on his confidence, but unfortunately it's made him think he has supernatural powers.

'Good. Nicole?'

'We're not going to let any bloody man fut up our lives again.'

'Robbie?'

'She means *fuck* up, Miss.'

'Thank you, Robbie, remember we don't use the F-word in school, because it's very rude. Now what was your resolution?'

'Not to use the F-word in school, Miss?'

'Good, excellent.'

Robbie smiles. He's less than four feet tall with hair shaved to his skull and no front teeth.

'What's the F-word?' asks Nikita.

'Never mind about that. What is your resolution?'

'What's a resolution?'

They're just six years old but some of them are still babies and some could order double vodkas in a pub and get away with it.

'Who can tell Nikita what a New Year's Resolution is? Day . . . ean?'

'It's when you stop smoking, Miss.'

'Yes, some people decide to give up something they do which is bad for them, like smoking. Some people make New Year's Resolutions not to kick people, Robbie,' Extremely unamused look. 'But it doesn't have to be about giving up. Some people might decide that they're going to try very hard to learn their spellings . . .'

Mr Batty is leaning out of the window of the staffroom.

The three witches are muttering round the biscuit canister.

'It's freezing cold in here and the smoke's blowing back in . . .' says Mrs Vane.

'I asked him to stand outside last term . . .' says Mrs Wates.

'Apparently, someone called the police about a suspicious man pacing up and down outside school gates . . .' says Miss Goodman.

Witchy hilarity.

'How long did you last?' I say.

Richard bumps his head on the bottom of the window as he turns.

'Twenty-eight hours,' he says, earnestly, as if I'm going to award him a sticker with a cartoon tiger saying 'Grrrreat!'.

'What about you?' Richard asks.

'I don't smoke.'

Richard smiles. I do like Richard. If only his skin wasn't so bad.

'Resolution?'

'To be kind and work harder,' I say in a sing-song voice. 'And no alcohol.' I add quietly.

The witches rip the paper off a packet of biscuits.

'Have one,' says Mrs Vane.

'No, thanks,' says Mrs Wates, pulling in her tummy.

'They're Go Aheads.'

'None at all?' says Richard.

I'm trying to read the biscuit packet at a disinterested distance. I wonder whether 'not more than 5% fat' means that there actually is 5% fat, which seems quite a lot of fat for a slimming biscuit.

'Biscuits?'

Quite a disgusting amount if you imagine a solid chunk of lard shaded onto the Fat column of a Biscuit Contents bar chart.

'Alcohol,' whispers Richard.

'None at all,' I say, trying to do a contented little smile of self-denial.

(The Baileys with my mother yesterday did not

count, because it was really a sauce for the ice cream. I did have a little bit more afterwards, but from a spoon, so more like that vitamin tonic she used to give me when I got my periods, except that tasted more like Campari, as far as I can remember.)

'Good Christmas?' Richard asks.

'Fine.'

I'd like to tell him everything because I know it would make him laugh, but not in an unkind way. Everyone gets pissed at New Year, don't they, he'd say, but none quite as spectacularly as you. Which would sound like a compliment. But I'm not going to tell him because he might start to hope that this was his chance.

And if that sounds like I think I'm some sort of siren of the First and Middle, I do not. I am plain. But Richard Batty is considerably plainer. I'm the sort of person of whom people say, she has a nice smile. But the best people could say about Richard is that he's a nice person. In the league tables, Richard would come below me. And league tables matter. We may not like them, but they're here to stay, as the headmaster's always telling us.

The stranger's arrival in the staffroom is heralded by the sudden silence of the witches. He is of average height, good looking, but it's not just that that makes him look wrong in here. He's young, too young for the suit he's wearing.

Middle age really must be creeping up if I think my colleagues look too young to be teachers.

10

The witches are fluttering.

Richard frowns, turns his back on the stranger.

'How's Andy?' he asks me, quite loudly, annoyed by another male on his patch.

Richard always asks how Andy is, as if we're all friends. Sometimes I think he's hoping that I'm going to say, 'Oh, he died.'

'Fine,' says the stranger, as he pings the lid off the catering tin of coffee and puts in a damp spoon. The witches stare. Damp spoon in coffee tin is very bad news. By the end of today there will be an anonymous Post-it note stuck on to the lid saying something like, 'Don't waste coffee! Dry that spoon!' in black felt-pen capitals.

'Andy's fine,' I say trying to divert the wafts of wrath away from the stranger.

'Yes I am,' says the stranger, smiling.

'Err, hello?' Richard says, as if it's a question.

'Andy,' says the stranger, holding his hand out towards me.

'Andy?'

It comes out as a bit of a yelp because I know several Andys already. There was a period during the sixties when every other boy child was called Andrew. There were four of them in my class at school. Names come and go like that. People call their sons Tom and Harry now, not Andrew and Richard.

But this Andy is not my generation. By rights, he should be called Kevin or Jason.

'I'm marrying an Andy,' I explain.

'Steady,' says the stranger. 'We've only just met!'

Near hysterical laughter from the witches.

The stranger winks at me. Do you know sometimes how you just know you're going to get on with someone, like you have a kind of understanding? I love that feeling.

'Are you working here?' I ask him.

'Supply,' he says.

'Ahh,' I say, as if that answers every question in the world.

'Lunch today?' says Richard trying to retrieve our conversation.

I have a salad bag of rocket, spinach and watercress in my briefcase plus a couple of rice cakes. The witches always bring a packed lunch and sit in a circle totting up calories. I look out of the window. The sun is trying to break through the wintry mist, but it really is too cold to start a detox today.

'Why don't you join us, Andy?'

'Sure,' says Andy.

Not like, are you sure? Like, sure, I'd love to.

Richard sniffs.

Is there anything more comforting than dipping a hot chip into the yolk of a runny fried egg?

'So, what did you get up to?' Richard asks.

We're sitting in the café bit of the nearby supermarket.

Two eggs and chips for £1.99. At least there's no

dairy, unless eggs count as dairy. I'm never sure. No red meat anyway, and no wheat except for the slice of white bread and marg on the side which is complimentary, and which I am not going to eat.

'This and that. What about you?'

'This and that. New Year?'

'Had a quiet one,' I lie.

Richard's face falls. I know he's imagining scented candles and sex on the carpet, with Jools' Hootenanie in the background, and I can't be bothered to put him out of his misery.

'How about you, Andy?'

I keep calling him Andy as if I'm teaching, or trying very hard not to forget his name and I must stop it.

'Snowboarding,' he says.

He's got a baked potato and salad. He's good at getting forkfuls of salad into his mouth. When I choose salad there's always a bit of raw red cabbage that goes in sideways and gets stuck so that I have to hook it out with my finger.

'You don't look like an Andy,' I say.

'You can call me something else if you like!'

Burst of over-enthusiastic laughter and particle of chip, which lands on Richard's tie. Must get hold of myself.

'How about New Andy?'

'Like New Labour!' says Richard, discreetly wiping his tie with his jacket sleeve.

'All style and no substance,' says New Andy,

who's very much the centre of attention so I don't think he's noticed.

'Oh I wouldn't say that . . .' I begin, looking at his over-large jacket, his spiky hair, his frankly gorgeous face, which looks a bit like that actor with the funny Welsh name which is not pronounced Joan. He is smiling because he didn't really mean it about style.

'Did you go away?' I ask Richard.

'Skiing in Klosters,' he says.

The bottle of HP I've been holding upside down over my chips suddenly discharges half its contents.

'Only joking,' says Richard. 'I was with Mum.'

'How *is* she?' I ask.

'Hard to tell,' he replies.

There's a silence as we all chew our food trying to think of somewhere to go from here.

'What's snowboarding like?'

'Fast,' says Andy. 'Are you going to make a chip butty with your bread?'

'I wasn't,' I say. But now that he's said it, I rather fancy the idea.

'Can I have it?'

'You help yourself,' I say, relieved he's taken the wheat temptation out of my hands.

Every time I speak to him I sound like my mother but I've worked out that he cannot be less than twenty-four, which makes the gap only twelve years at the outside. If you're careful with the age you pick that doesn't sound too bad. For instance,

14

thirty-six and twenty-four is fine, quite exciting. It's when you get to forty and twenty-eight that it starts sounding desperate. Sixty and forty-eight is a bad one too. One with a bus pass, the other still playing football on Saturday mornings.

'What brings you to this part of the world?' I ask him.

'I was brought up round here.'

I suspect a broken relationship, a period of recuperation at home (he's still young and won't be able to keep up the rent on an inner-city flat by himself).

'There's a lot to recommend the suburbs,' says Richard.

'There is,' I agree, and then I can't think of a single thing.

'The schools are better,' says Andy.

'They are,' Richard and I leap on this.

'And there's the tube,' says Richard.

'There's the tube,' I repeat.

'And don't forget the Chiltern Line,' says Richard. 'Ten minutes to Marylebone.'

I know for a fact that Richard has not been into town since he took his mother to see Gene Pitney at the Palladium in 1998.

The methane produced by a classroom of six-year-old boys should be harvested in some eco-friendly way to heat the water or something. It's the bum side of the job (Richard's joke, not mine). There's the salary aspect too that could do with improving and class size, of course, but if I had a choice of no farting or no above-inflation increase in salary for the rest of my life, the farting ban would probably win out. But you very rarely get stark choices like that in life.

Fern, my classroom assistant, believes in visualizing yourself out of your problems. She takes charge while I stand in the materials cupboard, breathing deeply and imagining myself in the Alps.

The sky is clear blue, there's been an overnight fall of powdery snow. My nose is too cold to smell anything. Miraculously, I can snowboard. In fact, I am quite good at it, which is remarkable since even as a child I could not manage two roller skates at the same time. I'm zipping down the mountain, there's a crowd cheering me on, the noise of shouting is becoming almost—

'Emergency, Miss!' Geri's screaming at me. 'Robbie has thrown paint all over Ethan!'

I summon my extremely unamused face and burst out of the materials cupboard. Fern is wonderful at alternatives but she doesn't do discipline.

Ethan has blue paint on his hair, yellow on his school sweatshirt.

'Robbie, put the paint down immediately!'

'It wasn't me!'

'It was, it was, it was!' chorus the others.

I hold both hands above my head. A couple of the girls who are paying attention notice and do the same. Gradually the whole class catches on, and

16

after a few minutes we are all standing there with our hands stretched up, wonderfully silent. Try it next time, you're surrounded by thirty over-excited five and six year olds. It works. But only if you don't do it very often.

'Ethan, what happened?' I say when we've all calmed down.

'Well', says Ethan, glancing at Robbie, who's got him fixed with a threatening stare, 'Robbie was getting some water to mix with the paint and . . .'

Ethan falters in his story, I suspect because Robbie didn't have a chance to rehearse the whole thing with him.

'. . . I accidentally tripped over a chair, and the paint sort of threw itself over him,' says Robbie.

'That's a good story, Robbie, but paint doesn't just throw itself—'

'It does if it's magic, Miss, and Ethan made it magic because he's got a wand at home . . .'

He should really have stuck to the 'I tripped' story.

'Robbie, go and sit in Miss Goodman's class.'

Miss Goodman is head of the First School and teaches Reception. She never smiles. The children are still young enough to be completely terrified of her. So am I, as a matter of fact.

Going to sit in Miss Goodman's class is the ultimate deterrent and I've employed it on day one. I am a failure. Still, I've set the rules for the term. If I threaten, they'll know I mean it.

Gwyneth's crying.

'What's the matter?'

'My boyfriend's in there all on his own!'

I didn't realize they were an item.

It won't last. She's a nice, middle-class girl and he's, well, just not suitable, as my mother used to say with pursed lips when I was a teenager.

'Miss?'

'Yes, Geri?'

'Are we doing dancing?'

'Not today. Today we are seeing how many different shades of colour we can make with one colour mixed with white.'

'You were dancing in the cupboard . . .'

'I wasn't.'

'You were!'

'Can I remind all of you that children are not allowed in the materials cupboard?'

CHAPTER 2

'The Americans have suffered their first casualty in fighting near the Tora Bora cave complex . . .'

The reporter is standing next to a large khaki tent. He's wearing a short-sleeved shirt which shows off his tan.

'Tora Bora sounds like some romantic place in a novel, doesn't it?' I say.

'What happened to the dreadful Afghan winters everyone was going on about last year?' Michelle asks, putting a glass of white wine on the nest of tables next to me.

'Do you remember those shaggy coats people wore in the seventies which smelled? Weren't they called Afghans?'

'Afghan coats,' says Michelle, like they've reminded her of something nice. 'That must be where they came from.'

'Why do you think all the burkas were blue?'

'Pardon?' says Michelle.

'All the burkas the women used to wear in Afghanistan when it was still the Taliban. They were all quite a nice shade of lavender.'

'. . . For the Six O'clock News, Bagram airbase,' says the reporter.

'I wonder how he manages to iron his shirts,' says Michelle.

Tuesday night is girls' night. Towards the end of last year, when we were sluggish with work-party white wine and Ferrero Rocher, we resolved to do something healthy or improving on our evenings together, but today is our first day back at work and we're both too exhausted to go to the gym.

Michelle's suggestion is that we delay the official start of the New Year until next week and go out for a pizza. I offer my bag of spinach, rocket and watercress salad to be eaten in front of the News. We compromise with a frozen deep-dish pepperoni, which is in a buy-one-get-one-free promotion at Safeway, so feels quite virtuous, News on in the background, and both of us testing the samples of Age Reversal Under Eye cream Michelle got in her Christmas-is-for-Giving freebie from the manufacturers.

'There's a supply teacher at school and guess what he's called?'

'Andy?' says Michelle.

'How did you know?' I'm slightly irritated with her spoiling my new piece of information.

'Well, either it had to be something really ordinary, or it had to be something weird, and I knew you'd have rung me if it was something weird.'

Michelle has known me for twenty-four years.

We met on the first day of big school. New Andy may just have been born.

'I suppose you know what he looks like as well?' I say, with a touch of adolescent sarcasm. I sometimes wonder if you stay the same age as you were when you met someone.

'Attractive and a bit too young for you,' says Michelle.

'Too young? How do you work that out?'

'Because you're sitting with your hands clasped round your knees trying to make yourself look like a teenager at a slumber party,' says Michelle.

I sit up properly.

'I'm going to be a grandmother,' she says, unable to hold back her piece of momentous news a second longer.

'What?'

'Do you think I'd win a competition for glamorous grans?'

She makes a kind of vampy face, but it doesn't work with the thick layer of white cream she's got under her eyes.

'What competition's that?'

'I don't have a pacific competition in mind,' says Michelle, impatiently.

There are several words she always gets wrong, but this is not the time to correct her.

'Anyway, forget that bit,' she says, regretting she's mentioned competitions in the first place. She knows what I'm like. 'What do you think?'

'Michaela's pregnant?' I stutter.

'Four months.'

'But she's so young . . .'

Michelle just looks at me. Michelle was pregnant at fifteen.

'I didn't mean . . . I just meant, it makes me feel so old.'

'Shall we have the other pizza?' Michelle says comfortingly.

'No,' I say.

'It was free . . .'

'But it'll take half an hour to cook and then we won't want it.'

'I put it in the oven when I took the other one out,' says Michelle.

'Shame to waste it then,' I say.

Michelle gives me first choice of the slices. It's her way of being sympathetic because she thinks I'm depressed by Michaela's news which I'm not, actually.

I know it makes me sound even more desperately broody than people already imagine I am, but the truth is, I'm not sure whether I would want to be a mother anyway. I love children, but I love not having to see them at the end of the day. I love being able to go out to a movie if I want to, without making any kind of arrangement. Not that I ever do, because I usually go to movies with Michelle and she's got three girls, so we have to fit round their schedules. But I like having the option. Frankly, what with my sister's children, and Michelle's, and now

Michaela's baby, I haven't got a lot of love left over for any children of my own, or time, or money.

Of our own, I should say, because Andy would be involved. (Not New Andy, obviously.)

'What does Andy think?' my mother asked the other day.

'Not interested,' I told her.

'Is she happy?' I remember to ask Michelle. This is Michaela we're talking about, my first and favourite goddaughter.

'She's put herself on the housing list and she's going to ask you to be godmother.'

'Oh, that's nice.'

'Are you called grandgodmother when you're godmother to your godchild's child?' Michelle wonders.

'No such word,' I say firmly.

I am definitely the expert where words are concerned.

Total silence required for *Eastenders*. If you've seen magazines in your supermarket with cover stories like STEVE AND MEL LOVERS AGAIN and wondered who is so keen on soap opera that they seriously buy magazines which detail the background stories as if the characters really exist, then look no further than Michelle.

'It's so true to life,' Michelle says.

If Michelle's life were a soap opera, Michelle would be played by Michelle Collins, which would make it easy for the director, especially if her character were called Michelle too.

Ironically, Michelle's life could easily be a soap opera, but if it were, I don't know who would play me.

Michelle got pregnant at fifteen by her one true love who was almost immediately killed in a motorbike accident. She then married his brother and had another child, but he never got over the fact that she loved his dead brother more, so he left her for a barmaid, whose husband murdered him, leaving Michelle a widow twice over by the age of twenty-two, and her mother-in-law denouncing her to anyone who'd listen. Around that time, her parents' timeshare in the Canaries was engulfed in a freak mud slide burying them alive, but, as Michelle put it, every cloud has a silver lining, and even though they hadn't spoken since the first pregnancy, they'd forgotten to change their will and so she got everything including the house in Hatch End. Two evenings a week I looked after the kids so that she could do a hairdressing diploma for which she was awarded a distinction, even though some of her early cuts were a bit experimental. She had an affair with the teacher, but left him when it turned out he was sleeping with three of the other students, two of them male. After that, there was the AIDS scare, and the court case for assault. I think Michelle got a suspended sentence because she's so tiny and the judge didn't know she'd been Home Counties junior karate champion in the third form. She fell in love with the lawyer who defended her, and he left his wife for a while, but he'd been to public school and I think Michelle and her kids were a bit much for him after the sex wore off. The salon owner who gave her her first job told her he'd had a vasectomy, but she was pregnant again within weeks. She used the money he gave her for an abortion to buy a little van and set herself up as a mobile hairdresser–beautician, which, it turns out, she's really successful at. As Michelle always says, since she gave up men, it's been plain sailing, except for the VAT scare, and the hair dye with the wrong label on it, which wasn't her fault.

Course, she hasn't really given up men.

'So how's Andy?' Michelle asks as the snare drum beats into the title music.

'Andy?' I yelp.

Whilst appearing to concentrate on the screen I have been privately visualizing sharing glühwein and salted nuts with New Andy in a café at the foot of the piste, our snowboards leaning against our banquette. Slightly disconcertingly, we are gazing out of the steamed-up window at three little bundles of Gap fleece standing in a line on the nursery slope waiting for their first skiing lesson.

'Fine,' I say.

'Have you talked to him since . . . ?'

'I'm going to send him an e-mail.'

'Use my computer, if you like.'

'No thanks.'

I'm not that keen to have Michelle looking over my shoulder while I compose an apology to my fiancé.

Michelle suddenly does one of those giggles that you want to keep inside but just kind of bursts out.

'What?'

'Pole dancing with a crucifix!'

'It wasn't a crucifix.' I tell her crossly. 'It was the war memorial. I thought it was the bus stop.'

'No buses on New Year,' says Michelle.

'In the end we flagged down a minicab.'

'How much did that cost?'

'I think Andy paid.'

'We shouldn't have had that bottle of champagne,' says Michelle, wise now.

'It was two bottles.'

It was Michelle's fault, actually, because she didn't have a New Year's Eve Party to go to. She was the one who came up with the idea that I'd go round before-hand and we'd pretend to be in Tonga or Moscow or somewhere where it was already midnight at six in the evening.

'You were fine when you left here,' she says, trying to duck responsibility now.

Tiny snatches of the evening flash through my conscious mind when I least want them to. Just when I think I must have plumbed the depths of my embarrassment, I get a clear, bright memory of something new and hideous.

'I sang "Tie a Yellow Ribbon Round the Old Oak Tree",' I tell her.

'Did you remember all the words?' Michelle wants to know.

Is it more or less humiliating that I did? How does alcohol do that to you? You haven't heard a song for twenty years, you never liked it anyway, yet you find yourself belting it out to a group of serious semi-professional musicians you've never even met before.

'The thing you have to ask yourself,' says Michelle, 'is why you drink so much when you're with Andy.'

I hate it when she tries to get psychological.

Michelle doesn't understand because she's pretty. She's confident and fun and outrageous because she's good looking enough to get away with it. I'm confident and fun and outrageous if I've had three pints of Stella Artois, or the unit equivalent (which I count as six, although I secretly think it's probably more like nine).

I have an animated conversation about dim sum with the minicab driver who is Chinese. As I hand him the money, including a generous tip because he has no change and keeps saying, 'Nice lady, nice lady,' he hands me a piece of paper on which he has written, if I understand correctly, the name of a Chinese restaurant run by his family in Soho. I clutch it like prize money.

Andy loves Chinese but we have been a bit

disappointed with the crispy duck at our local recently.

I shall take him into town for our anniversary.

Sod the anniversary, I shall take him into town this weekend and treat him. As a way of saying sorry for my behaviour at New Year, and to show that I am not really entertaining silly fantasies about a bloke half my age.

Not that he knows that bit.

No-one does. Not even Michelle. It is my secret.

I open my home page.

My mouse glides over:

War on Terrorism latest

clicks on: **Ten hot looks for a cold climate**

I manage to resist the

What's your Attitude to Work? Quiz

There are no new messages in my Inbox.

Click on COMPOSE.

Dear Andy.

Hi Andy!

Hi!

Never know how to start e-mails. Andy just dives straight in as if he's in the middle of a conversation. No, hello, dear, or even Lydia—

Dearest Andy

No, because he'll think I'm drunk if I start getting sentimental, which I am not. Not really. It was only one bottle and there were two of us and we ate two pizzas.

Dear Andy

I'm looking forward to the quiz tomorrow. Assume we're still on. Do you fancy Chinese meal at the weekend, because I've got the name of a fantastic restaurant? My treat!

By the way, my New Year's Resolutions are:

1. Never demonstrate pole dancing. (I don't know if you wondered, but I knew how to because of a programme on Channel 5, but that was indoors!)
2. Never sing in the company of people who can sing, particularly Eurovision Hits. (Sorry about making the fat woman take off her shoes for Sandie Shaw. It wasn't actually my glass. Did she have to have stitches?)
3. Never try to join in reels unless I have previously learnt the steps. (Sorry about your kilt. Funny that I didn't know you were Scottish when you think

about it. I should have guessed because of St Andrew. Anyway, it looked very smart. Nothing against kilts per se, I've actually got one myself that my mother bought in the Edinburgh Wool Shop sale. Not keen on them at weddings, though, are you?)

4. Never drink alcohol.

There may be other things. I won't do those either. See you at the quiz.

LXX

Yes, I'm happy with that. Think it strikes exactly the right balance between remorse and not getting it all out of proportion.
  Click on SEND

CHAPTER 3

We're on Couples' *Who Wants to be a Millionaire?* and the question's worth £125,000.

'How are you feeling?' asks Chris Tarrant.

'Fine,' says Andy, with a slight get-on-with-it quality in his voice which won't go down well with the viewers at home.

'Lydia?'

'Nervous,' I say, because that's what you're meant to say. Andy doesn't understand these things.

'OK,' says Chris, 'I've got Andy and the lovely Lydia playing for £125,000. Have a look at this.'

The lights dim.

'Which band had a hit with "Tie a Yellow Ribbon Round the Old Oak Tree" in 1973?'

A Chickory Tip B Bucks Fizz
C Dawn D The Mamas and the Pappas

'Any ideas?' says Chris.

'I'm thinking Chicory Tip,' says Andy.

'No,' I hiss. 'It's Dawn.'

'I'm sure it's Chicory Tip . . .' Andy persists.

How come he's suddenly the expert on trivia? I do the trivia questions. That's the whole point of me. He's the one who does dates and geography and proper subjects.

'It's Dawn,' I say.

'You've got no lifelines left,' says Chris. 'You can go home with £64,000, which will help with the wedding, or you can play for £125,000.'

I wish Andy had said something a bit more imaginative about what we were going to do with the money. Every time we win a bigger cheque, Chris brings the wedding up again, and it's beginning to make us look ridiculous. It's not as if we're the sort of people who will have *OK!* and *Hello!* vying for the rights. The only picture of our wedding in the press will be in smudged black and white in the *Gazette* alongside the 'Always in our thoughts' messages to dead relatives.

Also, if we hadn't asked the audience about Gail's first husband in *Coronation Street*, which I knew but Andy didn't trust me on, then we would have that lifeline left now, and I'm sure at least 75% would back me on Dawn.

'Dawn? I've never heard of Dawn,' says Andy.

'*You've* never heard of Hear'say!' I say, exchanging a cheeky glance with Chris.

'Hearsay?' Andy repeats. He's never heard of them.

'They're not even married yet, but they're arguing already,' says Chris with a big grin to camera.

32

'If you don't believe me, then let's take the money,' I say.

'I've got a real feeling about Chicory Tip,' says Andy.

The more he says it, the more I'm getting doubts. It was Dawn, wasn't it? I know they definitely did 'Knock Three Times on the Ceiling'. God, maybe I'm wrong.

'Chicory Tip sounds right to me,' says Andy.

'It's not Chicory Tip. They did . . .'

Suddenly I can't remember the name of the song that Chicory Tip did. I could hum the intro. The intro went on for ages. But what was it called?

'Which group had a hit with "Tie a Yellow Ribbon Round the Old Oak Tree"?'

'Chicory Tip,' says Andy.

'Hang on!' I say.

'Final answer?' says Chris.

'No!' I'm screaming, but nothing's coming out of my mouth.

'Final answer,' says Andy.

A bell rings.

'Andy and the lovely Lydia have got £64,000, they can win £125,000 if the answer's right. But we're out of time . . .'

The audience laughs.

I cannot bring myself to look at Andy.

'Find out tomorrow . . .' says Chris.

The doorbell rings again.

Normally on *Millionaire*, it's a hooter.

I wake up sweating profusely.

'OK, OK,' I shout, getting out of bed with the duvet still wrapped around me, which proves a bit of a problem going downstairs because I've got a wrought-iron spiral staircase from my landing straight into my living room and the duvet gets all tangled up in it.

'What are you doing?' Michelle's saying on the other side of the front door. I remember that she promised to deliver my car back.

'I'm stuck,' I call.

'I'll shove the key through the box. I'm late for my lymph drainage, and Michaela's on a double yellow.'

'What if I can't free myself?' I call, sitting down on the second-to-top step. I can feel the cold metal pattern imprinting on my bum. I'm clammy all over but also shivery, from a combination of the dream and last night's wine. How much did I have? I tug at the duvet, but it only makes things worse. I'm almost weepy with hangover and failure and bloody Andy losing us all that money over Chicory Tip. Chicory Tip, for God's sake! At least if you're going to lose on *Millionaire*, do it with the orbits of the planets, or something Biblical.

'Who sang "Tie a Yellow Ribbon"?' I shout to Michelle.

'Tony Orlando and Dawn.'

I was right!

We were not on *Millionaire* and we have not actually lost any money.

34

If I go back up the staircase the duvet will come with me.

There is no need to get to the door because Michelle has pushed my car key through and it is waiting for me on the mat.

Michelle was right. We should postpone the official start of the New Year until next week. That way I can start my detox properly, on a Monday when it's easier to keep to resolutions.

My clock says I have just ten minutes to shower and dress, but I have done it in six before, and anyway, I always set the clock five minutes fast to give me the impression that I have to hurry.

If the traffic's not too bad, I may even be early.

The more I relax, slow down and schedule in time for pure enjoyment, the more I accomplish every day!

Fern told me I should say this to myself in times of stress, while kneading my kidneys.

I'm not actually sure where my kidneys are.

Think I am meant to say it out loud.

The children in the back of the Volvo in front are staring at me. I jig around a bit in my seat, pretending that I'm singing along to the radio, which has the added advantage of a random massage of most of my back.

Amazingly the words go quite well with the rhythm of 'Murder on the Dance Floor'.

The more I slow down da da,
And schedule

In time for pure enjoyment. Hey Hey
The more I accomplish every day, hey hey!

The Volvo kids are watching very intently as if lip reading when I remember that this may have been one of the life affirmations I was meant to write down.

I scrabble around in the glove compartment for a piece of paper.

The more I . . .

The biro has dried up but if I press hard enough the impression of the words stays on the paper which must count.

The car behind is beeping at me.

There's air and tarmac where the Volvo was.

I only just make it through the green light. In fact, it's red when I go through but several cars follow me, so that's all right.

The biro is rolling round the floor. I reach down with one hand to pick it up because Andy once told me that a fatal accident can be caused by a can of Coke rolling around the floor and getting stuck under the brake pedal. Debris on floor while car is in motion is second only to talking on mobile phone in Andy's directory of car crimes, but how much harm could a biro do?

Beep! Beep!

Oh F off your F-ing self!

Four hundred children watch me attempt to reverse into my space three times.

Then there's not enough room to open the driver door, so I have to squeeze across to the passenger side, and my extra long and rather chic jersey skirt is all twisted round my knees. I have to unwind myself like a telephone flex before I can walk.

The more time I spend reciting Fern's bloody affirmations, the more hassled and stressed I become, and in any case is Fern a good advisor given the fact that she hasn't even noticed that Robbie is practising his kick-boxing in the line-up which she's doing because I'm late, silly cow!

'Thanks, Fern, you're wonderful,' I tell her.

At the school gate, Ethan is standing with his father refusing to come in.

Ethan has forgotten his lunch box.

'Sorry,' says his father, 'but my wife's unwell. She usually does all this. Can I drop it in later?'

'*Before* lunch, Dad,' says Ethan.

'Nothing serious, I hope?'

I was only making conversation but his face mutates from flustered to stricken and I wish I'd never asked.

'Sorry about the paint, by the way. In Ethan's hair.'

He's just staring at me.

'Blue paint in hair, yellow on jumper?' I say.

'My gran picked me up yesterday. She washed them,' Ethan explains.

So, absolutely no need for me to have mentioned it at all.

'How did he get paint in his hair?' says his father, connecting at last.

'Something to do with my wand,' says Ethan.

'No harm done, anyway!' I say, turning the child round by his shoulders.

'There was an owl on our roof this morning,' Ethan tells me as we run in together.

I shiver. I seem to remember my mother telling me once that owls in the day time are bad omens, but, knowing Ethan, it was probably a pigeon.

'Miss, Robbie just kissed Gwyneth!'

Geri races up to me as we enter the classroom.

'Don't tell tales, Geri.'

'But he DID.'

'Robbie?'

'It's a free country,' he says.

'Yes, but you mustn't kiss anyone who doesn't want to be kissed.'

I can't get into another discussion about benefits accruing from responsibility. Last time I heard myself sounding just like Tony Blair.

'She wanted it.'

Gwyneth smiles.

'No kissing in school,' I tell them, firmly.

'Not even if we get married?' says Robbie.

The thing I love about Year One is that they know so much, and so little at the same time.

'Kissing's against school rules,' I say, gently.

'What about blow jobs?' says Dean.

'That is not a very good start to the day, is it?'

'My brother says it is.'

'Are you married, Miss?' asks Ethan.

'No, Ethan, I'm not.'

'I'll marry you,' he says.

'I'll bear that in mind.'

I've had seven proposals since I started teaching Year One.

'Marriage is just another word for prison, isn't it, Miss?' says Nicole.

'No way would I marry you, Miss,' says Robbie.

'Oh, really? Why's that?'

'Because you smell.'

That's rich from a champion farter.

'My mum sometimes smells like you, Miss,' says Nicole consolingly.

I nip into the materials cupboard and sniff my armpits. I can't possibly smell this soon after a shower? I think he means my breath. Even though I've consumed a whole box of Tic Tacs for breakfast, my mouth still has the sourness of alcohol and pepperoni.

I wonder if Nicole's mum is drinking because step dad 3 is back or because he's gone again.

'Are you having a ciggie, Miss,' asks Geri.

'No.'

'Can I remind you all,' I say, as I come out with an armful of paper, 'that children are not allowed in the materials cupboard.'

'Miss?'

'Yes?'

'Forgotten.'

Some of them just like putting their hands in the air whether they've got a question or not.

'Miss?'

I hate the word Miss. Especially with a hangover. It makes me think of Misanthropy, Mistake, and particularly, Miss Goodman, who is the portrait in my mental attic. The woman I will turn into if I don't get married.

'Yes?'

'Are we wrapping up presents?'

'No. We're not wrapping presents. We are investigating different kinds of paper.'

I get them to sit in a circle and I put all the paper in the middle.

'Can anyone think of some words to describe paper? Robbie, leave it alone for the moment.'

'Toilet roll, Miss.'

'Yes, that's a type of paper. Can you think of some words that tell us what toilet paper looks like, or feels like. You can feel it later, Robbie.'

Too late. There is now a streamer of Apricot Andrex right across the classroom.

'Anyone got any ideas?'

Several little heads duck down, several tongues come out of mouths.

'Miss?'

'Yes, Dean.'

'Pooey?'

A Mexican wave of giggles goes round the circle.

'I meant before you use it.'

40

'I know, I know, I know.'

'Yes, Geri?'

'Soft, strong and very long!'

'Very good.'

'Any others?'

Blank faces.

'That's what it says on television,' says Geri defensively.

Better not push it because I can't think of any other properties myself right now.

Absorbent! That's a good one, but might be worth saving until we get to the kitchen towel.

'Would somebody like to choose a different piece of paper and tell us something about it?'

No volunteers.

'What do we call this sort of paper?'

'Newspaper,' says Dean with a yawn.

'Has anyone seen one of these at home?'

Only four out of thirty hands go up.

I don't know why I'm shocked. If I'm honest, I only ever look at the TV listings.

'What is a newspaper like?'

'It's black and white and red all over,' Robbie volunteers.

'Excellent. That's a joke as well, isn't it, Robbie? Do you know why it's funny? Stop that.'

'Don't know.'

'It's funny because a newspaper is black and white, and we read it. So it's read as well. The reading sort of read. Not the colour sort of red. Yes, Dean?'

'My dad's newspaper is black and white and red *coloured*.'

OK, so it's a joke from a pre-tabloid cracker, but we don't want to go there.

'What other words describe newspaper? Oh, look, here's Ms Green. Can you help us?'

Fern thinks for a moment.

'Recyclable?'

Thanks a million, Fern.

'Does anyone know what recycling is? Yes, Gwyneth?'

'It's when you put newspaper outside in a green box.'

'Good. And does anyone know what happens to all that old newspaper?'

'It gets all soggy because the bloody van never comes when it's supposed to,' says Nicole.

'What happens is they make new newspaper. So they won't have to cut down so many trees. Now, if you've been listening, Robbie, you might have an answer to my next question. Which is where does paper come from?'

Getting further and further away from properties, but never mind. Lesson plans are my weak spot. That's what the Ofsted inspector said. Bastard!

'Yes, Dean?'

'Why do they make new newspaper, when they've thrown away all the old newspaper?'

He's a very bright child.

I think of the hours I spent with his brother

42

Wayne trying to get him to write his name correctly. The memory is sepia-coloured now and tinged with nostalgia.

'You OK?' Richard Batty asks.

We are kneeling on our staffroom chairs with our heads out of the window. A large drop of water from the damaged guttering above the window explodes right next to my eye.

Richard Batty lights his second cigarette from the tip of his first. What is it in cigarettes that makes them stay burning even in a downpour?

'Fine, thanks.'

'You look a bit tired.'

'Late night.'

'I like your hair like that.'

Normally I tie it back, but today it is hanging round my face.

I've had quite a few hair styles in my time, especially during my twenties when Michelle was doing her course. My hair is naturally brown, and these days, I have a plain bob, which even Michelle finds hard to make 'interesting' although she's always trying to tempt me with a Mahogany tint, or Chestnut low lights.

'Thanks. Is New Andy here today?'

Oops. Bit of a give-away connecting him with the loose hair.

'I don't suppose we'll be seeing him again until someone gets sick,' Richard says, with a little smile and a satisfied drag on his Rothmans.

43

I shoot a glance back at the witches. Miss Goodman has put her coat on as a non-verbal protest about the open window. I wish a prolonged virus on all of them, but they are in cackling rude health and I've risked nits for nothing.

CHAPTER 4

There are two new messages in my Inbox which gives me a little fillip of excitement, a bit like getting an envelope in the post with handwriting you don't recognize. Actually, these days it's more often than not a charity appeal, and the handwriting is computer generated just to fool you, but at least you sometimes get a free pen.

Reduce Ageing and Burn Off Fat
Still single?

Is it just me, or does everyone get unsolicited e-mail that uncannily taps into their current insecurities? It's almost as if my mother is out there in cyberspace spookily directing the spam. My mother is an avid silver surfer, as a matter of fact.

Click on COMPOSE.

Hi! Usual time? Usual place? L

I've probably given the wrong impression of my

boyfriend, Andy. Is boyfriend the right word for someone who's over forty? We are engaged but partner sounds ridiculous if you don't even live together.

Obviously we will after we're married, or sooner, if Honey goes. It's awful to wish death on any living thing, even a dog, but Honey is extremely old. I've always slightly suspected that Andy popped the question because Honey was at veterinary hospital and he felt a bit lonely. But she bounced back.

Bounced probably isn't the right word.

I ought actually to be grateful to Honey because she was instrumental in our getting together, but ever since I was knocked over and bitten by a boxer as a child, I am not comfortable around dogs. I've noticed the world divides into people who say 'he was only playing' when I tell them, and people who say, 'I can't stand dogs either.'

If I'm absolutely honest, I didn't particularly like the look of Andy when I saw him sitting in Nando's forecourt in the O2 Centre on Finchley Road, and I secretly wished that I'd been firmer about just meeting for a coffee. But, as he rightly pointed out, a cappuccino in Starbucks is almost the same price as a chicken meal, and then you haven't eaten.

He was a bit more ginger than I had expected, but I hadn't been entirely truthful either. I expect that we were both a bit disappointed. Which is why Nando's turned out to be a good choice, because if it had just been coffee we wouldn't have had to make the effort, and it turns out we have quite a lot in common.

For instance, we both chose the hottest piri piri option (I could see he was impressed by that. Men, are. At university, my popularity seemed to be largely dependent on my ability to down the strongest vindaloo on the Star of India menu).

Also, we both love doing quizzes. Really. I can't ignore a quiz. Even if it's one about calcium designed for five-year-old children on the back of a cereal packet. There's still a small buzz of satisfaction as I turn the packet upside down to read that I've got the correct answers. Not if I've forgotten to fold down the bag inside, obviously.

Andy is more enthusiastic about comic operetta than my ideal date would be, but I'm more interested than he is in Pilates, yoga and jazz dance (all classes I've signed up for in the last couple of years).

As our date progressed and I realized that Andy's idea of healthy living consists of holidays with the Ramblers' Association and eating two Shredded Wheat each morning, my enthusiasm for physical activity increased. I even managed to drop Egyptian Dancing into the conversation. Only that I was thinking of trying it.

I sensed that Andy was calculating that while I wasn't much of a looker, I would probably be quite fun in bed with all that fitness and flexibility.

I began to wonder whether he had hair on his shoulders.

★   ★   ★

I don't honestly know, however, whether we would have made it to another date, if it hadn't been for Honey's incontinence. We exchanged e-mail addresses, but I would not have contacted him, because on the tube home I convinced myself that he was a stalker. Not as mad as it sounds, by the way, because when I got out at my stop, I caught a glimpse of him sitting in the next carriage down, and he quickly put his *Evening Standard* up in front of his face.

Michelle reasoned that it was perfectly possible that he lived further down the line – why else would anyone suggest meeting on the Finchley Road? – but I thought that was too coincidental. Admittedly, I was in the middle of the latest Nicci French.

When Andy's head appeared by chance over my fence the following Sunday, I was a bit spooked. Oddly, the fact that he had a dog, especially a lolloping old Labrador, made him seem softer, somehow. And he was carrying a plastic glove to clear the poo up with.

'You're easily pleased,' Michelle said, when I told her after.

Turns out he didn't have hair on his shoulders.

Having a relationship makes life easier. You don't get the pity. There's someone to do the barbecue if you decide to throw a spontaneous party in summer. When the children in your class ask you if you have a boyfriend, you can say yes, full stop. No further questions. A husband would be even better.

We don't even have to see each other that often.

I didn't mean that to sound like it did.

My job involves a lot of preparation, and twice a week I go to my health club or see Michelle. Twice a week, Andy rehearses with the Metropolitan Opera which is an amateur company named after the tube line that divides the sprawling north London suburb in which most of its members live. We have a tacit agreement that he doesn't talk about it, and I don't tell him about the amusing things the children in my class have said.

During the week our only real fixture is quiz night.

Last year, Andy and I were regional champions in the North Herts and Middlesex league, which is pretty amazing since it's just the two of us, and we have never resorted to the use of mobile phones. Andy is brilliant at facts, I am brilliant at trivia. We make an almost unbeatable team.

Andy and the lovely Lydia.

That is what the publican called me the night of our second date when we first won and it stuck. And so did we.

We have not seen each other since he dropped me back home after New Year, and I waved the taxi down the street, then woke my elderly neighbours up trying to get my key into their lock.

He has not replied to my e-mails either, but he often doesn't, so there is really nothing to worry about. Everyone gets drunk at New Year, don't they? I will not even bring it up.

'Broken any resolutions yet?'

'Never make any,' says Andy. 'How about you?'

'I feel much better without it,' I tell him solemnly.

'Good,' says Andy.

So that's that.

'How was rehearsal?' I ask him, as if I am interested,

'We've decided to go for *Cosi fan tutte*.'

'*Cosi fan tutte*? by Mozart?'

'Full marks.'

'Bit more difficult than Gilbert and Sullivan.'

'Mozart was not considered highbrow in his time,' says Andy.

'I was there when you rented the video of *Amadeus*,' I say.

'Testing, testing,' says the publican into his mike.

'Who received the best-actor Oscar in the film?' I whisper.

'Tom something?' says Andy.

'No, actually it was F. Murray Abraham,' I tell him. 'The bloke who played the baddie.'

'Salieri?'

'One two, one two,' says the publican.

'Did anyone mention New Year's Eve?'

It just slipped out.

'No,' Andy says.

'I'm really sorry.'

'You got drunk. You tried to play the bagpipes. End of story,' says Andy, fidgeting a bit in case we miss the first question.

God, the bagpipes! What can have possessed me? The irony is I hate the sound of bagpipes, but I think I must have seen one of the presenters on *Blue Peter* try it once.

So that's that.

I'm sure there's something further to be said, but I don't know what it is.

Differences between men and women:

1. Bearing grudges.

If Andy were a woman sitting next to me, the silence would imply that I have not yet paid my penance, and that I need to prove myself in some way before being forgiven. But it is quite possible that Andy is thinking nothing at all. When a man says he's thinking about nothing, he often really does mean it. If a woman says nothing when you ask her what she's thinking, it means there is an agenda as long as your arm.

I think it must be genetic. If you tell a six-year-old boy off, he's forgiven you by the end of the next playtime. If you tell off a girl, she'll scowl at you until the end of term.

★   ★   ★

What do I see in Andy? Michelle's always making me list the pros and cons as if he's a spending decision. The trouble with Michelle is that she's never had a relationship that lasted beyond the first trimester, so she doesn't know about the matter of just getting along, which is all most people want.

He's good looking enough, intelligent enough. Presentable, is my mother's word. He's sensible with his money, but not fundamentally mean like so many men. And when we win a quiz and he smiles at me, it feels zingily right. When we win, Andy and I are 'in love', which is great because it happens every week, so it's a bit like renewing our vows, like celebrities do in *Hello!* magazine when they're stuck for a bit of cash. Without the flowers and the priest and Caribbean island and all that stuff, obviously, although the publican is Irish, and this week, because he's had a crate of Malibu delivered by mistake, he's got an offer on cocktails and he's wearing a Hawaiian shirt.

We win! We are in love, and I have redeemed myself, if I needed redeeming, because I knew that the most populous city in North America was Mexico City, not New York.

And Andy's supposed to be the expert on geography!

I didn't tell him that Richard Batty read it out of a Key Stage 2 book the other day. I just sort of sat there smiling, as if it was my native intelligence.

I do have native intelligence as a matter of fact. It makes me good at knowing what sort of answer they're looking for. For instance, I know that the answer is unlikely to be New York because that's what everyone would think. So even if I hadn't had inside knowledge, I might well have guessed Mexico City.

Actually, I probably would have said Chicago or Miami, if I'm being totally honest.

Our prize is a bottle of Malibu, which is fine because I can put it into the next tombola at school, and will feel like I'm doing something for charity. Last week it was a big jar of pickled eggs, which Andy appropriated because he said he knew someone who liked them. He confessed later he'd been referring to Honey but didn't want to say in case Paddy was offended. I think pickled eggs is probably worse than dog food, myself, but it's the winning that counts not the taking prizes!

'Mexico City!' says Andy, admiringly, as he bends forward to take the first slurp of his second pint without lifting the glass from the table.

Does everyone have particular habits that their partner finds almost intolerably irritating? This bending forward and slurping is one of Andy's that fills me with a kind of seething inner rage, only for a second or so, so not really worth drawing to his attention and, in fact, totally irrational on my part, since it's not unsanitary or antisocial. It's just that pints are for picking up. I'm the sort of person who likes to chink glasses whether a toast is called for or not. What does it matter if it foams all over your fingers? Andy cannot bear to spill a drop.

This is the point where the 'in love' changes to 'loving someone', although it doesn't feel like I thought it would.

It's not what it's like in the movies, but then they do not make movies about plain people falling in love. They do not make movies about plain women full stop. Even when they do, they use Michelle Pfeiffer. *Mother Teresa, The Movie* would star Michelle Pfeiffer although Robin Williams would actually be a better likeness, and what's he really done since *Mrs Doubtfire*?

Michelle (Pfriend not Pfeiffer, obviously) says my problem is that I want my life to be like *Barefoot in the Park*. Nobody gets Robert Redford, she says, not even Demi Moore in *Indecent Proposal*, but that doesn't mean you have to settle for Woody Harrelson.

Andy is nothing like Woody Harrelson, by the way, and I believe some women find Woody attractive. As they do Andy. In the league tables Andy would probably come above me.

And anyway, I haven't fancied Robert Redford since I was a teenager.

It's been Gary Lineker for some time. Since Italia '90, as a matter of fact. Michelle, who doesn't like football, thinks I'm joking. Which is fine because I don't want her knowing all my thoughts.

It was that smile when he'd scored a goal.

It just looked like pure happiness.

'Are you coming in?' Andy asks as I park outside his flat.

'Not tonight,' I say. 'I've got a lot of preparation for tomorrow.'

'Go on,' says Andy.

He's had two pints of Boddingtons and he's looking at me in a slightly predatory way. Andy is quite highly sexed, which is another one of his plus points. None of that really-it's-fine, it-doesn't-matter, there's-probably-too-much at-stake, we've-drunk-too-much, not-slept-enough, it's-a-much-commoner-problem-than-you-think and a-cuddle-is-sometimes-just-as-intimate stuff for us.

'I've locked Honey in the kitchen,' he says.

This is Andy's version of soft music and champagne cooling in an ice bucket.

'OK, then,' I say, switching off the engine.

The first time I came to Andy's flat, he opened the door and said, 'As you can see, I'm a minimalist.'

Which made me laugh more than the remark demanded. We had just won our first quiz. I was over-excited and nervous.

Andy's interpretation of minimalist is no comfortable furniture and lots of wires everywhere. Did I mention that Andy was in computers? He's the kind of brains end of a website design company, which means that he is quite rich, on paper. (What does he need to do with the paper to get the money? I've never really understood finance, and there comes a point when you're too old to ask.)

There is an orange-and-brown-tartan sofa left behind by the previous owner, which is so seventies it would have some value as a retro item if it were in good condition, but as Andy says a bit tearily, there's really no point in buying a new one while Honey is still around. You can't criticize a man for not expressing his emotions and then haul him round IKEA every other weekend, can you?

The other piece of furniture is a pouffe with a woven pattern, which his mother threw out when she got the free footstool with the sofa from Courts. (What is the correct pronunciation of that word, by the way? Is it poof, like homosexual, or is it poofay, which Andy's mother calls it, because she thinks it sounds more refined? I sometimes wonder whether she knows that couple who live in the other half of her semi-detached are gay. She always refers to them as the boys next door, with an indulgent smile as if they're *Men Behaving Badly* flat-share types.)

I bought Andy one of those blobby oil light things for Christmas, as a kind of ironic statement, but he has not taken it out of its box. Andy is just not interested in interior design, which is another plus because it means that I will have as free a hand in our new house as Laurence and Diarmuid do on television. Not *Changing Rooms*, obviously. (See what we can do for £500? Yes, I do.

Tie-dye a sheet and paint your floor grey.) I mean *Home Front*, where money's no object to curving cupboards painted chartreuse and cobalt kitchen surfaces custom-made of volcanic rock. Michelle's videoing it so we can see what sort of house they haven't done yet, which might just influence my plans about what and where to buy.

'How about Rickmansworth?' I ask Andy, as he puts his arms around me.

I'd love a cup of coffee, but I daren't venture into the kitchen. Not that Honey would ever bite, but she does jump up and try to lick my face, and even though these days, she doesn't reach much further than my knees, that would still mean a trip to the dry-cleaners with these trousers.

'Meteorologically, it's the coldest place in Britain,' Andy replies as if it's a quiz question. I don't know whether this is because he genuinely thinks that I have asked him one, or if it's his way of ducking the issue.

'It can't be,' I say. 'There must be places in Scotland colder than Rickmansworth. Or Yorkshire.'

'I read it somewhere,' says Andy. He kisses me.

He's not bad at kissing. Quite dry. People who say that dogs are like their owners or vice versa, are wrong about Andy. Quite urgent. I kiss him back. We topple onto the bed.

'Shall we?' I ask.

Andy's undoing his zip, undoing mine, sighing in a quite passionate way.

'Rickmansworth?' I say, trying to sit up.

It's not as if it's the first time it's come up. We discussed Rickmansworth on Christmas Day. It's still on the Metropolitan Line, so easy for Andy's commute, but feels a bit more like the country than Harrow, which, if we're ever thinking of . . . as soon as that bit loomed, we moved on to the third type of brandy butter. Andy's family Christmas always involves a taste test of some sort, which I was asked to buy for this year, partly because I'm nearly one of the family, and partly because nobody could face Andy's different brands of stuffing mix again.

'Rickmansworth,' Andy murmurs, sort of muffled.

His face is so close to mine, I can see my reflection in his eyes.

'Have you forgiven me for snogging the paramedics?' I whisper.

'Paramedics, mmm,' he says.

'I think they're used to it at New Year,' I say.

'New Year,' Andy echoes.

'All forgiven?'

'All forgiven.'

Andy has a condition that means that when his mind is on sex, he is incapable of conversation except to repeat the last words of any sentence I utter. I call it penis brain.

Sometimes I find it quite flattering, actually.

CHAPTER 5

The sun is shining in through my bedroom window. I must remember never to drink again because mornings are so much better. In my twenties, I used to be able to drink anyone under the table and still be bright and buzzy at work the next day, but when I turned thirty, I started having to get good at making up excuses for being late. This morning, I'm so clear-headed, I can't imagine why I ever drink alcohol at all.

Not drinking allows me not to sleep at Andy's. I've always found the sleeping together bit of having a relationship the most difficult. Not the sex. I really mean the sleeping. There's the question of different body heats, the way the bottom sheet always seems to ruck up when there's two of you, and the fact that I like to sleep with the curtains open, and Andy has to be in blackout.

Then there's the snoring. Finding out that he snores like a pig was bad enough, but finding out that I do was worse. Nobody ever mentioned it before Andy, which meant that I felt bad about the present and doubly bad when I thought about past boyfriends snickering at me behind my back. The more Andy told me not to worry about it, the more I badgered him to demonstrate the exact volume. In the end we agreed to do impersonations of each other's snores. He was shocked by how ferociously loud his were compared to mine. I did make him go first, which was probably a bit sneaky.

Not drinking allows me to drive home when the roads are virtually empty, which, for some reason, always makes me feel as if I am in a movie. Not drinking means I can stop at the petrol station and buy a Cadbury's Creme Egg at one o'clock in the morning.

Not drinking allows me to participate fully in the morning after, which Year One is spending with Jonah, a man from Senegal, who has come to school today to play the drums with us.

There are a few minutes at the end for our questions.

'What is the difference between Senegal and England?' Gwyneth reads out one of the questions we have prepared earlier.

Jonah thinks about this one for quite some time. So long that I wonder whether he has in fact heard.

'I expect there are lots of differences between our two countries,' I say, in a loud clear voice.

Jonah smiles, almost to himself, closes his eyes, then laughs silently.

I wonder if the constant drumming is doing him any good.

'Senegal and England. Two very different countries. It's probably hard to know where to begin,' I prompt.

'In England,' says Jonah, 'everyone is in a big hurry. In Senegal we take our time.'

I like Jonah's attitude, but I was hoping for something we could put in our Differences between England and West Africa wall chart.

The bell goes.

The children scramble to their feet, looking hungrily in the direction of their lunch boxes.

'Before we all rush off to lunch, can we all thank Jonah very much for coming to see us today.'

I start off the clapping.

Then I take a picture of Jonah and the class with the school's new digital camera.

'OK. Go and wash your hands, then line up.'

'I expect the weather's a bit better anyway,' I say as I help Jonah carry his drums to his car. It's pouring with rain.

'It rains,' says Jonah. 'It rains every day, for two whole months.'

'But then it's nice and sunny.'

'Too hot.'

'I always wanted to go to Africa,' I tell him.

'Why?' he asks.

To travel and help people, obviously, but I don't want to sound colonial.

'To teach,' I say. 'In a different place. With different values and climate.'

'To help the poor?' he says.

'Well, yes, sort of,' I stammer.

'I always wanted to come to England.'

'Why's that?' I ask.

'To get rich,' he says, with a wonderfully calm smile.

'How far do you think Senegal can go in the World Cup?' I ask him.

I know they qualified because the African Nations' Cup was on late-night television a while back.

'Let's put it this way,' he says, suddenly animated, 'Argentina's not in our group.'

We shake hands, glad to have found some common ground.

'They've got me helping out with drama,' says New Andy.

'Oh dear,' I say.

'I am an actor.'

I laugh, then realize that he's not joking.

Is it the age difference?

'Why do they call actors resting when they're not working, instead of unemployed?' says Richard, cracking open his sandwich packet, which I notice is a very good example of a rectangular prism. Usually the only one I can think of is a Toblerone box. A faint smell of boiled egg drifts across the table.

We didn't really want Richard in our gang today, but he caught us trying to sneak out of the side gate.

'It's ironic, Richard,' I say.

The mortified look on his face shames me because Richard is a loyal friend. Also, I'm not keen on people who use 'ironic' to mean the joke's not very funny.

Richard eats his sandwich quite fast, then scrapes his chair back noisily.

'Work to do,' he says, sensing he's not wanted.

'See you later!' I say breezily, as if it's quite normal for him to leave first.

Outside the window, he stops and lights a cigarette, then blows the first smoke out, smiles, and waves brightly at us.

'Have you got digital TV?' asks New Andy.

'I have.'

Treated myself to a widescreen television last birthday. It's the first time I've been asked, and I feel rather grown up.

'There's a Kurosawa film on FilmFour tonight.'

'It's my gym night,' I tell him.

It isn't really a lie, because frankly I would rather work out for three hours than watch some Japanese art movie in black and white.

'Maybe some other time, if you're not doing anything. It's just that my folks don't have nonterrestrial,' says Andy.

'I think I can make an exception for Kawasaka,' I say quickly.

In a list of ten sentences I am least likely to utter, this would come pretty near the top.

'To be honest, I never actually go to the gym,' I add.

'I've been bad lately, I used to go three times a week when I was in town,' says New Andy.

'. . . on Thursdays. Tuesdays and weekends are all I seem to be able to manage.'

'Which gym?'

'The one down the road.'

I should offer to show him round. You get a free sports towel if you introduce a new member.

'Any good?'

'Depends what you're looking for,' I say enigmatically.

If I thought he might be there, all lean in cycling shorts, I would never even bother to spend the time thinking about going, before sensing the onset of a cold and deciding it was sensible to give it a miss.

So does he want to come round to watch Kawa what'sit or not? I'm not sure how to ask.

My mobile phone rings.

'Is that Lydia?' says a male voice I do not immediately recognize.

Am I the only person in the world who wonders what I've done wrong when I answer the phone to an unfamiliar male voice?

'Yes?' I admit.

'I have Joanna on the line for you,' says the voice.

Alas my love you do me wrong to cast me off discourteously . . .

'Lydia. Thank God I've tracked you down!'

I feel instantly guilty, as if I have been deliberately difficult to get hold of.

'What is it?'

My tone of voice is so urgent that New Andy looks up over his second chocolate mousse.

'Emergency,' says my sister.

I imagine an ambulance with my mother in it and lots of drips and things.

'Bloody au pair's let us down,' says Joanna. 'That really is the last one from Eastern Europe. Thing is, we've got a dinner party and I absolutely can't have the children wandering in and out and screaming the place down, so would you come over?'

'When?'

'Tonight. I know it's short notice, Lyd, but I absolutely can't cancel, I've got the food ordered.'

'I'm sorry, I've got other plans.'

'What plans?'

'Seeing Andy.'

Rather pleased with myself about that one. True, but doesn't make me look uncool.

'Bring him too!' she says, magnanimously. 'Listen, could you make it by seven because I've got a hair appointment and I need someone to let the girls in. Actually don't bring Andy. He wouldn't fit in and the children don't like him.'

'What girls?'

'The caterers.'

'How many people are you having?'

'Just six, but it makes such a difference, especially mid week.'

'But where will the children be?'

'God! Well remembered! Look could you pick them up from school on your way over? I'll get Kim to call the school now and tell them it'll be you.'

'But—'

'Don't worry if you're a bit late. I pay them enough.'

'I'm sorry, but I can't tonight,' I say.

And all but my lady Greensleeves . . .

No point in ringing back because I know Kim, who is as loyal to Joanna as any gay man could be to a woman, won't let me through.

'I guess that's a no?' says New Andy.

'This afternoon we are going to have a writers' workshop.'

Six hands go in the air.

· 'Nikita?'

'What's a writers' workshop?'

'I was hoping someone would ask me that.'

I smile at her.

'A writers' workshop is when we write a story together.'

All I remember from school about writing a story was that it had to have a beginning, a middle and an end. Our teacher used to read us *How the Elephant got his Trunk* by Rudyard Kipling. The rhythm of the words (great, grey, green, greasy Limpopo River! I haven't heard it for thirty years but it's still there!) became almost as automatic as the Lord's Prayer, but easier to understand. (Why was God's name Hello? Did you have to say 'Hello!' twice when you met him?)

I thought for a long time that all you had to do to write a story was choose an animal and make up some weird reason why it looked like it did. My story 'How the Rabbit Got Its Ears' won the school prize. My parents were called in after 'How the Boxer Dog got its tail cut off'.

I found a story about a whale by Ted Hughes in a children's anthology the other day. He obviously had the same idea. His whale was a root growing in the ground. But that's Ted Hughes for you.

'How do we start a story? Anyone got any ideas?'

'Paper?' Nicole offers.

There's an unusual logic to Nicole's thinking, because she always suspects that I'm asking trick questions.

'Yes, we'll need some paper,' I say. 'And a pencil,' I add quickly, to stop us getting sidetracked on the technicalities.

'Or the computer,' says Dean.

'Quite. Once we've sorted out what materials we're going to use for writing our story, how are we going to start thinking about what to write?'

'Once upon a time?'

'Very good, Gwyneth. A lot of stories start like that, don't they? Another way is to start thinking about who's going to be in the story. The characters. Can anyone think of any characters they'd like to include in our story?'

'Owls,' says Ethan.

'Monsters,' says Robbie.

'A princess,' says Nikita.

'Girls and boys,' says Geri.

How refreshingly traditional!

'A mummy,' says Dean.

'Good, Dean. A mummy for the boys and girls.'

'Not a mummy. The Mummy,' he says. 'Like *The Mummy Returns* . . .'

I'm sure it's a 15.

I write all the suggestions on the whiteboard.

'Right now, let's give our characters some names. Robbie. Can you think of a name for the monster?'

'Sulley?' he says.

'Let's try to think of our own names, not ones we've heard in movies.'

I hate Disney. I hate the way children's imaginations have been Disneyfied with the full cooperation of their parents who seem to think that because Disney cannot be avoided, it must be embraced.

'I know! I know!'

'Yes, Robbie?'

'Dean, Miss.'

'I don't think Dean's a very good name for a monster,' I lie. 'I think we should think of a name that doesn't already belong to someone in the class.'

'You said our own names, Miss.'

'Miss? Dean just said the F-word.'

'Don't tell tales, Geri.'

'But he did.'

'What's the F-word?' asks Nikita.

'My brother's got *Monsters, Inc.* on video,' says Dean.

'Don't be silly, it's not even in the cinema yet,' I tell him.

He gives me one of his knowing looks.

If I start on piracy, we'll only get sidetracked by *Peter Pan*. Disney's version, obviously.

'Ethan. What would you like to call the owl?'

'Hedwig,' he says.

'How about a name that's not already in a book,' I say brightly.

'Andy,' says Ethan.

'Andy?'

'It's my dad's name.'

He's on the verge of tears because I haven't let him have Hedwig. I can't make him think of another one.

'OK, so we've got an owl called Andy, and a monster called Dean, some boys and girls and The Mummy.'

'And a princess,' says Nikita.

'What would you like to call the princess?'

'Barbie,' she says, after some thought.

My mind is like a Radio 4 game show trying to concoct a narrative out of these disparate parts.

'I wonder what will happen in our story?'

I think I'll leave them with that thought. It's almost going-home time.

'The Mummy unleashes unspeakable evil and they all die,' says Dean.

'Push your chairs under your tables quietly, please, and get your coats. What's the matter, Gwyneth?'

'I don't want Barbie to die,' she says.

'She won't,' I assure her.

'How do you know?'

'Because it's a story. Anything we want can happen.'

The usual groups have collected in the playground to pick up their charges.

The Bash Street Mums, who smoke and allow their toddlers to peer through our windows and make faces at their siblings if I forget to put the blinds down for the last quarter of an hour of class. I'm always very nice to them because they can tend towards violence. Robbie's mother came to blows with Dean's just before Christmas after Dean cut the sleeves off Robbie's uniform sweatshirt. I felt slightly responsible because we'd been doing a Christmas collage for the hall and I'd asked them to use a variety of materials. A little further away stands a group of Neurotic

70

Mothers who always hand in very neat home-work and worry about SATS and next to them the Harassed Childminders (this is not a nanny sort of catchment) with babies sleeping in double pushchairs. Then there are the Embarrassed Dads whose bond of minority, unemployment and sports talk, is strong enough to overcome differences of colour and class. Collecting round the gates are the Suburban Martyrs, insufficiently acknowledged women of the PTA who spend the little free time they have devising and creating fund-raising activities for the school. To them we owe the Christmas Fayre, the Summer Fun Day and the annual Auction of Promises. 'Have Fun and Help to Raise Money for Your School!' shout the posters one of them gets her husband, who's got the local Kall Kwik franchise, to print off. The numbers that turn out barely make all the work worth it. But that doesn't put them off. In fact it drives them on to further feats of joyless self-sacrifice like craft evenings where they fill jam jars with bath salts and decorate bargain picture frames with sequins.

I know I should be more grateful.

The usual parents are late. I don't mind because it's stopped raining. Standing in the playground after school amid kids charging around pretending to be aeroplanes is a nice bit of the day, and a necessary transition between the random and relentless noise of the classroom to the measured tones of Radio 4.

I listen to Radio 4 on the way home because I feel I should at my age, and to have Capital on all the time would be like going into the newsagent's and buying *Hello! OK!* and *Heat* when you should get the *Guardian* with the Education Supplement. (To be honest, even when I do buy the *Guardian*, I only read *G2* magazine, which is really just like *Heat* in black and white with articles about single mothers so that they can print a picture of Liz Hurley.)

The playground is suddenly silent, as if a tornado has swept through and blown everything just beyond earshot, leaving only the memory of noise, and Ethan, who's got stuck at the top of the climbing frame and doesn't quite trust his flying ability.

'I've left Nimbus 2000 at home,' he explains as I jump him down.

I'm about to go to the office to look up his emergency numbers when his father arrives out of breath, and full of apologies.

'No problem,' I tell him. 'Ethan's a good boy.'

His father takes his lunch box with one hand and puts his other hand on the little boy's shoulder. Ethan moves towards him and they walk away as if he's stuck to the outside of his father's leg. If they were a photograph they could be the cover of a Tony Parsons novel, if he ever wanted a change from shoes.

'Guess what? I'm writing a book,' says Ethan.

CHAPTER 6

Beep Beep Beep Beep Beep Beeeeep!
'BBC Radio 4. The News at Four o'clock.'

'Statistics released today by a government think-tank show a further decline in manufacturing output . . .'

I'm not an expert on economics but whenever someone says that Britain is becoming a service economy, I know they're talking about my sister Joanna. Joanna employs a huge number of people to do all the chores that ordinary people do for themselves. Joanna has a cleaner and a gardener, which is not unusual for someone in her income bracket, but she also has someone who does her ironing, and a cook, who also does the shopping except when there's a dinner party, when Joanna gets in caterers. She has an interior designer, a garden designer, a closetologist (apparently it's someone who sorts out your cupboards twice a year. Everyone in New York has one), a real Chinese feng shui expert (must remember to take that piece of paper the minicab driver gave me because when I discovered it in my coat pocket stuck to a Starburst that had gone squishy, the restaurant he had recommended was written in Chinese characters). Then there's her personal trainer, personal shopper, Korean manicurist, hair stylist and colourist.

Joanna is not the sort of person who goes to the GP. She has a whole army of -ists and -icians and -paths on call, whether she's ill or not, as well as a chiropractor, an Indian head masseur, and, recently, a reiki master. I'm sure it won't be long before the plastic surgeons of Harley Street welcome a new customer, because the last time I saw her she greeted me by sticking her face very close to mine and saying, 'Tell me honestly. Chemical Peel or Botox?'

As soon as Joanna's got an idea in her head, she does something about it. She had only had three months trying for a baby when she lost patience with her body and went for IVF. The result was twins Cy and Ry, which was typical of her efficiency. Why have two pregnancies when you can do it in one? An instant family, as she put it, sitting up in bed after the Caesarian, in a bower of wisteria, with a simple vase of blue irises changed daily on the bedside table. Knowing they were boys, she had sorted the arrangements beforehand with her florist, because she'd find congenital deformity easier to look at than blue carnations.

Joanna is something very big in Third World

Debt. Her husband is something even bigger in venture capital. They own a house in Notting Hill which is worth something mad like two million pounds. When Joanna was interviewed in the *Financial Times* she attributed her success to an ability to delegate. 'Trust the people around you to do the job,' was her advice. The interviewer did not ask her what she did when the people around her let her down, but I expect she would have said something like, 'I always have backup ready,' by which she would have meant me.

The children used to have two nannies, one for day and one for night, but now they're at school, they just have an au pair, or me, depending on how badly Joanna has treated the au pair.

Would it be very old-fashioned of me to say that I don't think Cy and Ry would need to see their paediatrician, psychologist, neurologist or cranial osteopath if Joanna were to spend a little bit more time with them?

Time, says Joanna, is one luxury I do not have.

Actually it would be me being horrid. I have so many negative thoughts about Joanna that I am putty in her hands when it comes to baby-sitting because I feel so guilty. I love her very much too. And I adore the children, especially during the holidays. Midweek, they can be a bit wearing. The last thing you want when you've been dealing with children all day long is more children to deal with (see what I mean about being a mother?).

'. . . BBC Radio 4 News.'

'Which one am I, Cy or Ry?' says Ry.

'Ry. Why?'

'We're identical twins.'

'No, you're not. You have dark hair and Cy has fair. You don't even look very similar.'

'I mean our names!' says Ry.

'Oh I see,' I say. I did think it a little peculiar of Joanna myself, actually. Not just the rhyme, but the names themselves. Unless they see it written down, everyone thinks Cy is short for Simon, so Ry gets asked if he's short for Ryman. It creates problems they could do without. She wanted Cy because she thought it was the sort of name cool American artists from the 1950s were called. She had a bit of a shock when someone told her it was short for Cyril. I wonder what Ry's short for? I don't think she's dared ask.

Joanna, of course, doesn't know what it is like to have an odd name. Not that my name is particularly odd nowadays because it's in fashion, but I was the only one I knew when I was growing up, and I was Lydia Dustbin for so long, that in the end everyone forgot that it was a puerile joke, not my real name, and shortened it to Dusty, or Bin, if they didn't like me. Nobody has called me that for some time, thankfully, especially in the wake of September 11th.

'What do you say?' I ask Cy, when I've finally got them strapped in the back seats and eating Creme

76

Eggs, which they spotted as they went through the glove compartment.

'What?'

'I've come all this way across town to pick you up from school. I've given you chocolate. What do you say?'

'Were you going to eat them all yourself?'

'Not all at once,' I say.

'Four Creme Eggs all by yourself?'

The petrol station had an offer on a box of six.

'You might say thank you. Or sorry for hiding.'

'We didn't know it was going to be *you* picking us up,' says Cy, not unreasonably.

'You shouldn't treat Jana any differently from the way you treat me,' I tell them, all politically correct.

'It's not Jana any more,' says Ry.

'It's Nadia,' says Cy.

'Nadia, then.'

'But she hits us.'

'Have you told your mother that Nadia hits you?' I ask, feeling suddenly protective. They are just seven years old after all.

'Yes, but she doesn't believe us.'

The cruelty of my sister!

'Well, she'll believe me.'

Seven years old is not quite old enough to know about rear-view mirrors and the fact that you should leave your exchange of triumphant grins until your attentive aunt is concentrating on the road ahead.

'Only kidding,' I say.

'What?'

'Well, you were only kidding, weren't you?'

'How did you know?'

'I have eyes in the back of my head,' I tell him, which is a mistake because then they're both scrabbling through my ponytail.

Is there anything more indulgent than sitting on the toilet reading glossy magazines listening to the chink and murmur of a dinner party going on downstairs? It takes me back to my childhood, only then I was hiding in the only room with a lock, with a copy of *Jackie* and curls of vanilla-flavoured tobacco smoke from my parents' Christmas cheese and wine party drifting up through the bathroom floorboards.

Even then, Joanna was the sophisticated one who knew how to hand round prawn and mushroom vol-au-vents and little bowls of silverskin onions. I never seemed to have enough hands to offer the grown-ups a cocktail sausage and a napkin at the same time. Where are you supposed to put the bowl while you hand over the napkin? Not the arm of the sofa, anyway.

Nowadays, Joanna gets a waitress to hand round the canapés, but even as a guest, I can't do glass, handbag and food altogether, especially if there's dipping sauce involved. If I do manage without spattering a pair of shoes, I'm bound to be the one who's chatting away with a flake of filo glued to my top lip, or a porcini-speckled incisor.

Cy and Ry are in bed competing for a five-pounds-for-the-one-who-goes-to-sleep-first prize, which I think is worth it for the peace, and, frankly, it's less than two copies of *Harpers and Queen*, which I shall read sitting here for free, as well as *Tatler*, *Vogue* and *Elle Decoration* at no extra cost. Nevertheless, I can't get over the feeling that it's bad to bribe children. I put down the magazine guiltily and pretend to be trying to go, when Joanna comes into her *en suite* to tidy her hair.

If my life were a film, which it wouldn't be because nothing ever happens, Joanna would be played by Kristin Scott Thomas. She has a fragile English beauty that's hung on a skeleton of steel. But she's not just beautiful. She knows how to put on make-up without looking orange, how to spray perfume so that it follows her around rather than announcing her arrival like a liveried herald at a ball. She makes good, quick jokes, she has an instant grasp of the complexities of conversation, she can quote any number of poets, politicians, playwrights, and yet she still knows exactly when to defer to her husband or guests. If she was anyone else's sister, I would hate her. But since she is mine, I am just crazily proud of her.

I should tell you that Joanna is really good to me. She bought me my car. If it had been up to me,

I wouldn't have chosen one of the new Beetles in lime green, but that's mainly because I would have been pushed to afford a second-hand Corsa with nought-per-cent finance. She bought me my purple Power Mac and my fondant pink Smeg fridge. In fact, she's always buying me hugely expensive items in amusing colours.

I sometimes wonder if she missed out on childhood, or if I got a double dose, like I did chickenpox.

'That's it. I'm ringing Lester first thing tomorrow.'

Joanna's speaking to my reflection in the mirror whilst peering at the top of my head and miraculously applying a coat of mascara to her eyelashes without smudging.

'Lester?'

'My colourist. You're going grey!'

I touch the bit she is staring at, as if that will restore its colour.

'It's just Creme Egg.'

She looks at me oddly.

'Creme Egg?' she says, pronouncing the cream the French way, as if it's a new styling product.

'Doesn't matter,' I say, remembering that the boys are not supposed to have sugar.

'Come down when you're ready,' she tells me, as she wafts out of the bathroom. 'It will be nice for you to meet some new people.'

Joanna always manages to make it sound like she's doing me a favour when I babysit at zero minutes' notice.

'This is my sister Lydia!'

'Hello!'

'Drink?' Joanna's husband Vladimir asks.

Vladimir sounds Russian, but is in fact American. It's the sort of exotic but eminently sensible combination that Joanna goes for. They honeymooned in India, ferried from luxury hotel to Maharaja's palace in a white convertible Bentley. In the movie, Vladimir would be a younger Michael Douglas because of the Slav cheekbones and the sheer wealth. Even though I can see that Vladimir is perfect for Joanna, I don't really like him. He thinks I drink too much, which he wouldn't if he were a real Russian.

'Water, please. Sparkling, if you have it.'

It's worth it just to see the surprise in his slightly dangerous eyes.

'Lydia's simply brilliant with the boys,' Joanna says, as the guests look at me, waiting for my presence to be explained. 'I won't bore you all with our au pair nightmare . . .'

Cue three other couples relating their staff horror stories, which includes one couple who recently found their fourteen-year-old son giving cunnilingus to the French art student who does the ironing.

'While she was ironing?' I ask, trying to picture it.

The assembled company stares at me.

★　　★　　★

81

London dinner-party conversation is more like conjugating verbs than actually talking. It goes something like this:

My Croatian au pair has such hangovers she can't get the children up for school,

Your French ironing lady has sex with your son,

His Macedonian gardener digs up a rare camellia,

Her Jamaican cleaner polishes a stripped oak table,

Our Irish nanny expects us to pay for her abortion,

Your gay interior designers import the wrong stone flagging,

Their extraordinarily plain sister makes embarrassing social gaffes.

'Greg Andrews.' The very tall and very bald man who I am seated next to at dinner offers me his hand to shake. 'What do you do?'

'I'm a belly dancer.'

'Where do you dance?'

'Actually I'm a teacher, but when you say you're a teacher people say how interesting and then turn away.'

He's looking at me as if waiting for a clue.

'Wait a minute. You teach belly dancing?'

'I have signed up for an Egyptian dancing course . . .'

'In Cairo?'

'Sudbury Hill.'

I wonder when his hair fell out. Did he just wake up one morning and there it was on the pillow, or did it thin gradually? When he got to the last strand or two, did he just pull them out decisively, or did he let them linger like a fond memory?

I should ask him what he does, but he's clearly Canadian with his soft accent and his name. I once went out with a Canadian called Bernard, but half his ice hockey team were called Greg.

'What do you do, Lydia?' says the anorexic woman across the table.

'I'm a teacher.'

'How interesting.'

'We're very lucky in British Columbia—' Greg begins.

'Oh,' I hold up my hand, as if I've heard a noise. 'That sounds like one of the boys. Excuse me.'

My napkin falls to the floor of course. Greg is all solicitousness replacing it by my plate.

I am the subject of loud, fond conversation for the length of the first flight of stairs.

'Aren't you lucky, Joanna?'

'We are SO lucky.'

'She's marvellous.'

'I bet she's wonderful with children.'

'Oh, she is . . .'

Of course, neither Cy nor Ry has stirred. When

83

seven-year-old boys finally go to sleep, they really do go to sleep, not that Joanna or Vladimir would know that. They're breathing so quietly I test their foreheads to check that they're still warm, and pull up their duvets. Then I resume my position on the toilet with the glossies until I hear the guests taking their leave.

'Do say goodbye to Linda for us.'

'I will!'

Sound of door closing.

I can't hear Joanna and Vlad sigh with satisfaction as they stand for a moment with their backs pressed against the front door surveying their immaculately minimalist hall, now empty of people as well as furniture and coat hooks, but I do get the beginning of the post mortem.

'Did he say anything about the second tranche to you?'

'No, but I did wonder about "technical glitches" . . .'

They both laugh with a mean abandon that sounds quite different from the murmurings of civilized amusement which have drifted up the stairs accompanying the aroma of ground coffee.

I wonder if Baldy realizes that his finances are about to be frozen while Vladimir renegotiates the deal. Is he now anxiously asking his stick-thin partner in the back of the taxi, 'Do you think we've bought some time?'

I can't seem to muster any sympathy for him.

I went off Canadians after Bernard, who pronounced it BerNARD as if plain Bernud wasn't bad enough.

Vladimir calls it restructuring the loan. You have to be a euphemism expert in finance. I wonder if he knows that they call him The Impaler. Course he must. He's probably proud of it, like Joanna was when she told me with an excited little giggle which made me wonder slightly about their sex life.

The traffic lights are red at Acton and the bloke in the Audi next to me is talking on his mobile phone. He's confident looking. The sort of person who uses a mobile phone for a chat, not just to let his wife know he's going to be late. Is he speaking to his wife? I wonder. He's talking through a big pleased-with-himself smile which makes me suspect there's a mistress somewhere in town, whom he's left lying in scarlet silk sheets, still smelling of him, whispering down the phone about the things they've done together. Or the things they'll do next time. Is it her flat, I wonder, or his? The Audi is a convertible model which means he must have money, doesn't it? Not that you can necessarily tell anything from a car.

His eyes meet mine for a fraction of a second, catching me watching him. I shrug my shoulders trying to indicate that I know I am not the sort of person who normally drives a lime-green Beetle. He frowns, looks back to the road, shoves the gearstick into first, revs the engine slightly as the cross traffic stops, then chucks the phone down on the seat next to him. He's impatient to be gone. A lime-green Beetle is the sort of car his mistress would drive. Perhaps she actually does and I am an unwanted reminder of his double life.

I stick my tongue out as his car cuts in front of me as three lanes go to two. For all he knows, I could have a lover too, or several. I could be a dominatrix with a sports bag full of leather and whips in the irritatingly small boot of this car. Or, I could be a private midwife dashing through the night to get to a home birth. Or an A&E consultant called in to perform an emergency, life-saving operation. Lime green's not a colour you'd automatically associate with the medical profession, but my usual work car might be in for a service.

I could be a very important person.

Actually, he probably wasn't thinking anything at all.

Differences between men and women:
2. Back stories.

This is why I would normally rather go out for an Indian meal with Michelle than Andy. With Andy, there is a little discussion about whether raita comes gratis with the poppadoms, and whether we're hungry enough for an aloo gobi on the side. Then Andy starts off his pint of Kingfisher while it's still on the table, and we generally test each other on quiz questions. When we come out of the restaurant, the only comment Andy is likely to make is, 'Nice, but not cheap,' or 'What does Taj Mahal mean in Hindi?'

With Michelle, we order everything we fancy, chat non-stop, get quite drunk, eat coconut ice cream out of a coconut half shell, which neither of us actually likes very much, but you need something sweet after all that lager. When we leave the restaurant, after much hilarity with the waiter trying to get our arms into the sleeves of our coats, we talk all the way home about the history of the couple at the next table whose conversation we have been listening in to whilst conducting an increasingly loud one of our own.

Some of the semi-detached suburban houses lining the dual carriageway still have lights on. I wonder about all the lives that are going on behind all the net curtains. Are they all as complicated and sordid as those of the people Michelle and I always seem to end up sitting next to? Is that how normal lives are? Is my life one of the most boring in the world? Do women who sit next to me and Andy in Indian restaurants travel home frustrated, as if they've been to see a romantic comedy at the cinema which did not make them laugh or cry?

If my life were a film, who would play me?

This is what I mean about having moments when you wonder what it's all about.

I don't know why it always gets me on the A40.

CHAPTER 7

My mother (who is called Grace, a name which is very much back in fashion), is in a sulk because she was trying to pretend that it's her first time in the bridal department of Debenhams, but the assistant gave it away with 'Oh! Hello again!' after the initial 'Do you need any help?'

Also, I don't like any of the dresses she has picked out.

I don't like white or ivory or cream. Too sacrificial. I don't like anything with lace or little pearls on it. There's nothing worse than the metallic grey colour they call oyster. Even white is better than the wedding dresses designed for women who don't like white. I'm talking crimson velvet bodice and white satin skirt, or gold all over, or, worse, pink.

I don't, actually, like long dresses at all because they remind me of those paralympic fairy dolls you stick on the top of the Christmas tree who have a normal plastic torso and a paper cone covered with net instead of legs. I have quite good legs. They are my best feature. The only time Joanna is ever envious of me is when I'm wearing pedal-pushers. But you cannot wear pedal-pushers to a wedding, or even a miniskirt. I could just about get away with it from the waist down. But you can't wear a mini with a thirty-six-year-old face, unless you're Liz Hurley. Not that she, of course, is getting married.

'I think I'll just buy a nice dress from Monsoon,' I say. 'Something bright,' I add, to show willing.

'Don't know why you're bothering to get married at all,' says my mother.

'Marriage is not just about dresses,' I say.

'I just want you to look lovely,' she says, despairingly.

'But even if I have half a mile of tulle swathed around me and a headdress of real diamonds, I am not going to look lovely, am I? Let's face it,' I tell her in the café over a cheese scone that's so dry it crumbles to a heap of sand on my plate. 'What I'll look like is someone trying to look lovely, and everyone will say, "Doesn't she look beautiful?" but feel sorry for me behind my back. The tiara will make it worse.'

'I wish you weren't so hard on yourself,' Mum says.

She makes it sound like a criticism. My mother makes most things sound like a criticism. If I volunteer to go and see her on a Sunday, she'll say, 'All right then, but I can't cook you lunch,' as if the visit is for my benefit not hers.

Now she's implying that it's my fault that I'm

not pretty because I'm too hard on myself, when in fact it must be something to do with her. She is pretty, but she gave all her pretty genes to Joanna, although to be fair, she couldn't have known that she was going to have another girl later.

'I'm only being honest,' I reply, in that terse, uptight way I have only with her.

'You've got a lovely smile,' she says. 'If only you'd let us see it occasionally.'

'I do smile,' I tell her, crossly.

Just not with you.

My mobile rings.

'Lyd! Hi! Look, dashing, but I've had a word with—'

My sister makes a noise that's halfway between a sneeze and being stabbed with something very sharp.

'Are you all right?'

'Fine. Busy. She says that the characters mean "Woman reckless with money . . ."'

The penny drops. Joanna has shown my minicab card with the Chinese characters to her feng shui expert, whose name most people would pronounce Jung Choo, but Joanna is the sort of person who says words in foreign languages properly. She always puts on a real French accent for *fait accompli* for instance, and *duvet*.

'. . . which is an odd name for a restaurant . . .'

That's the last time I tip a minicab driver.

'Shall I have Kim do a search for synonyms?'

'No. It's fine. Joanna?'

'Yes?'

She's still there, but impatient.

'Do you know a really good Chinese restaurant?'

She has a quick word with someone in the background.

'Somewhere called Mr Kong.'

'That was Joanna,' I say to my mother.

'How is she?'

'Busy.'

'Joanna's always busy. Usually I talk to her nice young man,' says Mum. She's always preferred Joanna.

I say I've got a headache rather than face John Lewis in Brent Cross. And then I feel guilty, even though she says she's got plenty to do. I drop her home and she doesn't invite me in. I can see from the way she hurries up the front garden path that she's as eager to be rid of me as I am of her.

At the front door, she turns and gives me a forlorn little wave of disappointment or dismissal. It's hard to tell at this distance.

As usual, our outing has left me feeling unhappier than I was when we met. The lid of my Pandora's box of insecurities has not quite been prised off, but it has been tampered with, and uncomfortable questions, sensing a way out, are tapping away inside.

Is my general hatred of wedding dresses significant in a non-sartorial way?

Is marriage just something else in a long line of things that I think will make me happy, but ultimately disappoint? I'm thinking of the Tinkerbell outfit when I was six, and the denim jacket when I was sixteen.

In my early thirties I thought getting a boyfriend would do it.

My advert read:

Not very attractive woman, good legs, seeks man for fun and games. No Canadians.

I got fifty-seven replies, two of them, oddly, from women.

Michelle started calling it Soul Destroyers after five of the six guys I arranged to meet were disasters (apart from the one who pretended not to see me, there were three serious nerds and one recovering alcoholic, which I felt should have been mentioned even though we were only meeting in Starbucks).

If it hadn't been for Andy, I would have had to do another ad ruling out PlayStation 2.

When we started seeing each other regularly I realized that having a boyfriend wasn't enough after all. It had to be marriage. Unless it was marriage, then I would always be thinking, If we're not getting married, when's it going to end? And How old do you have to be before you're an old maid? That sort of thing.

Michelle advised me to leave brochures for Sandals resorts lying casually around my living room, but it did sound a bit precipitate, when Andy was idly flipping through, to start going on about weddings on a beach wearing nothing but your swimming trunks. We'd just won a couples' quiz in Pinner and I think it was the euphoria which made me think that avoiding the expense of a morning suit would clinch it for him.

We split up for a while. To be fair on Andy, he wasn't afraid of commitment in the unspecific lager advert sort of way that a lot of men are. He was wary because his first marriage to a hairdresser called Tina ended after eighteen months when he was twenty-four. I think this is why he's always been suspicious of Michelle.

I'd be lying if I said that his divorced status wasn't one of his major attractions.

How desperate would you have to be to sleep with a man in his forties who hadn't been married at least once? I've done it and believe me, desperate.

I missed the quizzes and the sex, but most of all I missed having a boyfriend. You can only do 'I've just split up with someone', for so long.

I was on the point of Soul Mates again, or even the one in the *Financial Times* (only because it's called Affairs of the Heart, which sounds like one of those great American funny weepy women's movies starring Sissy Spacek), when Michelle bumped into Andy in Safeway late-night shopping one Friday and he asked after me. Being my best friend, she told him that there was someone I seemed to be getting quite serious about, and the next day, he arrived at the door with a mixed bouquet from a bucket outside the garage and a proposal. Would I like to go to the quiz?

'I have another question for you,' he said in bed afterwards.

Michelle says I should have phoned a friend before giving him my answer.

It wasn't what she had intended when she'd chatted to him by the 3-for-2 promotion.

I ring my mother when I get home.
   'Feeling better?' she says.
   'Yes, sorry about that.'
   There's a long silence.
   'I'm online . . .' she finally says.
   'Oh. OK. Bye then.'
   'Lydia . . .'
   'Yes?'
   'Anything wrong?'
   'NO, I'M FINE!'
   I was until I rang you.

What does she find to chat about all day on the Internet? And who to? Does she know that there are a lot of weirdos out there who pretend to be younger than they are? If they think they're talking to a well-off widow, which she probably makes out she is, they might pretend to be older than they are. There are even people these days, apparently, who hack into your e-mail and then become friends by pretending to have an uncannily similar life to yours. Which is why Andy is always changing his e-mail address, although, frankly, there's not a lot of mileage you could get out of 'Quiz? Usual time? Usual place?'

She's old enough to look after herself, anyway.

But for how long?

When my mother asks why I'm so grumpy, I sometimes want to tell her, it's because you're getting old. And realistically, let's face it, you won't be able to live in your three-bed semi on your own for ever, silver surfing all day and going to the bridge club three evenings a week. And what is going to happen then? It's going to be me, isn't it? I'm the one who's going to have to look after you, and it's not that I can't cope with incontinence, it's just that old people get so unreasonable and negative, and you're negative at the best of times. And if you want to know, I find the prospect ABSOLUTELY TERRIFYING, as a matter of fact.

Of course I say nothing and just seethe silently.

CHAPTER 8

'Why did you choose this place?' Andy asks, sucking the top off his pint.

Why does he have to have Carlsberg anyway, when the cool media types at the next table, one of whom looks familiar, are drinking Tsing Tao from the bottle?

'The other evening when I got a minicab back from Michelle's . . .'

The minicab anecdote is quite funny in retrospect, Richard Batty thought so, and the media types would enjoy it too, I think.

They're all catching up on media gossip. The one I vaguely recognize knows the *maître d'* well enough to call him by his first name, which is apparently Edwin. A surprisingly un-Chinese name.

'I had this Chinese driver . . .' I continue, before realizing that if I'm not careful I'm going to have to reveal that I was drunk.

'. . . and it reminded me that we hadn't had Chinese for a while.'

'Good plan,' says Andy.

Newsnight. That's where I know her from. Or is it GMTV? I'm never properly awake for either.

'What does Hong Kong mean?' Andy's looking at the menu.

'Fragrant Harbour.'

'Correct.'

I sip my Jasmine tea.

'I've always wanted to go there,' I say.

I've never actually thought about going to Hong Kong until now, but it's something grown-up people say, isn't it?

Somebody the media types know is bonking a junior minister.

'I'm sworn to secrecy,' says media woman.

She smiles at me as I try to look away without her noticing. I think she's used to having people recognize her. I'm tempted to jump in with my suggestion as her friends start to guess.

'Name of the last Governor's wife?' Andy asks.

'Lavender Patten.'

Now I've missed the minister's name.

Next door, they're all saying, 'No!'

'Amazing,' says Andy.

For a moment, I think he's heard and is about to tell me.

'I knew it was something flowery, but I would have guessed Daffodil,' he says.

What cool media people eat is scallops on the half shell, prawn and coriander rolls, Emperor chicken. yam and aubergine fritters, and some off-menu greens I don't recognize.

We've stuck with the quarter crispy aromatic duck and things we know.

'You get what you pay for,' Andy says appreciatively, which makes me feel better about the expense of it, which he seemed to disapprove of at first, even though I'm the one who's paying.

Probably seakale, or something. What is seakale anyway?

'They're asking for newly weds on *Millionaire*,' I tell Andy.

'Are they?'

'Shall we try?'

Apparently if the Secretary of State for Transport makes one more gaffe, he's out. It's official.

'We're not married yet,' says Andy.

'It includes people who are going to be married by the date of the programme.'

The media woman thinks he might survive longer because he's such a friend of Tony Blair.

'It must increase the odds of getting through, mustn't it? How many newly wed couples can there be per season?'

That appeals to the player in Andy.

'Go on then,' he says, picking up his beer and clinking it against my handleless china cup.

Shattered glass and beer all over our main course.

Edwin's very nice about it, even though I don't think you're supposed to have Sweet and Sour Pork in a place like this.

★   ★   ★

98

'I am Don Alfonso, by the way,' says Andy, when they've changed the tablecloth.

'Remind me which one that is?'

Best to be circumspect. He gets annoyed when I confuse a tenor with a baritone. I think baritones have a bit of a chip on their shoulder because of the Three You Know Whats which we're not allowed to mention in Andy's presence, let alone play on the car CD.

'It is, of course, a bass part,' says Andy. 'But I have the lowest register of the bass baritones . . .'

'You'll be ideal then.'

'Not ideal, by any stroke of the imagination,' says Andy, with a little smile.

The *Gazette* commented of Andy's performance in *HMS Pinafore* that he attacked the role with gusto.

'Isn't it stretch? Any stretch of the imagination?' I ask.

One of the media types is telling them all about a survival course he's been on where they pretend to kidnap you.

'Basically, the plot goes like this . . .'

I nod at Andy as if I'm interested.

'Don Alfonso sets out to test the fickleness of women. He lays a bet with Guglielmo and Ferrando . . .'

I shall have to ask Joanna for the correct pronunciation.

'I was elected leader of my group,' says the media type who's got his back to me, 'but unfortunately my strategy led to us all being summarily executed!'

Laughter from the media table.

'. . . they disguise themselves,' says Andy.

'As what?'

'Albanians.'

'You'll have to get a badly fitting leather jacket.'

'Eighteenth-century version,' says Andy.

'I'm not buying you any more tights,' I tell him.

I sometimes wonder about Andy. It's not the first pair.

Even if I haven't spent the evening with him, I can tell how much Andy has had to drink by how randy he is. One pint makes him wink occasionally, two and his legs press against mine on the tube back, three, his arm goes round my shoulder and four, he's trying to touch my breast under cover of my jacket, too drunk to realize that it's quite obvious what he's doing to the man in a suit sitting opposite who's talking on his mobile phone.

'There's something wrong with the tube . . . again,' Suit's saying. 'I'm on a semi-fast to Watford now, but I had to wait an age.'

I know for a fact that this isn't true. I watched several trains leave Baker Street as I waited for Andy to emerge from the Gents.

Suit sees me glaring at him and retaliates by staring at my chest. I'm wearing a stretchy pink v-neck by Jasper Conran at Debenhams, and I can tell without looking down that one of my nipples is erect, and one is still soft, and I'm a bit old to get away with that sort of asymmetry in public.

Is this going to be my life?

Andy's fallen asleep, and I'm lying wide awake and sober next to him. We've had good sex. He even said I love you when he came, which was nice, although when he doesn't open his eyes I always suspect he's thinking about someone else.

Is this how it's going to be?

My car is outside and I have not drunk alcohol. I could go home.

I'm feeling less and less ready for sleep, and in the pitch darkness of Andy's bedroom, the question of whether I should go home is mutating from simple choice to existential dilemma.

What does it say about me that I don't want to wake up next to my lover on Sunday morning?

What does it say about our relationship?

Would it be worse to be lying alone in bed on Saturday night, free, independent, with the curtains open, but without sex or marriage?

Old maid, unmarried daughter, spinster of the parish?

On balance, yes it would be worse.

I look at Andy's sleeping face, and I feel warm and protective towards him. Men look so vulnerable asleep, and he's in the snore-free bit of the cycle.

But I'm still going to go home.

★   ★   ★

There's a tanker discharging in the all-night petrol station, which means they're not allowed to serve customers.

Since when was a Creme Egg a safety risk? It's not as if I'm asking for matches, or even cigarettes.

Last summer they had a proper hold-up with a gun. I later recognized the perpetrator from his photo in the *Gazette* as one of the first boys I ever taught. He only got eighteen months because he'd nicked the gun from Woolworths (it was silver with a red handle which must have made him look about as terrifying as the Milky Bar Kid, but it's difficult to see at night). He's served his sentence now, because I saw him the other day behind the counter in a kebab shop. I suppose that counts as rehabilitation.

The all-night teenager refuses to meet my eyes through the window but that may be because I have shouted and there is actually a sound link.

'I'd settle for a Crunchie!'

No sense of humour either.

The services on the A40 have run out of Creme Eggs, even though it's over two months to Easter, which must mean that it's not just me. I choose a Bounty ice cream instead, and the coconut reminds me that there is a bottle of Malibu standing on the small pine cupboard next to my television.

★   ★   ★

102

Seems a shame to open it for just a glass. And I don't really like the taste.

I have created a new liqueur coffee!

How to make a Caribbean coffee:

1. Make a mug of black coffee
2. Add a good slug of Malibu
3. Float cream on top if you have any.

Unfortunately, I don't. But it tastes all right without, especially after Chinese. Actually, I'm surprised Chinese restaurants don't pay more attention to the desserts. It's always lychees or banana in batter. If they did Caribbean coffee instead of those orange wedges which are refreshing but difficult to extract from between your teeth, they'd be onto a real money-spinner. I might suggest it to Edwin next time.

Is Malibu actually in the Caribbean?
Think it's actually in Los Angeles, so better call it Californian Coffee. Which sounds healthy and sunshiny and not very alcoholic, although Americans tend not to be very keen on caffeine.

Oops! I remember telling one of the Suburban Martyrs that I had a bottle of Malibu for their next tombola as a gesture of goodwill when none of the dates proposed for the PTA meeting suited me.

Have to buy another one anyway, so doesn't matter if I drink a little more, but just half a mug this time.

What's a respectable length of time for a New Year's Resolution? Probably forty days, which I've almost managed. Or is that Lent? Logically, New Year must officially be over by Lent because you've got to find something else to give up then.

Not that Andy actually appears particularly bothered.

Probably suspects I've broken it.

Oh ye of little faith!

Or he's trying to lull me into a false sense of security, like he did with the swear box. Then presented me with a bill for £14.20.

Am I an alcoholic? Did I drive home from Andy's because I had a subconscious desire to drink my bottle of Malibu?

Not that I'm going to drink the whole bottle.

It only looks quite a long way down because the neck bit of the bottle is thinner.

I can't be, because otherwise I would have drunk it before.

Anyway, we all need to relax once in a while. It's lovely just lying here on my nice Laura Ashley sofa, in my knocked-through living room with my Jeff Banks' carpet that looks like sisal but is much easier on bare feet, and the stencilled dado rail

I did myself. Only one wall. It's not as easy as it looks on *Changing Rooms*.

In Malibu veritas! Or is it *in Malibo*? I've forgotten almost all of my O level Latin.
   Eureka!
   Which is Greek I think.
   The answer to my existential dilemma actually is nothing to do with whether I can stand to be married to Andy for the rest of my life, it's about being worried about giving up my nice home! I feel secure here. I know where the floor creaks in the bathroom.
   But – here's a thought – what if Andy were to cash in all his paper? Perhaps we could afford to buy another place altogether, and I could keep this place as a second home? A huge percentage of people our age have them now, although Joanna's got three, which makes a difference to the statistics.

Caribbean Coffee would probably have Bacardi in it, which I don't think would work.
   Anyway, haven't got any Bacardi.
   Actually, Malibu has Bacardi in it. Never read the label before. So is it in California or Jamaica?
   Very confusing.

How about Malibu for our honeymoon? California or Jamaica. Doesn't matter to me. Or one week in Malibu, one week in the Rockies, or the Grand Canyon, if we have to compromise.
   Where is Las Vegas anyway? We could try

gambling. With a strictly limited amount of cash. Have to leave our credit cards behind although I'm usually lucky the first time I play a game.

I could be a mascot for some rich bloke who's shooting craps. Can it really be as simple as throwing a seven?

He might offer Andy a million dollars to sleep with me!

My mouse glides over:
  Bush: Axis of Evil
and clicks on:
  The Bottom Line

  She's got the most talked about derriere in the world and there's plenty of speculation about how she's achieved it . . .

Why am I sitting at my computer?
  How did I get here?

Mmmm. Malibu Coffee. That's the best name for it. Why didn't I think of that before?

There are no new messages in my Inbox.

  Click on COMPOSE.

Dear Andy,

Here's a quiz for you.

If Robert Redford offered you a million dollars to sleep with me would you:

a) take the money and disappear?
b) share the money with me?
c) refuse?

My anxieties about our forthcoming rather depend on you furnishing a response to this question. There may be a d) I haven't thought of. Oh yes!

d) give me all the money? Not really!

My position is that a million dollars is a lot, although not enough to buy a house in Notting Hill. And there is the question of his skin which has gone rather odd as he's got older. I don't know why he hasn't had a chemical peel.

By the way is a million more or less than you are worth on paper? I think I ought to know. If only for legal reasons. We could have a prenup, if you want, although frankly I'm finding it difficult enough to choose a dress.

Whilst we're on the subject, do you act-ually love me, or do you just say it:

a) after sex?
b) when you're about to come?
c) after sex (post, as opposed to wanting it)?

I'll tell you why it matters. It matters because we've never talked about children, which would be normal, wouldn't it?

Certainly something to think about.

What about Malibu for our honeymoon?

I've invented a new liqueur coffee, by the way.

Sometimes you need the clarity that alcohol can bring. I would never use the word furnish normally.

Anyway, New Year must end in time for Lent.

Lxxxxxxxxxxxxxxxxxxxxxxxxxxxxxxxxxxxxxxxxxxxx

Yes, that seems to set it all out in a not-too-heavy way.

Click SEND.

CHAPTER 9

Joanna is receiving the Whitbread Prize for a book she has written in her spare time, and I am at the reception, which is taking place in the school hall. Everyone keeps asking me if I'm proud of her, and of course I am, but I can't seem to remember the title, and every sentence I utter involves having to allude to it. Finally, the cover flashes up on stage behind the interview she is doing with Carol Smillie, I see that the book is called simply *How to Be*.

Of course it is.

I wake up slumped on my keyboard with the sensation that I have very definitely done something I should not have done.

There is one new entry in my Sent Messages Box.

Malibu

Maybe it's not as bad I think.

I open it and read it through.

It is in fact worse.

There are no new messages in my Inbox. Yet.

If only I knew a computer expert, I could hack into

Andy's Inbox and delete **Malibu**, but Andy is the only computer expert I know.

'Promise me one thing,' says Michelle.

'What?'

'Never click on SEND when you're drunk. You should have had that as your New Year's Resolution. When you're pissed you have this uncontrollable urge to tell it like it is, don't you? You just can't stop yourself.'

'Better than getting pregnant every time, though.'

Not very nice, I know, but she's not exactly being sensitive and I'm regretting showing her my Sent Messages.

'I didn't realize you were so bothered about the question of children,' she says, reading through *Malibu* again.

'I'm not.'

I sign out and shut down.

For Lent I am going to give up discussing my personal life with Michelle. She is worse than my mother. And she's staring at me now with a concerned look, trying to make me crack and contradict myself.

'Do you want to see Michaela's ultrasound?' Michelle asks.

'Go on then.'

It's like one of those pictures from the Hubble telescope which looks like a bit of cloud but tells scientists that the universe is dramatically older than they thought.

'Beautiful, isn't she?'

'Does she know it's a girl?'

'Well, you can't see anything, can you?'

'No.'

I can't really make out which bit is the head, let alone whether there's a penis.

'They're ninety-nine per cent certain. And shall I tell you a secret?'

'Don't if it's Michaela's secret . . .'

'She's going to call her Lydia!'

'No!'

'Only as a second name.'

I stare at the black-and-white Polaroid, feeling soppy about my little namesake. A tear comes to my eye, which I blink away so that Michelle won't see.

'By the way, Malibu Coffee's been around ages,' says Michelle.

CHAPTER 10

'If I have two apples and two oranges in my fruit bowl how many pieces of fruit do I have altogether? Yes, Nikita?'

'What's a fruit bowl?'

'Dean. Can you tell us all the answer to Nikita's question because we can't all hear what you're saying?'

'Five.'

'Why five?'

'Because you told us the other day. Five pieces of fruit, you said.'

I'd give a lot for them all to be this quick. But not as much as I'd give to keep Personal, Social and Health Education out of the Numeracy Hour. We have ground to cover.

'Well remembered. We should all eat five portions of fruit or vegetables every day. What's the matter, Gwyneth?'

'My mum only put one apple in my lunch box.'

'That's fine.'

'I'm supposed to have five!'

'One apple is absolutely fine at lunchtime. In

112

fact, anyone who has an apple in their lunch box can write their name in the Happy Book. After lunch!' I say, as there's movement in the lunch box trolley direction.

The Happy Book is an exercise book with an orange cover which says Happy Book on the front in letters I cut out of different coloured paper. They can write their name if I say so. It is an honour I bestow rarely, or when I'm desperate. Simple thing, but it does magically make them happy and means they have to practise their handwriting. At the end of the week we count up the names and the person with the most gets a sticker saying Terrific!

'What about a banana?' Robbie asks.

'Celine Dion goes into a bar. The bartender says, "Why the long face?"' says New Andy, biting into his double cheeseburger.

I smile weakly.

'What's up?'

There's a little smear of ketchup at the side of his mouth that I would love to lick away. But I don't tell him that.

'Hungover.'

'I never drink on Sunday evenings,' he says.

'Nor do I. This was Saturday.'

'Wow. A two-day hangover.'

'You'll understand when you get to my age,' I tell him.

Let's have it out there. I'm too old for him. And

that's before we even start on league tables. And I am spoken for anyway.

We've both gone for the vegetarian option, which I'm counting as two portions of vegetables. I asked Richard Batty about chips but apparently they're not eligible, which seems a bit mean of the Government, since it's the only vegetable most of the kids ever see.

The roasted-vegetable lasagne has been heated up in a microwave. The top, which is so hard it's as if the pasta hasn't been cooked, eventually yields up a bubbling interior.

My dilemma is whether to keep the blisteringly hot slice of courgette in my mouth, or spit it into a tissue.

Unfortunately I do not have a tissue.

Richard offers the saucer from his teacup.

The three of us look at the toothmarked vegetable circle like the thing in *Alien*. Richard pours me a glass of water, but the damage is done. There are soft loose bits of skin in the roof of my mouth and my taste buds have been destroyed.

'I'm not supposed to be eating dairy or wheat, anyway,' I say, dismally tapping the unforgiving crust with my fork.

'Food intolerance?' asks New Andy.

'Possibly,' I say, because detox sounds as if I want to look like Carol Vorderman. I've never really got it with Carol Vorderman. So, she can do sums. I think it's a male thing.

'Can I get you something else?' Richard's asking.

'No thanks.'

I'm sore now, and grumpy, like a child with a grazed knee after the initial thrill of showing everyone the blood has worn off.

I wish there was a Happy Book for grown-ups.

I have drawn rough approximations of an owl, a boy, a girl, a princess, a monster and the Mummy on the whiteboard.

'So, we've got our characters. The next thing we need to think about is what happens. What happens? Does anyone have any ideas? Yes, Geri?'

'Forgotten.'

I am going to have to make suggestions.

'Sometimes it helps to ask a question. A question like what if . . . ? What if one of our characters were to meet another one of our characters . . . yes, Gwyneth?'

'What if Barbie meets a handsome prince?'

'There isn't a handsome prince,' Geri points out.

'Nicole?'

'What if Barbie meets the Mummy?'

I doubt we'll sell it to Nora Ephron but it will do.

'What happens when the beautiful princess Barbie meets the ugly old Mummy?'

'Do they become secret lovers?' asks Ethan.

He must have heard it on television. Normally the only secrets Ethan knows about are wishes, and he can never keep those to himself.

'That's girls' stuff,' Dean sneers.

'So what do you think happened, Dean?'

'The Mummy smashed through the wall of Barbie's house, and Barbie was still in bed and then . . .'

I'm on the edge of my seat wondering at which point to censor. He can certainly hold an audience.

'. . . and the Mummy says, "Get up, you lazy cow, because you've got to help me save the world," because, guess what?'

'What?'

'He wasn't really the Mummy, he was really a Power Ranger but, guess what? He was disguised as the Ultimate Killer so all the baddies in the world would be tricked and he went up against the monsters and the world was saved.'

'Wow! What an exciting story! Did everyone like Dean's story?'

General awed nodding.

'Miss?'

'Yes, Gwyneth?'

'I'm frightened.'

Conveying atmosphere is really more Year Two, than Year One. We're making marvellous progress.

Beep Beep Beep Beep Beep Beeeeep!

'BBC Radio 4. The News at Five o'clock.'

'Aid agencies estimate that two million people may die . . .'

It's always two million, isn't it, whether it's starving children in Malawi, or a four-bed house in Notting Hill? Two million for the new BBC corporate branding, two million for each of this week's Lottery jackpot winners.

I wonder whether I'd be happy if I won two million pounds. Obviously it would make a significant difference to a teacher's salary, but would it be enough? I wouldn't be able to buy a house in Notting Hill, for instance, not when you take stamp duty into account. But would I really want one?

I could certainly travel for a few years. I've always wanted to travel, but I've never had the bottle, or money, to do it alone. But with only two million, I'd still need to work at the end of it, unless I got to grips with a Personal Pension Plan, or an Investment Portfolio or something like that. I've never really understood how those things work, and there comes a time when you're a bit old to ask.

Sounds ungrateful, I know, but I think it would have to be five million if I really wanted to take the money worries out of my life.

Would I actually feel any different though?

Is Elton John happy?

And why, with all that money, can he still not get a wig that looks natural or just accept that he's bald?

'. . . It's two minutes past five.' I think it's the voice. Exactly the same tone for the collapse of the World Trade Center as for the Queen's Jubilee concert tickets. During the beeps I get myself revved up for what's happening in the world. And then my mind wanders.

CHAPTER 11

My Inbox has three new messages.

Lose weight AND save money!

Don't put off a promising career!

Re: Malibu

I delete the first two before opening Andy's inevitable reply.

L. I ignored the first two e-mails, but after this last one I feel it's only fair to tell you that you're sending these to the wrong person. Sorry to finish our relationship like this.
   With very best wishes for the future. A.

Very best wishes?
   Fair?
   Finish our relationship?
   He may be good at computers, but nobody

is allowed to call off an engagement by e-mail. No way.

Click REPLY.

Oh come on! One e-mail and that's it? L
Click SEND.

A new message appears almost instantly.

L. Perhaps I didn't make it clear enough. I am the wrong person. But you cannot marry him. A

Is it a joke, or has he been drinking? Neither option likely at this time of day.

Much more likely to have been something I said or did at our last meeting.

It was a good meal.

I paid.

We had sex afterwards.

It wasn't even my fault about the broken glass this time.

Was it the tights? L

Look, I'm trying to end this gracefully, but you're making it difficult now. Good-bye. AX

I wonder if he means anything by the kiss, or whether it's just automatic. Or perhaps he feels sorry for me.

'Shell?'

'Lyd, I'm halfway through a Reviving Facial.'

'Listen to this.'

I read both e-mails.

'Sounds like he's chucking you.'

'That's what I thought.'

'Sorry.'

'You don't sound at all sorry,' I snap.

'Don't blame yourself.'

'Why didn't he have the balls to tell me face to face?'

'Plenty more fish, Lyd. Look, I'm sorry, I really am, but I'm exfoliating.'

Michelle is an expert on Visage and Revitalift and any number of age-reducing serums with V in the name. Who makes up the names? And what are Activa Cell and Q10? Did I miss something, or did they just appear one day, and get accepted into common parlance as if they'd always been there, like Vitamin C?

We don't talk about wrinkles, say the adverts, but Michelle spends her whole day talking about wrinkles. I sometimes catch her zooming in on my neck, although since I've always followed her beauty regimes, I shouldn't have to worry. But it doesn't work like that. Cosmetics are addictive. Once you start, you can't go back to soap and water, never. Nobody tells you that bit.

Not that it matters now, because I have been dumped.

If I had known how to use concealer properly, would it have made any difference?

I'm in the corner shop for the *Guardian* and the *Evening Standard* and a bar of chocolate to cheer me up.

OK! has Posh on the cover so I buy that too and Mr Patel has got an offer on New Flavour Cranberry Breezers and cranberry is very purifying.

If I'd kept to the detox, would it have made a difference?

I re-read the exchange of e-mails.

Wrong person?

I wonder if Andy has flipped? Possible first sign of CJD? Andy's always viewed health guidance as a kind of dare. Beef on the bone was the only time I've heard him mention human rights.

Would I still marry him if he had CJD?

Horrible, but probably not.

Even more horrible, being a tragic widow has a certain appeal.

Not that I appear to have the choice any more.

That goodbye is pretty final.

Why should he have the last word?

Click REPLY.

Fine. You only just beat me to it. L

Check that I am not drunk. Not possible on two alcopops.

Click SEND.

I wait, expecting myself to burst into tears, or wail, or throw something. But nothing happens.

Middle

Middle

CHAPTER 12

February

I am lovable, desirable, sexy and altogether magnificent.

Fern says I should repeat these words to myself all day, until they enter my subconscious. However, I keep interrupting myself. I am lovable, but not to someone who is prepared to let an ancient Labrador lick his face. (What meat do they use for the meaty chunks in dog food, by the way? Is it beef? Is it tested for BSE? I mean, if infected meat got into the human food chain, it must have got into the dog one, and that's another place that Andy could have contracted CJD. Not that he actually eats it, but there must be traces in Honey's saliva.)

I am lovable, desirable, sexy and altogether magnificent!

Not sure about magnificent. Sounds a bit large. Sounds like the sort of adjective they use to describe Dawn French.

I think it must have been an American book

Fern got this from. The English version might have an alternative I would find easier to say (even to myself). Like I am lovable to the people who've known me a long time, I have quite good legs, and even though I do have mean thoughts, I am not a bad person really.

I reverse into my parking space at the first attempt, so it must be having some effect.

'How's Andy these days?' asks Richard Batty.

'We split up.'

'Oh. Sorry.'

His hands are actually shaking as he lights his cigarette then ducks his head quickly out of the window.

The witches pretend to be engaged in another conversation, but I know they can barely contain their *schadenfreude*.

'Oh dear, are you back on Slim Fast?' says Mrs Vane.

'It's too easy to cheat on the Internet,' says Mrs Wates, 'and I just don't have the time for Weightwatchers.'

'Have you tried Slim Fast, Lydia?'

I duck my head out of the window.

'How are you feeling?' Richard asks, concerned.

'Fine, actually. Bit humiliating, but . . .'

'He was the one who ended it?'

Richard's astonishment is really very comforting. If only his skin weren't so bad.

'He only just beat me to it,' I say, with a smile.

126

The more I say it, the truer it sounds.

Perhaps that's because it actually IS true?

'The only thing I miss is doing the quiz,' I elaborate, which doesn't sound quite as true, but possibly will with repetition.

Andy has had the absolute EFFRONTERY to send me two of his usual, Usual Time, Usual Place? e-mails. To which, on Michelle's advice, I have not replied.

'I think I need a new quiz partner,' I sigh.

I should have waited until Richard exhaled because now he's choking which is not how he's practised this moment, I know.

'If he's not interested, count me in,' says New Andy, whose face has popped out of the window on the other side of Richard's.

'No, no, I absolutely am interested,' says Richard.

Damn him!

'What about your mother?' I ask.

'She'll be fine if she's got a pad on. She probably won't even notice, to be honest.'

'Did you see the moguls?' I ask New Andy, bending further over so that I can talk to him below Richard's cloud of smoke.

I'm an official Winter Olympics fan. I have bags under my eyes in the morning, and a whole new vocabulary: Snowboarding, Three Hills, Luge, Skeleton and Half Pipe. I love them all. And I am probably one of the only people in the UK who's glad that Salt Lake City is so far west that most of the events don't start until after midnight. I get the same excitement staying up after my bedtime, that I used to as a kid when my dad sometimes let me watch the ice-skating with him. The judges were eccentric then too. They used to stand on the ice and hold up a mark in each hand. My dad sometimes used to shout at them, even though his knowledge of ice-skating was rudimentary.

Frankly, it's the Winter Olympics that have made Andy's rejection almost bearable.

The only thing I can't be doing with is the curling. It's just too similar to darts.

My mouse glides over:

US Foreign Policy 'absolutist and simplistic'

and:

Pop Idol **And then there were three!**

There are no new messages in my Inbox.

Click on COMPOSE.

Dear Andy. In the circumstances, I think it's only fair that I take over the quiz team. I have found a new partner. L

Fast work! But I think you should talk about this. A

My phone rings.

'Lydia?' says Andy.

'Andy?'

'About the quiz . . .'

Deep breath.

I go over what I've rehearsed with Michelle for if he ever has the NERVE to call. I'm meant to put the phone down now. But I can't have rehearsed it enough. Anyway, he'd probably think I'd just dropped the phone, which I sometimes do, and ring back.

'I'm sorry, but I've already asked someone else.' A little bit croaky at first, but gaining in confidence as I go on.

'Someone else?' he says.

He does actually sound a little sad, and he's not much of an actor (the *Gazette*'s words, not mine).

'You can't really expect to behave as you have and still be in my team,' I say more gently.

'I thought it was our team.'

Bloody hell! 'So did I!'

I put down the phone.

I had the last word AND I put down the phone.

Michelle will be proud of me.

Actually, I enjoyed it.

I almost wish he'd ring again, so that I can put it down again.

I wonder if he will ring again?

The phone rings.

'Yes?' Suitably abrupt and unforgiving voice.

'Am I speaking to Lydia?'

'Kim, Goodness me, you work late, Joanna is so lucky—'

Alas my love . . .

'Lucky! That's about the last thing I feel at the moment. Look, Vlad found a joint in Ingeborg's room and sacked her.'

'The nice Dutch girl?'

'If it were up to me, I'd turn a blind eye, but you know how Vlad is about smoking.'

'Was it the tobacco or the grass he objected to?'

'Didn't taste like grass actually, tasted like Moroccan Black. I think I was more interested in the nicotine.'

'Joanna?'

'I smoked it in the back garden when Vlad was in Chicago. For God's sake don't tell, Lyd. I needed a giggle. I wouldn't have dared if it had been Europe, but with Chicago I thought even if he calls this minute and tells me he's on his way, I still have five hours. I've been brushing my teeth almost constantly since, and everything had to go to the dry-cleaner. You won't tell, will you?'

What I want to say is, Of course I won't tell, but if you fancied a giggle, why didn't you invite me round? We could have had a bottle of white wine, or a jug of Pimm's, like we used to do when you were at Oxford, sitting out on the flat roof below your window, our giggles ringing out over the Broad, and people looking up, trying to see where the laughter was coming from.

What I say is, 'So what do you want?'

'Ever been to Legoland?' says Joanna.

I'm not usually keen on theme parks, but it will

130

be a way of spending some time with my sister, whom I suddenly feel enormously fond of.

'Bring Andy!' she adds.

'We've split up.'

'Oh. Well, you know what they say . . .'

'Yes, they go on about fish, which doesn't actually make sense metaphorically or literally, because there are not shoals of unattached marriageable men out there, and, according to Radio 4, the cod stocks are almost exhausted.'

I think just by having it on in the car you absorb a certain number of facts.

I put the phone down on Joanna. Which isn't quite as pleasurable as with Andy, but serves her right for fish, even though she didn't in fact mention fish now I come to think of it.

I ought to ring her back, but I'm loath to get on the phone again in case Andy rings and I can put the phone down on him again.

Perhaps he's been trying to ring all the time I was speaking to Joanna.

If I want to be sure not to miss putting the phone down on him again, I shall have to get call waiting.

And caller ID.

The reporter is walking towards the camera across a dusty airstrip where there are helicopters taking off.

'The message from Washington is that America is prepared to act alone on its "war on terrorism" whether or not its Nato allies support it . . .'

I wonder why they do that walking towards the camera thing. I wonder how often the cameraman trips over because he can't look behind him.

'Who do you think will win?' asks Michelle.

'I don't know if it's a war that can be won,' I say.

'*Pop Idol*. Dur!'

I hate the way parents pick up on the phrases their children use.

'Gareth. Definitely.'

'Why?'

'Because he's got a stutter. Darius is too cheesy and Will looks a bit gay to me. Not that I mind. Some of my best friends are gay. But isn't it a bit weird for a teeny idol?'

Actually I don't know any gay people except for the couple who live next door to Andy's mother, and then it's only pleasantries over the fence on summer barbecue nights.

'Who's gay?' asks Michelle.

I can't remember either of their names.

'Kim,' I say. 'Joanna's secretary.'

'Well, I've joined friendsreunited.com,' says Michelle.

It's typical of Michelle to do something new without telling me. She does it with diets too. She always gets a head start on the Pounds Lost Bar Chart.

'Friendsreunited.com?'

'It's this website where you can get back in touch with—'

'I know what it is, but we *are* in touch with everyone we knew at school. We never moved away or got exciting careers, and nor did anyone else. I saw Sophie Fitt in Safeway the other day . . .'

'I thought she went to New York with that actor.'

'Well, she's back. Her step dad's got prostate trouble.'

'She always thought she was somebody.'

'So, who have you been in touch with?' I pretend not to be interested.

'Do you remember Declan?'

'Where's Declan these days?' I yawn.

'West London,' Michelle says, like it's a move up.

'Probably Wormwood Scrubs. For God's sake, don't get involved with Declan.'

'That's what my mother used to say.'

'Boys called Declan are invariably bad. Anyone else?'

I am interested, damn it!

'There's Andy.'

She hesitates before saying his name, like she's being sensitive about my feelings.

'Which one?'

'Not sure. He remembers so much about me, I didn't dare ask. He says I turned him down for a snog at the Cricket Pavilion Disco and he never got over it.'

'That was Sandy Andy.'

'Are you sure?'

'Well, it wasn't Randy Andy.'

'How do you know?'

'Because you never turned him down.'

'Stop!'

'And it wasn't Handy Andy, either.'

Michelle blushes.

'And it wasn't Andy Pandy, because he was a pouf. So, by a process of deduction . . .'

'Sandy Andy,' says Michelle, with a wistful look in her eye as if he's a long-lost first love when in fact she was always vile to him.

'He's a personal banker down the NatWest,' I tell her. 'And he's married to Mandy.'

'Cheeky bugger,' says Michelle. 'Which Mandy?'

CHAPTER 13

'In these stressful days, it is very good to relax with a football,' says the woman who's doing the demonstration.

The lights are dimmed. I'm trying to visualize myself floating with the help of the background whale music.

Frankly, the football doesn't work for me. Does she mean lying with it against the small of your back, like a hot-water bottle, or kicking it around the garden?

I open my eyes.

She actually means putting your feet in a washing-up bowl filled with hot water and aroma-therapy bath salts.

I think she's Swedish or Swiss or something. Herbal remedies are far more plausible sold with a foreign accent. If this woman came from Liverpool, I very much doubt whether I would be circling the Herbal Foot Bath on my order sheet and imagining that my life's problems are about to be solved by a simple credit-card transaction. And a trip to Homebase, because I wouldn't want to use the same bowl I wash salad in.

I wonder whether Fern actually realizes that this is really a Tupperware party but with no Tupperware.

My mother got straight into Tupperware after my father died.

'I was never allowed before,' she used to say to the assembled neighbours in our living room, as if Tupperware had been a burning ambition denied her by marriage.

Still, very nice of Fern to invite me. My friends are rallying round.

There's a large woman sitting diagonally opposite me whom I vaguely recognize. I smile at her. She blanks me.

I've done this before with people I think I know, but have in fact only seen on television. I said hello to Dermot Murnaghan when I went to the races with Michelle when we won free entry in the pub quiz but Andy was too honest to take the day off work. You don't expect to see a newsreader in that type of place. He was very nice and twinkly about it even when I couldn't stop myself telling him that I thought he was the best newsreader of all time and my mother thought so too (which was actually a lie because my mother prefers Michael Buerk). My horse had just come in at 5 to 1 and I was a bit light-headed after the champagne and prawn sandwiches.

Michelle says she thinks they probably love it anyway.

'If a stranger came up to you and told you, *you*

were gorgeous,' she says, 'secretly, you wouldn't mind a little invasion of your privacy, would you?'

The fat woman does not look famous.

'This gel,' says the Swede, rubbing a little on everyone's forearm, 'will help to rebalance your hormones, boost your immune system and soften your skin. It's good for hot flushes . . .' She looks around the room. Several of the women look away, as if she's pointed at them and shouted, 'Menopause!'

'It is also an insect repellent, it has mild disinfectant properties and, of course, it is marvellous at relieving stress.'

'But can it take the rubbish out and check my tyre pressure?' I whisper to Fern.

She's not amused. Laughter, as far as Fern's concerned, is about the production of natural pheremones from utilizing the muscles in your face, or something. She tells me this whenever I say something like, You've got to laugh, haven't you?

It's really an alternative version of my mother informing me crossly that, 'Smiling is actually good for you, Lydia. It's been scientifically proved.'

I circle the Rescue Me Gel with my recycled pencil.

Actually, Fern and my mother would get on very well. Perhaps I should introduce them.

Funny how you see people differently when you go to their house.

Fern's is a surprisingly normal semi-detached. I expected more of a teepee feel to it, but it's as MFI as the next person, except that she's got a Buddha on the mantelpiece where everyone else has a clock, and the whale music is coming from a perfectly conventional mini sound system.

It's a bit too loud, as a matter of fact. The whales could almost be in the room with us, which makes it pretty crowded because there are already seven women not including the demonstrator.

Oh my God, I do recognize the fat woman. I think she is the one who trod on someone else's glass at New Year. Must have healed up, though, unless she's got a dressing under her ankle boot.

'I didn't know you knew Fiordiligi?' I whisper to Fern.

'I'm a recent recruit. It's about expanding personal horizons, isn't it?' says Fern.

'And being able to sing,' I say. 'So you know Andy?'

'Andy?'

'Don Alfonso.'

'There's certainly a Don,' says Fern.

It's my turn for the head massage.

Very nice.

Very relaxing.

A bit vigorous.

Ow!

'You couldn't turn the whales down a bit, could you?' I ask Fern, but she doesn't hear.

138

'COULD YOU TURN THE WHALES DOWN?'

'But they're—'

'Pardon?'

'They're VERY RELAXING!'

'Now, does anyone have any questions?' says the Swede.

'Can you PLEASE stop thumping my head?'

Fern puts it down to the amount of coffee I drink.

I feel so guilty I buy an essential oil burner and a long-handled brush for dry scrubbing my skin as well as my products. Fern, as host, gets freebies to the value of ten per cent of what everyone spends.

'Would you like to host a presentation?' the Swede asks me, as she makes a note of my expiry date.

Are you crazy? I've already spent my holiday savings on smelly things I will never use!

'I'd love to,' I say, because if I agree Fern gets a bonus bottle of Seawood Foamer, and, in the circumstances, it's the least I can do.

It won't be too bad. I'll just invite my mother and Joanna, who'll buy the entire range, and then I'll get so many freebies, I'll have to buy a bigger bathroom cabinet. Or clear out the present one.

CHAPTER 14

'Can anyone think of a word we might use to describe Andy?'

'Nice?'

'Let's think of something other than nice. Nice doesn't really mean anything.'

'Fluffy?'

'Good.'

'Friendly?'

'Very good!'

'Feathery?'

'Excellent! Yes, Robbie?'

'He can fly?'

'Yes, he can fly. He's a fluffy, friendly, feathery owl who can fly.'

I don't think I'll bother them with winged.

I write all the words on the whiteboard.

'Does anyone know what these words are called? Words that describe things?'

'F-words?' suggests Nicole, her face screwed up with the effort of trying to deduce the answer from the clue. Definitely a useful quiz-team member of the future.

'They're called adjectives. Words that describe things and people are called adjectives. Can anyone think of any other adjectives? Yes, Ethan?'

'My dad can fly, Miss.'

'I don't think so, Ethan.'

'He can, Miss. He really can.'

'Can anyone else think of any adjectives? Dean?'

'Wicked?'

'Very good. Now on your worksheet, there are four pictures of things and I want you to write one adjective describing each one.'

Heads duck down, tongues reach for noses. I can almost see the thought bubbles above their heads. I wander round looking at what they're writing.

'Miss?'

'Yes, Ethan?'

'What does elope mean?'

'Where did you hear it, Ethan?'

Always a good idea to establish the word you're defining is the word they are asking about. I recently got myself tied in knots with paedophile when I could have just said 'one by one' if I'd asked him to repeat the question.

'My mum has *eloped* with someone she met at karate.'

'I see. Well, you know, I'm not really sure what it means. I may have to ask your father. Is he picking you up today?'

'Yes.'

'How are you feeling?'

141

'I had McDonald's for BREAKFAST!' he beams.

'I borrowed the Genius edition of Trivial Pursuit from a friend,' says Richard in the queue for the till.

'You'll be fine. Honestly, you know loads.'

I choose the Bumper All Day Breakfast. They give you a little flag for your table, so that the woman from the kitchen in the blue-checked overall doesn't have to shout it out, and make you feel like a pig when everyone looks in your direction.

Sod the detox. I think I actually felt worse without the toxins.

According to Fern's Swede, that's all part of it. It's got to get worse before it gets better, she said when I complained of a headache after the massage.

Michelle says the same about facials, as if it's a self-evident fact of life.

I think it's a con perpetrated by alternative therapists and beauticians. If you come out in a rash after a treatment, then you're so relieved when it gets better that you forget what you were actually like before. So, you think you're better, because it's definitely better than a rash, but in fact, you're probably just about the same.

'Have either of you had a marriage break-up?' I ask Richard and New Andy.

'I was engaged. But only for two weeks, so it wasn't that bad,' says Richard.

'I meant, in your class.'

I didn't know Richard had been engaged.

'I've got seven single mothers . . .'

'We've all got single mothers,' I say, 'but what about dads?'

'Never had a single dad,' says Richard.

'I've had several,' says New Andy, with a wink.

'And?'

'Just make sure you don't fall in love, all vulnerable and needy . . .'

'Actually, I'm fine.'

'I meant him.' Another wink.

Fall in love with Ethan's dad? It would never have crossed my mind.

Though, actually, it would solve quite a lot of problems in one go.

Ethan is a dear little boy. We get on well, so no worries there. I'm sure he would grow to love me, and Cy and Ry would be fine once they got used to it. His father is sweet too. And quite good looking. Out of my league in normal circumstances, but I could be key in helping them both build up their self-esteem . . . Is it unethical to marry the parent of one of your pupils? Not if it wasn't you who broke up the family, surely? I could change schools. I have been meaning to get round to a career move. I could probably get deputy head if I wanted to. Senior teacher, definitely. So the ethics won't even be an issue by the time the divorce papers come through.

On the other hand, could I stand always being second best? Second-best daughter, second-best wife? Is it a role I'm drawn to, because of Joanna?

New Andy cracks open his third sandwich rectangular prism.

'I don't know where you put it,' I tell him.

'As the bishop said to the choirboy,' he replies.

Oh my God! New Andy is gay!

I must have known all along subconsciously.

We get on, New Andy and I, just like single women always do with gay men in contemporary novels. Hooray! If our friendship continues to flourish, very soon I shall truly be able to say that some of my best friends are gay!

'ANYONE FOR THE BUMPER BREAK-FAST?'

My tote bag has blocked the flag.

I blame my mother. If I put my bag on the floor when we're eating out, her eyes keep flicking anxiously down, and it makes conversation difficult.

What does Ethan's mother look like? Think she's exotic and slim.

I can't do exotic, but I can eat only the egg and the beans (for fibre) and give the meat bits to New Andy, even though he's bound to say something about slipping him a sausage.

Ethan's dad is certainly more suitable in every way.

'Question number one. What would you use a bodkin for?'

Richard has already written down 'darning'.

On the other side of the room Andy is chewing the top of his biro. That's another thing I don't like about him. He keeps spitting out yellow bits of plastic and the end of the pen's all wet when you want to write an answer down.

Actually, I think he's got a nerve turning up.

He'll be hopeless without me.

The second round is called Sons and Daughters. He might just get Beatrice and Eugenie, but I doubt whether he knows Peter and Zara, let alone Connor and Isabella, Phoenix Chi, Anais, Lennon and Gene.

Richard is very impressive at countries of the former Soviet Union.

I am almost perfect on Musicals except I miss *Carousel* (I know the connection with Liverpool Football Club is 'You'll Never Walk Alone', but I can't get *Guys and Dolls* out of my head. As soon as Sky Masterson appears in the final question, I know it's wrong but they want the papers back in straight away).

Richard does not slurp from the top of his glass, partly because it's a tomato juice, and those little bottles have such a minute quantity in, they'd barely reach the halfway mark on the wineglass.

★   ★   ★

We win!

'Let's hear it for Richard and Lydia,' says the publican, in the voice of the man who says One Hundred and Eighty on television darts.

I've become plain Lydia for now. It's too soon after our break up to be lovely with someone else.

The prize is a pair of T-shirts with Smirnoff written on.

The usual crowd clap a bit grudgingly.

I've shown the world I can win without Andy. I've shown Andy I can win without Andy. (So good he turned up, in fact.)

I look at Richard.

We have won!

We are in love!

That can't be right.

Even though he knew the Trent was the third longest river in England when most people would have thought the Ouse, I do not want to sleep with him, therefore this feeling I have cannot be what 'in love' feels like.

Very curious.

CHAPTER 15

'Oh, I thought I said,' says Joanna.

'No, you didn't.'

'Thing is, I've got a Honey Moo massage in the Mongolian yurt at two o'clock, and Mimi's picking me up.'

'Who's Mimi?'

'My new best friend.'

Joanna has a new best friend almost every week. They've usually got something useful like a Lear jet or a private island.

'You know, once you've got used to travelling by helicopter, you don't want to go any other way,' says Joanna.

'Can't you take the twins with you? They'd love the ride. They could run around the grounds.'

'Thing is, there's a lake, and it's meant to be relaxing for me. Goodness knows, I get little enough of that,' says Joanna. 'Anyway, isn't there a helicopter ride at Legoland?'

'If you don't mind waiting an hour.'

'That was the height of summer. I'm sure there won't be many people mad enough to queue in this weather,' says Joanna.

'You know I hate theme parks.'

'You enjoyed Sea World.'

'Only because it was Florida. It was warm. There were beaches.'

Still, I'm reminded that Joanna paid for the whole trip.

'Why can't I ever be your new best friend?'

My voice sounds croaky, because I've got a silly childish urge to cry.

'You are my old best friend,' says Joanna. 'My oldest best friend, and my best best friend.'

She hugs me tight.

'But I never see you,' I smile through my tears.

'Come to dinner next week.'

'I hate your dinner parties.'

'Well, come to lunch. As a matter of fact, why don't you stay over tonight, and come to lunch tomorrow? Greg's coming.'

'Greg?'

'He's asked Vlad twice about your job.'

'I thought Vlad was shafting him?'

'No that was the stick woman. Greg's our new next-door neighbour.'

'But he's Canadian!'

'Well, you know what they say . . .' says Joanna with a wink.

'No, what do THEY say?'

'Oh sorry, I was thinking about his baldness. That's most women's objection. Anyway, I must run. Have a wonderful time!'

Joanna knows that I would never just stomp out

of the house slamming the front door and get into my stupid lime-green car and screech off in a cloud of pulverized rubber. For one thing, I'm a cautious driver. For another, there are two small boys with no front teeth grinning at me from between the banisters.

'There are going to be ground rules,' I say.

'Ohhh . . .'

'Otherwise we'll stay here.'

'OK.'

They are capable of being sweet and acquiescent. But only in captivity.

'And don't try to smash down the model village this time. You're not at home.'

There are lights on in many of the houses which haven't yet been compulsorily purchased at the side of the A40. So I am not the only one doing nothing on Saturday night.

Legoland is closed in February. We didn't find out until we reached the entrance, although I should probably have been alerted by the absence of a queue. Vlad offered me his ticket to the Opera to make up for it, but it was *Cosi fan tutte*.

My mouse glides over:

Paralysed woman's delight at being allowed to die

and clicks on:

Get Ready for the Oscars!

I score above average in the Oscar History Quiz.

149

There are three messages in my Inbox.

They're all from Andy. The headings are:

Well done!

I miss you!

Can we try again?

Number 1 says:

Well done at the quiz. Did you get **Carousel**? If I've offended in some way, sorry. You've certainly made your point. Back to normal next week?

Number 2 says:

L. I miss you. I expect you're cross with me, but in my favour, I needn't have written at all. How long would it have taken you to discover your mistake then? A

Number 3 says:

L. OK, so you're probably feeling like you've stood at a lit window in your underwear, but it was great underwear. Can we stay in touch? AX

Sometimes people have been driven insane by a broken heart. If it isn't CJD then Andy has depths I haven't even dreamed of.

'Have you voted yet?' says Michelle, as she opens the door.

I get the horrible guilty feeling I had the morning of the last election when I realized I had failed to fill in my electoral register form and inadvertently disenfranchised myself. And that was after several sessions trying to explain to a class of five- and six-year-olds that democracy meant more than just a day off because of the school being a polling station. I pretended to vote, of course. I don't mean actually going to the polling station, but wearing a T-shirt with a red rose on it and staying up late to watch Peter Snow. They increased their majority in my constituency, so it didn't really matter anyway.

Of course, it's not just a Saturday evening, it's *the* Saturday evening.

No wonder people are staying in up the A40.

Michelle hands me the phone and I ring Gareth's number.

'Gareth?' says Michelle.

'I thought we wanted Gareth.'

'But it's cool to like Will.'

'Says who?'

'Charlene.'

Normally I wouldn't set much store by Michelle's second daughter's advice, but she's probably right on this.

'But I don't like the way Will just stands there singing. Why doesn't he move around a bit more?'

'Will's going to win,' says Michelle.

'He won't need my vote then.'

Just like the real election.

'The tension's mounting. Crack open those Pringles,' says Michelle, as I hand her a bottle of Cava I picked up on the way over.

'How long till the results come in?'

'One hour and counting,' says Michelle.

'Can I show you something on the computer?'

I don't know how I missed the obvious when Michelle spots that the e-mail addresses are different straightaway.

Andy's latest e-mail address was meant to be easy to remember because it was just Andy with his age. But when I typed in **andy42@** . . ., I was forgetting that I'd known him three years. The real Andy's e-mail has **andy45@** . . . on it.

'Don't you use your address book?' Michelle wants to know, suddenly the expert because of Charlene's IT GCSE.

'Takes longer than typing it in,' I say.

Let's face it, some time-saving devices don't save time. Like toasted sandwich makers, for instance, if you include the washing-up. And I'm not keen on butter on both sides of the bread.

'How many Andys do you think there are in the world?' Michelle wonders.

I suddenly realize there is a God!

I will have a bit of explaining to do, but nothing compared to Robert Redford!

'That's before you count all the blokes who aren't called Andy, but just use it as their e-mail name . . .' says Michelle.

'Who on earth would . . . ?' I begin, but then I remember that Andy once did that, except he called himself Peter.

'Why Peter when you could have chosen any name in the whole world?' I asked him.

'I always wanted to be called Peter as a child,' he said.

Which I found rather endearing.

'Where are you off to?' Michelle asks.

'To see my fiancé.'

'You got rid of him . . .'

Nice of her to put it that way, although untrue in a bewildering number of respects.

Michelle never gave Andy a chance. Thing is, Michelle's pretty. Mum says it's what's inside that counts, but the first Soul Mates bloke walked out of the bar before we'd even spoken. He came in with his *Guardian* in hand, saw me, then looked at his watch and turned round again, as if he'd just remembered he was meant to be somewhere else.

Michelle says you should feel more for your fiancé than gratitude, but she doesn't know what it's like.

CHAPTER 16

Differences between men and women:
3. Birds of Prey.

I'm not talking about a pair of golden eagles nesting in a tree in the Lake District. That was one of the first news stories I remember watching on television. The country was gripped for about a week, and it was on *Blue Peter* and everything.

I wonder whatever happened to Goldie? And those pigs who ran away. They should do an animal version of *After They Were Famous*. I should write to the head of ITV and suggest it.

I'm talking about those little birds of prey you sometimes see hovering over fields when you're driving down the motorway.

Actually, I never do see them, and it doesn't really bother me, but every single man I've ever driven with has veered the car alarmingly while shouting, 'Look, a buzzard! See it? At least I think it's a buzzard. There! Over there! Or is it a sparrowhawk? There! There!'

In the end it's easier to strain my head back and shout 'Oh yes!' at the last moment, too late for him to ask me to point to where I think it is, but just in time to stop him going off the road.

We are on our way to Bournemouth, because it's where Andy used to come on holidays when he was little, and when we looked on the map, it wasn't much further than Brighton.

We are blowing away the cobwebs.

It was his idea, actually, after I told him how much stress I'd been under at school. He accepted totally that Richard Batty was thinking of starting his own quiz team and wanted to see how it was done.

At Fleet services Andy buys me *The Only Musicals Album You'll Ever Want* while I'm in the loo, and even encourages me to join in the chorus of 'Sit Down You're Rocking the Boat' as we by-pass Southampton.

I think I must be forgiven.

'How's *Cosi?*' I ask.

Opera buffs always say just *Cosi*, I've noticed, as if the opera is an old friend. I wonder why they never say *The Magic* or *Don* in the same way.

'Fiordiligi is on antibiotics for her foot, and Despina has issues about Tuesday evenings.'

'Issues?'

'She says it's no longer convenient.'

'Probably doesn't want to miss *Footballers' Wives*.'

'No?'

'You know, the fickleness of women!' I say.

'Perhaps I should offer to programme her video?' says Andy.

The words sound a little suggestive just hanging in the air over the gearstick. We both take our eyes off the road for a moment to look at each other. And then we start laughing.

Difference between men and women:

4. Videos.

It's actually nothing to do with whether we can or can't programme the video, women prefer to watch television programmes when they are on. Waiting until the weekend when you've got a bit of time to catch up with the week's viewing just doesn't do it. Anyway, who has that much time at the weekend? Once you've had a lie-in and caught up with your washing, it's Sunday night and then there's usually something decent on ITV. No point in videoing that while you watch your videos from the previous week. You'd never catch up.

'New Forest pony!' shouts Andy.

'Where?'

'There! No, there!'

'Oh right!'

'You can't see it now.'

Andy's plusses:

1. He is sexy. Maybe not objectively, but there's definitely a spark between us. Not the amazing electric current that makes me shift position on my sofa during *Match of the Day*, obviously, but more than I have with, say, Richard Batty. Which is why it was useful to see them side by side on quiz night. When a woman says to a man that she wouldn't want to spoil a friendship, she actually means that she doesn't fancy him. Not that Richard was necessarily asking for sex the other evening when he dropped me off. I think he was genuinely interested in my stencilling. 'I'm sorry I think it would spoil it,' was probably quite an odd thing to say, but he should have known better on a week night.

2. I am myself with Andy. I don't mean that he knows everything about me, thankfully, but I'm not always trying to second guess what he wants me to be. We are quite happy to stand on a pier in a freezing-cold seaside resort watching the wintry sun turn the western sky pale gold, and saying nothing at all. With Andy, I'm not always feeling that an appropriate remark is called for and I don't know what it is.

3. Occasionally, he does something spontaneous.

'If we didn't have to drive back, we could have a bottle of wine,' says Andy.

We are in one of those Italian restaurants you

don't really get any more in London, with whitebait for starters, and a dozen ways with a veal cutlet. On the walls are signed black-and-white pictures of yesteryear's celebrities like Max Bygraves and Kenny Ball.

I'm picking bits of wax off the candle in a Chianti bottle and debating in my mind if it would be too mean on Andy, who always drives when it's dark (or any other time if I can help it. He's much keener on the lime-green Beetle than me, not because of the colour, because of the engine which is apparently very good), to have a glass of red with Spaghetti alla Carbonara.

Is Andy trying to test my resolution?

Enough of the resolution! We are having a fresh start, blowing away the cobwebs, and total honesty is called for.

'I am having the occasional drink now,' I confess. 'Until Lent.'

In case he thinks that I've found it impossible to give up.

'I know,' he says.

'Oh?'

'Richard Batty bought you three pints of Stella,' he explains.

I'm flattered that he counted. Must have been watching me very carefully. I was sure I swapped the first empty when he was in the loo.

'In that case, I'll have a glass of red,' I say.

'Now that Honey's gone, there's no reason to go home tonight,' says Andy.

Oh God, he's not going to cry again.

During our separation, Honey has finally kicked the bucket, or the dog bowl, or whatever dogs kick.

I know I should be upset.

'So sad,' I say.

'If we weren't driving we could have a bottle,' says Andy.

Is he saying he doesn't want to drive? Too late, I'm halfway down my glass.

Unless he . . . surely not! Well, well. I thought it was a long way down the M3 just for the afternoon.

OK, so it's not spontaneous, but it's flattering that he's planned it anyway.

'What do you say to that?' Andy asks.

'What I say is, Waiter, can you bring us the wine list!'

'Oh, House'll do me fine,' says Andy.

Here we are, on a Dirty Weekend! Our room has a sea view, which they let us have without the supplement since it's February, and too cold for many clubbers. (Apparently, as well as being Retirement Capital of the South, Bournemouth is now the First Choice for the Youth of the South, on Saturday night. We've seen a few of them on the road from the restaurant, only the most reckless out with a bare midriff in this wind.)

We have tea- and coffee-making facilities, minia-ture soap and a sewing kit. Everything we could possibly need except clean knickers. I even dug a travel toothbrush out of my handbag which came from one of my mother's Luxury Christmas Crackers. (We had them on the 28th December, because she wasn't daft enough to pay full price, and just as well really, because the contents weren't much different from the Superior ones she bought the year before, except for the folding scissors – also in my handbag – and the magnetic address book in the shape of a credit card, which made a useful change from the pack of miniature playing cards made of paper.)

Using the same toothbrush makes it feel more like we're a couple than having sex does, in a funny kind of way.

We've shared a bed and a tent, but we've never actually been to a hotel together before. So it does have an illicit feel, even though you don't have to sign the register as Mr and Mrs Smith any more. Still, I would have done, if Andy hadn't taken charge.

We've had great sex, and finished in time to watch the last guest on *Parkinson*. Now Andy's snoring and I've crept out on to the balcony with his coat on.

I've still got that boiling-hot-after-sex feeling. If I were naked, there'd be clouds of steam coming off me like a satisfied customer emerging from the sauna in the Centre Parcs advert.

There's a silver path across the sea to the moon.

Does life get better than this?

I am in Bournemouth, with my lover (always felt a bit silly calling him that before, but now it's appropriate).

The sky is brilliant with stars.

I can hear the sigh of sea on sand.

I think this may be what happiness feels like.

Still haven't mentioned the ch word, but not the right time on a dirty weekend, especially so soon after Honey.

Are there people standing on balconies all over the world thinking about the meaning of life?

Are human beings united by a primitive wonder at the sea and the universe, and the sense of being part of something unimaginably huge, but nevertheless totally alone?

Is Andy 42 somewhere out there looking at the same moon?

How did he get into my perfect moment uninvited?

He probably doesn't even have a balcony, and even if he does, it's a pretty cold night.

It's perfectly possible that Andy 42 is just a normal guy who got a couple of mad e-mails from me, which was hardly his fault.

Anyway.

That's another story.

One day, I'll tell my Andy, and we'll laugh about it.

Or perhaps not.

You had to be there.

I'm standing in my underwear in a lit window, but I have my Andy's coat around me.

That has a nice metaphorical feel to it.

Anyway, nobody could see me unless they were on a boat.

Actually, it's freezing out here.

CHAPTER 17

How to make a Valentine's Card:

1. Outline the principle of reflective symmetry.
2. Fold a small piece of red card.
3. Demonstrate how cutting a half heart shape will give you a whole heart when you unfold. Put small red heart on one side.
4. Now, fold large rectangular piece of white card in half.
5. Cut two snips about two centimeters long and a centimetre apart into folded edge.
6. Push the hinge you have formed into inside of fold.
7. Stick your red heart onto the hinge with glue.
8. Write a message in your Valentine pop-up card!

'Miss?'

'Yes, Gwyneth.'

'My Valentine pop-up card doesn't open.'

'That's because you put too much glue on and

it's stuck together. Don't cry. Miss Green will help you do another one.'

'Miss?'

'Yes, Dean? Oh, that's lovely.'

'It's got a hole in it, Miss.'

'That's the pop-up bit.'

Trust him to spot the design fault.

'You don't get holes in ones you buy.'

'No, but I bet your mum will be happier with one you've made.'

'I'm not sending it to my mum.'

'Who's your Valentine?'

'Not telling.'

'You're quite right. Valentine's cards are normally secret, aren't they? What's the matter, Ethan?'

'I've written "love from Ethan", in my card.'

'Doesn't matter. I'm sure your mum would have a pretty good idea who it was from.'

'I'm not sending it to my mum. I don't know where she is.'

9. Make note not to bother with Mother's Day cards.

'Are we on for the quiz?' asks Richard Batty, incautiously shovelling a spoonful of shepherd's pie into his mouth, then making a big O with his lips as the microwaved mince sears through his mucous membranes.

'You bet,' I say. 'Andy asked if you wanted to

164

join us from now on. He was very impressed with Trent, I can tell you.'

You've got to be cruel to be kind, but I still feel terrible, especially since it's a bit cowardly to make the announcement when New Andy's around.

'Andy?' says Richard.

A bit of raw carrot has lodged in that funny gappy bit that's just beyond my mouth and not quite in my throat, so I just nod.

'You're back together?' says Richard, as cheerfully as a burnt mouth will allow.

Nod. Nod. Eyes beginning to water now.

'We are. Misunderstanding, really.' Cough, cough, cough!

'Are you all right?'

Paroxysm of coughing.

Eventually I have to put my finger in and dislodge the bit of carrot.

The tears are still pouring down my face, but I can breathe again. I put my hand on Richard's forearm. Not the salivary one that's been in my mouth, obviously.

'It's a bit difficult for me this week,' says Richard.

'Well, if you're sure.'

I wipe my eyes with the tissue he's handed me.

The coughing helped us through that slightly awkward patch, I think, and leaves Richard able to take his arm away from my hand as if I'm the one who's keen on him.

★   ★   ★

165

I am going to make a very nice dinner tomorrow evening. We missed the actual day because every other night these days seems to be a rehearsal night. I didn't mind because the curling was on, and it is actually much more interesting than darts, because there's ends and tactics and blocking stones and that's before you've realized what they're doing with the brooms.

The trouble with me and sport is that I start taking an interest because of fancying someone (not that I thought The Winter Olympics would really give me a chance with New Andy, but it's good to have something to chat about, and frankly, less expensive than subscribing to FilmFour), and as soon as I've figured out the rules, I'm hooked.

I got fourteen cards. Twelve of them anonymous with pop-up hearts inside, seven of those with back-to-front question marks, one from Richard Batty (postmark E Yorks. He always thinks it's going to fool me, but I know he has a sister in Hull. Still nice of him to make the effort in the circumstances), one from Andy, I think. Postmarked W1 which is where his office is. I purposely didn't send him one because last year he said that we don't need helium hearts and red roses to speak for us. Feel a bit bad now. Still, it is rather a crude card with a joke about harems. Probably all they had left in the garage. Where shopping's concerned, Andy is the opposite of most people who shop at the supermarket and take the opportunity to fill up with petrol on the way out.

Which is another reason to make him a very nutritious late-Valentine's dinner because he cannot possibly get all the vitamins he needs from Ginster's.

I'm not attempting *coeur à crème* with a raspberry coulis, or anything fancy like that, because I do not own a set of heart-shaped moulds, nor am I a good cook, although my mum did give me *Happy Days with the Naked Chef* at Christmas with a tag saying: 'We can all dream!'

I was thinking more asparagus dripping with organic butter, sushi and strawberries with melted chocolate on the side. Sensual, easy-to-prepare food you can eat with your fingers. That is what it says in all the magazines. Except *Hello!* of course. *Hello!* always seems to have a feature on ways with hake or chickpeas. The food section is definitely its weak spot.

I get the asparagus, but the sushi's got a reduced sticker on because the sell-by's today, which wouldn't bother me if it were anything other than raw fish.

I choose a tub of taramasalata and some ready cut crudités instead. Pringles are on a three for two, so better get six packets.

Damn! I've forgotten the strawberries which are right at the beginning of the shop. They've probably sold out anyway, so I'll buy a tub of strawberry cheesecake ice cream instead, which amazingly has no more calories per 100g than ordinary strawberry icecream. And saves melting the chocolate which I think you have to do in a bain-marie or something French.

And finally, champagne. Proper champagne, not pink. And for the main course, a full-bodied Rioja. And, in case we don't fancy red, a nice Sauvignon Blanc. If you buy six bottles you get the cheapest one free and a wine cooler worth £4.99 which seems too good an offer to miss. So two more reds and a white, and it's worth having the slightly pricier ones because they'll be cheaper on average.

The man in front of me in the queue has got Ajax powder. I didn't think they made it any more. Who would buy scourer when there's spray or mousse? You don't even have to bend over to clean the bath these days. You can just show it a convenient product.

And he's still on dry spaghetti, when there's fresh tortelloni with wonderful fillings like Parma Ham, basil and sundried tomato, or porcini and rocket, or spinach and ricotta. They all taste the same.

I should have done pasta myself. But we'll be fine with . . . Oops! Forgotten the main course.

My stuff's on the conveyor now and the woman behind has a mountainous trolley and an expression that says there'll be Till Rage if I nip back to the chilled compartment.

I'll order in a pizza and cut it in a heart shape in the kitchen when the bike arrives.

My total including savings is nearly a hundred pounds, which is not cheaper than going out, but it's only Valentine's Day once a year after all, and I get a 4p-off-per-litre petrol voucher.

I should really apply for the senior teacher's job that has come up in a first school in Pinner. I'm certainly experienced enough. It would certainly make the journey to work easier.

Now that marriage is back on, and I am a proper person again, it is the obvious next step on the career ladder.

I should spend the evenings when Andy's rehearsing looking in the *TES* and updating my CV.

There are two new messages in my Inbox.

More interest on your savings AND a lower mortgage!

Still single?

I delete both.

Tempting though the offers are, Andy and I practise safe surfing. Frankly the benefits that might be accrued by simplifying my finances would be vastly outweighed by Andy's fury if I were to succumb to a virus.

Who is stupid enough to play Casino Games?

Unless they let you win a little bit to encourage you. That would be the time to stop.

Friday night is not the best time to embark on:

How Smart Are You?

Especially since you have to set yourself against the clock. I'm sure I'll be smarter in the morning. Unless it's the same one I did the other day, in which case I could be very fast indeed. But that would be cheating. Although nobody would know.

There's only:

How Sexy Are You?

that I haven't done. For the obvious reason that I imagine the answer will be b) adequately.

I could do it and lie outrageously, but it might be undermining if I still got b).

I'm never sure about sexual fantasies. To be honest, I don't even know whether I'm genuinely having a fantasy or whether I'm just trying to imagine being gang-banged by a group of bikers because I once read it on a problem page and the psychologist said it was perfectly normal. They're always very polite about it actually, and not as smelly as you'd think they'd be under all that leather.

There is always Gary Lineker, but we're usually doing a charity cycle ride together, or playing a round of golf, and the pleasure just seems to be that we do get on remarkably well, although, I have noticed that he never mentions his wife.

Question 1 is about how I would flirt with a Brad Pitt lookalike barman.

Answer: I wouldn't.

I don't get it with Brad Pitt. To me he's the slightly mad son of Robert Redford, and I liked Robert Redford when he didn't have children, specifically no later than *The Sting*.

I wouldn't is not an option.

Do you have to fancy Brad Pitt in order to be sexy, or am I supposed to imagine someone else?

Try it with Gary Lineker, but I can't see him serving behind a bar, and if I substitute a health club reception desk, the options don't work.

Click on NEXT.

Are kitten heels sexier than stilettos?

I don't know. I never look sexy in heels, not because of my legs, which are my best feature, but because I always fall off. There are some women who are born to wear heels (Michelle) and others who go over on their ankles even if they're wearing trainers. I am in the second category.

The only time I wore a pair of heels for an evening, I got a stress fracture in my second metatarsal, which they can't put a plaster on, but was very painful none-the-less. Click on NEXT.

Now I have to choose between Tom Cruise, Robbie Williams or Craig David. Seems a bit limited. Why can't I choose who I want?

I know it's a cliché, but there *was* something about Tom Cruise in *Top Gun* (maybe it was the motorbike) but now he doesn't shave and he's so cagey about what happened with Nicole

171

Kidman, I just don't feel the same way any more.

Still, of the three, it's got to be him. I suspect it's the least sexy answer because the person setting it definitely favours rock stars, otherwise why would he/she have two in this category? Click on NEXT.

What's in my underwear drawer?

This may be a question about tidiness, rather than sexiness, because to be truly sexy, you wouldn't have to be someone who worries about tidiness, would you?

Perhaps I'm getting too psychological.

I'd be lying if I said there weren't pairs of tights with ladders which I have kept to wear under trousers in the winter, but I also have some brand-new high-waist white panties, which look very Cameron Diaz, and a purple lace Agent Provocateur bra which I won in a first-fifty-people-to-phone-in promotion. They sent the wrong size, and I was too embarrassed to return it, but the slim, pale-pink box is the best bit anyway. And it looks very provocative nestling among my nighties.

I wonder why Andy 42 mentioned underwear?

It does make it more difficult for me to contact him which would be only the polite thing to do.

In fact, very impolite not to contact him.

In the circumstances it's the least I can do.

A. Hello! Don't worry, not another mad one.

I just wanted to say sorry for barging into your Inbox, and thanks for alerting me. Life is crazy enough, isn't it? Hope you have a good one. L

Click SEND.

Feel altogether better. I think this must be what Fern means by closure.

There is, almost immediately, one new message in my Inbox.

Re: Hello!

I didn't mind. Did you make it up with the other A? A

Bloody cheek!

He's not the other A, you are! L

Is this flirting? Maybe I'm sexy after all!

He sounds a bit dull for you. A

You don't know anything about me. L

I know you're called Lydia. I know you like singing, dancing, Chinese food and quizzes. I know you don't really want to marry a man who wears a kilt, do you? A

That's really unfair. L

I'm sorry. A

Anyway, how do you know I'm called Lydia? L

I've just checked. All the other bits he could have got from the text.

Just a guess because your e-mail address is thelovelylydia A

It could be a red herring. Are you really called Andy? L

Would anyone call themselves Andy as a pseudonym? A

Point taken. I'm not lovely by the way. L

You sound lovely. A

We should probably finish here, because you'll only be disappointed. L

Disappointed? A

When we meet. L

Who said anything about meeting? A

Don't know why, but I just got a little thrill from my fingertips to the seat of the revolving chair I got from IKEA.

I think we ought to set some rules here. L

What are you like! A

Can I have a think about this and come back to you? L

Sure. Good night. AX

Good night. L

He's started Xing again.
   Very sensible to take a step back at this point.
   Michelle would be proud of me.
   Not that I am going to tell her.

CHAPTER 18

'Here's another starter for ten,' says Jeremy. My finger hovers above the buzzer.

'How many people are there in the world called Andy? And I'll accept to the nearest hundred.'

The team opposite exchange glances.

'No conferring,' Jeremy warns them.

Suddenly, I've got it. It has to be a trick question. I mean how could anyone possibly know the answer unless they've done a trawl through the birth registers of every English-speaking country, which is surely beyond the remit of any University course.

I buzz.

'Sudbury Hill, Lydia,' says a disembodied voice.

Jeremy looks at me from beneath one of his intimidating eyebrows. The other one makes a kind of roof above his eye like the Pizza Hut logo. Did it always do that, I wonder, even when he was a child, or has he developed it in front of the mirror?

'None,' I say, 'because they were all christened Andrew!'

'You've got three sitting next to you!' shouts Jeremy in sneering disbelief.

The camera zooms out to reveal that I am the only girl on the team. New Andy and Andy are sitting to my right, to my left there is a very large owl. Each has the word ANDY on the panel in front of him.

'The correct answer is, of course, two million,' says Jeremy.

I wake up feeling totally humiliated. Usually, I'm good at *University Challenge*. On one occasion, Andy and I got a clean sweep. We weren't even trying, but we were eating pasta in front of the telly (not spaghetti, obviously, or any of those long ones) and we just started jumping in.

Every single question right. Which was just as well because I'd forgotten to buy parmesan.

'Champagne,' calls Andy from the sofa. 'Are we celebrating something?'

I've set the glasses out and found a couple of red paper napkins left over from our Christmas mince pies and sherry party. I've even lit a candle, and sprayed my scatter cushions with Dioressence. The ambience in my knocked-through living room is distinctly romantic.

How are you supposed to cook asparagus?

It doesn't fit into any of my saucepans.

Are you meant to wait until the end bit goes soft and bend it in like spaghetti?

I shall chop it up and serve it as a vegetable. Or a warm salad, which sounds more professional.

How did salads, traditionally associated with hot weather, hard-boiled eggs and lettuce called iceberg suddenly get warm, by the way, with no consultation period? Why did no-one say, 'Warm? Are you crazy?' Instead, we all just meekly handed over £6.95 for a few wilted leaves and a soft-boiled egg as if we'd been doing it all our lives.

Damn! I've sliced the pizza in quarters and forgotten about the heart shape.

Actually, it's fine because quarters of a circle are almost heart shaped. All I have to do now is cut a simple couple of notches out of each edge, trim the corners (as they say on *Blue Peter*) and hey presto! There will be four hearts, which is better than one big one. Easier to eat, anyway.

This little wheel pizza knife is totally useless.

Perhaps I should apply the principle of reflective symmetry by folding the crust to make it even?

Think I'll leave it at two hearts.

Just unstick the fold.

And hey pres . . .

Thin crust does taste better but it's that little bit more fragile.

Wish I had ordered two regular pizzas instead of one giant because then I could have practised. Here's one I made earlier!

I take the pizza box through into the living room and open it with a flourish.

'Happy late Valentine's!'

'Did you tip the joker that delivered it in this state?' asks Andy.

I know it's the wrong way round. I'm the one who's meant to be in bed waiting for my lover on a Saturday night, and he's the one who's supposed to be watching the Premiership, but it works for us.

I do feel a bit disloyal to Gary, but I'm sure its only a matter of time before football goes back to the BBC.

We've had sex on my pine table. Champagne always seems to make Andy want to do it some-where different, although I think technically you're meant to be so carried away by passion that you don't worry about the washing-up first.

Still, a lot of men wouldn't do the washing-up at all. Especially not a saucepan that's black with burnt asparagus.

'How about July?' he said, neatly wrapping his condom in one of the red paper napkins afterwards.

'What?'

'July for our wedding.'

'After term breaks up?'

'Obviously.'

'Suits me,' I said, feeling warm all over.

Now he's asleep upstairs and I'm happily watching today's goals.

Does Andy 42 like football?

179

I do not want to know anything more about Andy 42.

Anyway, it's probably wrong to think about him while Andy is actually here. Even more wrong to talk. Especially since I'm practically a married woman.

Why wrong, though? It's not as if we're DOING anything.

There are no new messages in my Inbox.

CHAPTER 19

'Look, Miss!'

Dean opens his hand. On his surprisingly small and innocent-looking palm are at least five entangled, writhing worms. I don't look long enough to count exactly.

'Ugh! Put them outside at once.'

'But they're mini beasts, Miss.'

'You're right. They are. Well done, Dean. Shall we find something to put them in?'

Forgotten that half-term homework was to find a mini beast and make some observations.

Would not have had All Bran for breakfast if I had remembered.

'Has anyone else managed to find a mini beast?'

Ethan has a caterpillar in his sandwich bag.

'I thought he might get hungry. It's a long time to lunchtime, in caterpillar years,' he says.

Gwyneth has a square glass tank with assorted foliage and several stick insects inside.

'Are these your pets?' I ask her.

'No, I think they're Daddy's. He bought them at Pet Store yesterday.'

Typical competitive middle-class parents.

Our specimens are lined up on the table.

'Well, now. What we're going to do is think of some questions we can ask about mini beasts. Who's got a question?'

'Miss?'

'Yes, Geri?'

'Are you happy?'

'Yes, I am I think, thank you, Geri.'

'I didn't mean you. I meant my woodlouse.'

My passport has run out and I nip out in my lunchtime to get a new photo done because it would be a shame, in the unlikely event of Andy surprising me with a honeymoon in the Seychelles or somewhere, not to be able to travel.

There is a new booth in the ticket hall of the tube station. I wait while a gang of teenage girls get their underage travelcard pix. They look at me as if they know I am a teacher. And actually, they do, because I've taught two of them when they were innocent little angels with plaits. Didn't recognize them at first under the make-up. My extremely unamused expression now only elicits a nostril exhalation from the smoker and more defiant chewing from the one with bubblegum.

I step inside and pull the curtain across which gives the illusion that no-one can see me. Of course, they can, but not my face. A bit like an open coffin. But the other way round.

The coffee shop beside the station exit has turned into an internet café.

Click on COMPOSE.

Re: What are you like?

Put it this way. You know those photo booths where you get your passport photos done? Well these days you don't just get random flashes when you're least expecting them. Now there's a nice polite computer who talks you through, and shows you the image, and if you don't like it, you can readjust your expression and try again.

'If you're happy, press 1 to print', says your virtual friend. 'Or press 2 to try again.'

I'm the sort of person who presses 2 again and again until eventually, the computer says, 'Look, I'm sorry, but this is just the way you are, and there's nothing I can do about it.'

Think Steffi Graf on a bad day, with less expensive hair and heavier. I do have the legs, but I can't play tennis. And let's face it, if you take away the tennis, the little white skirt and that solemn way she smooths her hair back before she serves, you'd walk past her in the street, wouldn't you? OK, she pulled Andre Agassi, but take away the tennis from him and what have you got? You've got bald head and a mouthful of improbably perfect teeth.

Does that answer your question? L

Questions about our mini beasts.
I write a list on the board:

1. What does my mini beast like to eat?
2. Where does my mini beast like to sleep?
3. Where can you find my mini beast?

'Ethan, what does your mini beast like to eat?'
'Cabbage,' he says.
'That's right. Caterpillars do like to eat cabbage and sometimes if you're growing cabbages in your garden, caterpillars like to eat them a bit too much and there's no cabbage left for you to eat.'
'I hate cabbage,' says Robbie.
'All the more for the caterpillar.'
'He also eats strawberries and cherry pie,' says Ethan.
'You're thinking of the Very Hungry Caterpillar, aren't you? Does anyone remember reading that book last year? It was about a caterpillar turning into a butterfly, wasn't it? A beautiful colourful butterfly. Yes, Geri?'
'Will I turn into a butterfly if I eat cabbage?'
There are thirty innocent faces in front of me. If

I said yes, twenty-eight of them would probably eat cabbage happily for weeks.

It suddenly occurs to me that human beings do things the other way round from caterpillars. We are beautiful, colourful and quick when we are young and it's only when we eat and grow that we become sluggish and ugly.

I sometimes have moments like this at work which make me sad.

'No,' I sigh, 'I'm afraid you won't. But perhaps when we're writing a story next time, we can all imagine what it would be like to be a mini beast, a beautiful bright butterfly fluttering round a buddleia bush . . . Yes, Robbie?'

'Can I be a head lice?'

'Two head lice, one head louse.'

'I've got lots!'

I anticipate parental complaints.

CHAPTER 20

Michaela is already at a window table in Café Rouge. She doesn't look pregnant at all, which is a relief because we won't have to talk about babies all the time.

'Apparently babies are the new black,' I say, giving her a kiss. 'It's official. I think it became official when Kate Moss announced hers, although it must have been almost official with Liz Hurley . . .'

'Hello, Aunt Lyd,' says Michaela laughing.

I like Michaela best of all my godchildren, partly because I've known her the longest, and partly because she finds me gratifyingly hilarious.

'You don't have to call me Aunt Lyd any more if you don't want to,' I say. 'In fact, you never did have to. It was just something your mother started to annoy me.'

'I like calling you Aunt Lyd though.'

'Well, all right, you may continue, but I'm telling you now, if I ever hear the child calling me Great Aunt Lyd I shall cut off your book tokens. The same goes for Big Lydia and

Little Lydia, if you are really set on calling her that.'

'I am. Not just because of you.'

'Why not because of me?'

'I like the name.'

'But you must like the name because of its association with me.'

'Not really.'

'I don't see how you can separate them.'

'Will you be godmother anyway?' Michaela says. She's always been good at soothing ruffled feathers. Or smoothing them. Whatever it is you do to feathers.

'Oh, how lovely! Are you sure? I'm honoured,' I say, feigning surprise.

Actually, I think it was the name bit I was not meant to know.

I pick up the menu.

'What have they got which doesn't have listeria in it?'

'You know a lot about it.'

'Baby Lydia'll be my sixth,' I tell her.

'I'm thinking of Grace for a first name.'

'You can't!'

'Why?'

'It's my mother's name. If you're having Grace, you can't have Lydia,' I tell her firmly.

'Phoebe then.'

'Phoebe I like, but have you thought about when she's learning to spell? You put the child at a disadvantage in Reception and first impressions are important, even though they're not meant to be. Course they might have done away with baseline assessment by then . . .'

'You can teach her to write before she gets to school, like you did me,' says Michaela.

I'm touched she remembers.

'OK, but I don't want to push her too much. What does Adam think?'

'He prefers Courtney or Rachel, but I'm not sure that's just the names!'

A generation of children are to be called after *Friends*. Which is fine by me. Much more democratic than the royal family. Although, actually, do the royal family set the fashion or follow it? Were people starting to call their sons Harry before Diana did, and why aren't there more Williams?

'I mean about you being pregnant.'

'He's cool. Best to get it over with while we're young.'

'It was planned?'

'I am so not that stupid.'

It's official. I am middle aged. I come from the generation of women who spent their youth trying not to become pregnant.

Also, I do not regularly use the word so to emphasize a negative. I am past my sell-by date. I am uncool. I am *so not young* any more.

'Can we talk about something else?' Michaela asks. 'Don't you just hate the way you become a pregnant woman when you're pregnant?'

188

Her mobile phone rings with a text message. She texts back.

'Just Mum,' she says, looking up.

'Michelle?'

So she's doing texting now. She never tells me until she's got the hang of it. Then it's like 'Texting? Everyone does, don't they?' Well, actually, no. I don't even know how to. Actually, I don't even know whether you can on my mobile phone, and the boy behind the desk in Carphone Warehouse is an ex pupil so I can't ask him.

'What did she have to say for herself?' I ask.

'She just sent you her love,' says Michaela.

'I'm going to have the grilled goat's cheese . . .' I tell the waiter.

Might as well enjoy the benefits of not being pregnant and consume a few life-threatening mini beasts.

'. . . and a cappuccino.'

'Would you like chocolate on your cappuccino?'

'why else would I want a cappuccino?'

I notice Michaela's more embarrassed than amused by that one. Cappuccino can't be cool any more. Probably cool's not cool either. I hope we're not going back to bad instead of good, but only sometimes.

'Do you and all your friends chat to people on the Internet?' I ask Michaela, casually.

'You have to be careful,' says Michaela, giving me a probing sort of look.

'I know that,' I say.

The waiter returns with my coffee.

'Why exactly is it dangerous?' I ask Michaela. 'I mean, it's only like talking to a man on the train. You can always get off at the next stop if you think you've gone too far, can't you? Even if it means catching the next train and delaying your journey? It's inconvenient, yes, but hardly dangerous. I suppose if the next train is delayed because of signal failure and you end up missing the thing that was the reason you were on the train in the first place you'd have a problem, but it wouldn't matter that much, unless it was a funeral.'

'Or a wedding?' Michaela interrupts.

'I suppose it would have to be quite a good conversation to make it worth missing that for,' I say. 'And, in those circumstances, a pity to get off the train in the first place.'

'But what if he got off too?' asks Michaela.

'Who?'

'The bloke you were talking to?'

'You can't do that on the Internet, can you? Well, you can, but would it matter in the same way?'

'You've lost me,' says Michaela.

'The trouble with the railways is that you couldn't rely on there being another train,' I muse.

'If you're having difficulty booking tickets, you can always give me a bell . . .'

Michaela works in a travel agent on Station Road.

'Where are you going?'

'Exactly.' I smile at her.

'Just remember what your mother told you,' adds Michaela.

'Which thing in particular?'

'Don't talk to strangers,' says Michaela.

'Sometimes you can be more honest with a stranger, though, can't you, because it doesn't matter?'

'What are you like!' says Michaela, toying with her tisane in a way that makes me feel a bit immature sitting with a great wide cup of frothy milk in front of me.

How can I be both too old and too young at the same time?

There are no new messages in my Inbox.

Re: What are you like!

Just to let you know that I thought you were asking What are you like? rather than using this popular exclamation of dis-belief, which does not require an answer. As a matter of fact, I'm not keen on 'what are you like!'. Although I don't dislike it as much as 'You don't want to go there'. Funnily enough, as soon as I say I don't like using an expression, I find myself using it the whole time. 'As you do' is another one. And 'not' at the end of a sentence. And I'm so not a fan of 'so not' . . .

Hope all well. L

What I don't like is people who say, 'Try putting these words together: Go To There Don't Want We!' A

Glad I am it's so not just me! L

Up to any pole dancing recently been have you? A

Business your none of. L

On go words reversing we can't like this, we can? A

Not why? Easier makes it to the say things want you. L

Know about to you more I want. A

Enough you know me about. Wrong impressions think you got. About you what anyway? L

Think about this can I and back to you come. A

KO. L

Good night. AX

★   ★   ★

There is a programme about Tracey Emin on late-night television. She is everything I am not. She is so not ordinary. Even when she does ordinary things, they become extraordinary. Because she is an artist. Apparently she recently put a poster up on a lamp-post because she'd lost her cat and within minutes somebody had taken it down and offered it to The Saatchi Gallery.

I wonder if I ever met Tracey, would the encounter automatically be Art, or only if she videoed it? Would it depend on how long and where? If we brushed past each other on the tube, probably not. If we had an informal conversation in a bus shelter, perhaps.

There are a couple of questions I'd like to ask her.

1. At what point did your bed become art, and did you have a futon rolled up ready to use for when it happened?

2. Did you ever find your cat?

Would I then be an artist as well? Or just part of the installation?

CHAPTER 21

March

There are two messages in my Inbox.

Send Mother's Day flowers and get free chocs

I do not really believe my mother is directing the spam. And

Re: What are you like?

More Rusedski than Henman, I'm afraid, although I don't have his teeth. I can't play tennis either, but I do like to watch Wimbledon. A

So, in what way exactly do you resemble Rusedski? L

Hair thinning. And someone once told me I looked like the boy next door. A

Canadian? L

No. A

Thank goodness. Can't stand Canadians. L

Why? A

Ex-boyfriend. You don't want to go there.
L

Bastard! Surely nationality not to blame?
A

Well, in a way, yes, because they're so nice
and polite and politically correct, that
you don't expect them to be bastards. L

If I was in one of those photo booths, I
would probably press happy after the first
take. A

Are you happy? L

No, just boring. A

And a little bit arrogant if you think your
picture is so great first time. L

Maybe. A

Tell you what, why don't you get massively

drunk and then e-mail me? If you can remember to. L

Not drinking at the moment. Work. A

You ARE boring. As an alternative you could list three things you have done when drunk. Assume you're not teetotal or recovering alcoholic? L

Assume correctly. I will get back to you. AX

CHAPTER 22

'White chocolate and caviar? I don't know why we couldn't just have gone to the Harvester.'

'Mum, this is about the trendiest restaurant in the country,' I hiss at her. 'Joanna probably had to book it before Christmas. Can you just try to enjoy it for her sake.'

'Look at these prices!'

'The Harvester's not cheap.'

'But you know what you're getting. And they always have nice loos.'

'I'm sure the loos here will be fine.'

'Joanna's taking her time.'

'Can I get you a drink while you're waiting?' asks the waiter.

'No, thanks,' says Mum, as if he's trying to get her to invest in a timeshare.

He's very understanding. I think they must have brought in some off-duty nurses to be waiters for the day, perhaps expecting a number of elderly mothers feeling out of their depth with their successful offspring. I hope they're paying them better than the NHS, although in the NHS you don't get tips, apart from great big boxes of Milk Tray, which would make you sick along with the constant smell of disinfectant.

Joanna returns to the table looking peachy. She's so beautiful she can get away with jeans and a printed silk shirt even on Mother's Day.

'Is that Pucci?'

'I think it probably is,' says Joanna. 'Or Top Shop. Connie gets me some amazing stuff in the chain stores. It's the new chic, and costs virtually nothing.'

'Except you pay her.'

'Yes, but I'd pay her wherever, so the saving is considerable.'

Who am I to advise a debt expert about finance?

'I thought you'd both like to know that the wedding's going to be in July.'

'July? That doesn't leave much time,' says Mum.

'You're getting married!' says Joanna. 'Fast work!'

'To Andy.'

'Oh. I thought you'd found someone lovely. Never mind. Where's your list?'

'We're not having a list.'

'That's what you say now, but people really want to buy you things, and it's only fair on them. And you really don't want a whole load of Waterford Crystal, do you? Why don't you get Connie to sort it out?'

'It's not just the register office, it's the reception. They need a bit of notice for the table decorations or you end up with a dusty basket of artificial roses . . .' says Mum.

Thankfully, the waiter arrives with our starters.

'Marmalade,' says Mum. 'With duck!'

'What is the Harvester?' Joanna asks me, when we've dropped Mum off.

'You really don't want to go there.'

'I think we'd better next year.'

'No, I meant . . . doesn't matter. Do you think Mum's getting worse?'

'Worse? She seemed in the pink to me.'

Which makes us both laugh because Mum was very much in the pink. A deep fuchsia suit with a pale pink blouse, matching shoes and handbag.

Not much point in talking to Joanna about it anyway. She doesn't see Mum as often as I do. And Mum puts on a good show for her.

'Do you want to come in for a coffee?'

'Love to!'

I don't think Joanna's been to my house since just after I bought it and she brought her architect round to give me an estimate for the knocking through, except it wasn't called an estimate because we had to pretend that we were all friends until he realized that I was outside his price range. To be fair, his plans did involve taking it all down except the frontage, and building it back entirely in glass.

'Darling, you've made it so . . . cosy!' Joanna says.

'I knew you'd hate it.'

'No, it'll be lovely when it's finished.'

'It is finished.'

'You chose yellow for the walls? Suits the cottage style . . .'

'It's not cottage *style*. It is a cottage. I know you think it's hideous and nineties, but I like it.'

At least I did until about two minutes ago, and now I think it's hideous and nineties. Think I'll go to Homebase tomorrow after work and get some paint.

'Such a relief to be on my own!' says Joanna, plonking herself down on the sofa and kicking off her shoes in one balletic movement.

'Where are the boys?'

'Vlad's taken them on a field trip to Italy. They're doing the Romans at school. Do you know what they wanted to know?'

'Was there a McDonald's in Rome.'

'How did you know?'

'It's what they always ask.'

'I should spend more time with them, I really should.'

'Yes, you should.'

Serves her right for cottage style.

'God, you're lucky to have a little place of your own,' says Joanna.

'Lucky? Me?'

'Oh don't start, Lydia.'

I hate my sister.

'You're the one who started it. And you're the lucky one.'

'In what way?'

'Looks for start.'

'Looks aren't everything.'

'That's what good-looking people always say. When you're pretty, people take you serious-ly.'

'Not true.'

'Who'd put my bed in the Tate Modern?'

'What are you talking about?'

'Anyway, I've only got instant,' I tell her grumpi-ly.

'Instant will be perfect.'

I don't know why she has to do all this darling, lovely, perfect stuff for me. Does she even know she's doing it any more?

'I thought about Dad the other day,' I say, putting a mug of coffee down on the floor near her elegantly dangling hand.

'Really. Why?'

'I was at a kind of Tupperware party. And I thought, Mum actually replaced him with Tupperware . . . She even stored her picnic sets in his wardrobe. Why did she do that?'

'I think it's all about putting things in boxes,' says Joanna. 'Makes them easier to deal with.'

Which makes us laugh again, because she sounds just like one of Mum's demonstrations and she didn't mean it like that.

I love my sister.

'I couldn't remember his voice properly,' I tell her.

'But can you remember my voice when I'm not here?'

'Yes.'

'What's your strongest memory of him?' Joanna asks.

'Showing me places in an atlas.'

'Mine is making fires,' says Joanna. 'He really loved making a proper fire. I think it was his one little act of rebellion . . .'

'Of course, she got a living flame in before he was even cold. Why do you think Dad married Mum?' I ask.

'Because she was pretty. And pregnant.'

'No!' I can't imagine my mother being pregnant, but I suppose she must have been.

'Haven't you ever worked out the dates?'

'No.'

It's not something you do if you're not the oldest, is it?

'But it was the Swinging Sixties.'

'I don't think that reached as far as Kenton.'

'They wanted such different things. Dad would have been happy to buy an old camper van and take off round the world. Mum had her sights set on a semi-detached in Pinner.'

'Who do you think you're most like?' asks Joanna.

'Dad, of course. What?'

'Tupperware, marriage, a nice little house in the suburbs . . .' says Joanna.

'It wasn't actually Tupperware, it was aroma-therapy. Anyway, you're married.'

'I suppose so,' she admits. 'The trouble is, if you pretend you're happy with ordinary for long enough, you have a heart attack when you realize that you got it wrong, and now there's endless ordinariness stretching in front of you,' says Joanna.

'Is that what happened to Dad?'

My father had a coronary arrest on Platform 5 the week after he retired. He was on his way to the British Library. Nobody noticed until the rush hour was over. And by then it was too late. I've often stood in the place where he died and wondered what he was thinking about the moment before. The stationmaster told Mum that he had a smile on his face which she took to mean that he hadn't been in pain. But it might just as easily have been that the next train on the board was a Fast Aldgate, first stop Finchley Road.

'What do you think?' Joanna asks.

'I was in hospital at the time,' I remind her.

That was the worst moment. My mother and sister coming to my bedside with terrible stricken looks on their faces.

'Am I going to die?' I asked.

'No. You're going to be fine,' Joanna said.

'Dad's downstairs,' Mum added. 'He is dead though.'

I actually smiled because I was still in the relief-that-I-wasn't-going-to-die bit. And when I registered her words, I thought it must be her way of saying something else, like tired, buying a newspaper or some fruit. Something like that.

I may even have laughed.

Funny, us overlapping in the hospital.

He was alive when they brought him in, but he died a few minutes later. I thought afterwards that maybe his soul had passed through my ward on its way to heaven. Or wherever souls go.

I had to attend the funeral in a wheelchair which made it look as if I was attention seeking unless I explained about my operation. Which I hadn't wanted to do.

CHAPTER 23

There is one new message in my Inbox.

Re: Drinking

1. Chose 'The Green Green Grass of Home' on karaoke machine.
2. Cried, because words so moving.
3. Fell off podium.

Will this do? A

I don't know. It's really one episode, rather than three, isn't it? Did you know the words to 'Green Green Grass of Home'? L

You are quite keen on rules. And yes, sadly. A

Yes, I think that's probably sadder than knowing the words to 'Tie a Yellow Ribbon Round the Old Oak Tree', don't you? L

Definitely. At least in 'Tie a Yellow Ribbon', he's coming home with a smile on his face. Weird that they're both prison songs. A

Especially since they're the only prison songs I can think of. L

There's 'Take a Message to Mary' by the Everly Brothers. A

You're not in prison, are you? L

No. A

But you do like the Everlys? Not that it's technically a crime. L

If I say yes, will that count as embarrassing fact number 2? A

Not really. I borrowed their Greatest Hits from Mum and forgot to give it back. Never heard the last of it. In two ways, actually, because Mum went on and on, and so did the Everlys – that thing that happens with CDs when they stick for no reason at all. In case you're wondering, the song was 'Let it be Me'. Or 'Let It Be MMMMMMMMM', on my copy. L

Maybe it had fingermarks. You can get cleaner for CDs. A

You're not my mother, are you? L

No! A

Thank God! Don't mean to be mean, but I've had enough of her today. And of my infinitely more successful sister. I wish they would ban days where families have to get together, don't you? L

Absolutely. Starting with Christmas. A

But Mother's Day is the worst, because you can't even have a good old-fashioned family row like at Christmas. L

Is it Mother's Day today? Shit. Forgot to send mine a card. A

Will your mum do silently put-upon for the rest of the year? L

No. She's sweet, and so used to being generally ignored by men, she wouldn't expect me to do anything other than forget. Which makes it worse. A

Do you have a dad? L

What are you implying? Very much so. Flag-
pole in the front garden, shoes polished
every night. He was in the Army. A

Do you get on with him? L

That's a difficult question, isn't it? I
mean if you see your parents from somebody else's point of view you find them
laughable, but when they're yours, you
seem to spend your whole life trying to
please them. A

And failing. L

Quite. A

My dad would be pleased about my job, actually, but he died before he knew. Odd,
really, this is the second time I've talked
about him today and it's meant to be Mother's Day. L

What do you do? A

Hang on. I need several more embarrassing
facts from you before I spill anything more
about myself. If you can't do embarrassing

drunk stories, something like favourite film would be a start, and I mean real favourite. Not one by Kawasaki that makes you sound intelligent. L

Can I have a think about this and come back to you? A

Sure. L

Good night. AX

CHAPTER 24

It's World Book Day and everyone has come to school dressed as characters from their favourite books.

My class has almost equal numbers of Harry Potters and the characters left in their size at the Disney Store.

'Is Buzz Lightyear actually in a book?' I ask Dean.

'Yes. He's in the *Toy Story* annual.'

'So he is. You look very authentic!'

'What's authentic?' he asks suspiciously.

'True to life. Not that Buzz Lightyear is alive of course.'

'Who are you, Miss?'

'Guess?'

'Goldilocks?'

Fair enough. I have made a wig with thick plaits from a bathing cap and half a jumper's worth of yellow knitting wool.

'Actually, I'm Alice in Wonderland,' I tell him.

'You're a bit big,' he says.

I was hoping someone would say this. It's the

beauty of doing Alice as opposed to, say, Red Riding Hood.

'Alice has a bottle of potion that makes her big or small. And I'm Alice when she's big.'

'You still look stupid.'

'Says the superhero who's under four feet.'

I shouldn't really, but this swimming cap is very tight and hot.

'Actually, you all look fantastic! Ethan. Harry Potter, I presume.'

All the children except Ethan laugh.

'I'm Ron Weasley,' he says. 'Dad and I thought everyone would be Harry Potter.'

I did wonder about the jumper.

'Ron doesn't wear glasses,' says Robbie.

'Who are you, Robbie?'

'I'm Harry Potter.'

'So, where are your glasses? It doesn't matter, does it? Because we can use our imagination, which is what stories are all about. Now, because it's World Book Day, I thought we'd have a look at one of our favourite books.'

Quite pleased with that segue.

I have an extra-large book they make for classrooms. I hold it up.

'Who can tell me what the title of the book is? Robbie?'

'Ethan won't give me his glasses, Miss.'

Extremely unamused expression.

'Ethan give us your glasses, PLEASE!' says Robbie.

'Can anyone read the title to us?'

Ethan and Robbie both have their hands in the air. Robbie is wearing Ethan's glasses.

'Yes?'

'I can't see!' they shout in unison.

'Where are the three bears?' says Richard Batty.

'Where's Rudolph?' I counter.

'I'm Dumbledore.'

'I'm Alice in Wonderland.'

'I don't know how people with beards smoke,' says Richard.

'There aren't many people with three-foot-long beards made of cotton wool, are there, though?'

'Who's been eating my porridge?' says New Andy, joining us at our table.

'I'm Alice in Wonderland.'

There's no mistaking who he is supposed to be. I don't know what the headmaster thinks about him wearing a dress, especially a mini shift, half black, half white, and tights checked like a Grand Prix flag.

The witches were all highly amused. There's something about middle-aged women and drag.

'Who let the dogs out!' says Richard.

'Ha, ha. You're the first person who's said that today. Not.'

'Are we getting a team together for the Wine and Wisdom?' Richard Batty asks.

The posters went up this morning.

Wine and Wisdom
We provide the Wisdom (and nibbles!)
You provide the Wine (and corkscrews!)
Come along and Have Fun!

Of course, they don't provide the Wisdom, they provide the questions, but not a good idea to get pedantic with the Suburban Martyrs. One thing we can all agree on is that there might have been a good deal more Fun last year if the contestants had been able to open their Wine.

'Count me in!' says New Andy.

Richard and I stare at him. He's supply. Why on earth would he want to come to an after-school event?

'Not necessarily as much Fun as the poster claims,' I say.

'So that's three,' says Richard Batty. 'Shall I put Fern down?'

'Definitely. We can't manage without oriental religions.'

'And your Andy?'

'Of course.'

Last year, he was a bit of a hero pushing corks in. although the plastic ones that are increasingly common in non-vintage are virtually impossible to shift manually and he damaged a ligament in his thumb.

'So, that's five.'

'How many allowed?' asks New Andy.

'Maximum of eight,' says Richard.

'Wine and Wisdom, bit of a contradiction in terms,' says New Andy.

He is very young at times, but may be useful for filling in our Garage and Rap gaps.

'You don't have to be so black and white about it!' says Richard.

I can tell he's been waiting to say this all lunch, but the opportunity hasn't arisen.

'Hilarious!' says New Andy.

'*Five Minutes' Peace* is a story about a family of elephants called The Large Family. Can anyone tell me the name of one of the characters?'

Silence.

'What's the mummy elephant called?' I hint.

'Mrs Large?'

'Well done, Nicole.'

'It's a bit rude, isn't it, calling her Mrs Large?'

'Well, she is an elephant!'

'My dad calls my mum a fat cow and she thinks it's rude,' says Robbie.

'Because she's not a cow, dur brain,' says Dean.

'So, the characters in this story are Mrs Large and her three children, Lester, Laura and the Little One. And the question this story is asking is how is Mrs Large going to get her five minutes' peace?'

'Why does she want five minutes' peace?' asks Nikita.

Excellent interest in character's background.

'Well, sometimes children make a lot of noise and adults just need to get away from them for a short time.'

'Like you go to the materials cupboard?' says Geri.

'Miss? She's only just got up. She's had a whole night's sleep,' says Robbie.

Good reading of the subtext.

'Maybe Mr Large was snoring,' I say, trying to get them back to the point.

A round of giggles.

'Where does Mrs Large go to get her five minutes' peace?'

I turn to the relevant page, which shows an elephant in a bath with a tray full of comfort food beside her.

'She shouldn't eat cakes for breakfast, should she, Miss?'

'I suppose she shouldn't really.'

'She shouldn't leave the children by their own.'

'On their own. Perhaps not—'

'What if one of the children sets the house on fire?'

'They'd put it out with their trunks, dur brain.'

'You can't put water on a chip-pan fire. That fireman told us.'

'Elephants don't eat chips, do they, Miss?'

'Well . . .'

'Mrs Large,' says Ethan, after some consideration, 'is not really fit to be a mother at all, is she, Miss?'

★ ★ ★

215

The National Curriculum is very keen on encouraging lively literary analysis, and I think it's generally been a profitable day.

'We've thrown in a few surprises,' says the woman who's selling tickets for the Wine and Wisdom. 'I don't think you'll find it quite as easy as last year.'

'How exciting,' I say.

The Suburban Martyrs have thrown down the gauntlet. Our only response can be victory on the night.

'Do let me know if you'd like a hand with the nibbles,' I offer, to show willing, but she's already involved in a heated discussion on the relative merits of blind auctions and raffles.

'My dad wants to ask you a question,' says Ethan, taking my hand and dragging me across the playground.

There's a hint of an apology in Ethan's dad's smile even before I greet him and my heart sinks. I should never have offered to help in any way I could. Really, the marital problems of the parents are nothing to do with me, and sad though it is, he will have to work it out for himself. You have to ask yourself why a happily married woman was doing karate in the first place.

'Ethan is having a birthday party . . .'

'I know. I've been putting the invitations he brought in their reading folders.'

'Err. The thing is, he wants to invite you. You don't have to come, obviously, but I promised I'd ask. I know you like tea parties,' he says, shooting a glance up and down my blue shirtwaister and white bib apron.

At least someone has recognized me.

'It's very nice of you, Ethan,' I bend down to his level, 'but I'm afraid I'm busy.'

'But I'm having it on the first day of the holidays,' says Ethan.

'I'm sure you see enough of me at school!'

'No I don't. I'd like to see you all the time. At home too.'

So sweet!

'The thing is that I'm a bit old for parties.'

'My gran's coming and she's much older than you. I think. Dad, how old is Gran?'

'Oh, about sixty.'

'Are you younger than sixty?' Ethan demands.

His father smiles at me.

It's one of those adult smiles of complicity and understanding.

'You're as old as you feel,' I tell Ethan, which actually makes me sound like an old person who is pretending to be young. Probably the sort of thing Ethan's gran would say.

'Usually I feel about twenty-two,' I add hastily.

Another wonderful smile. Ethan's dad is really very attractive. How could anyone leave him for a karate teacher?

'I tell you what,' I hear myself saying, 'you let me know where it is, and if I'm passing, then I'll see if I can pop in . . .'

CHAPTER 25

Beep Beep Beep Beep Beep Beeeeep!
'BBC Radio 4. The News at Six o'clock.'
'Talks aimed at ending the siege of the Church of Nativity have broken down . . .'

I wonder why it is that if someone asks me how old I am, I always think twenty-two first?

I wonder how old Andy 42 is?

The obvious guess would be forty-two but he could be twenty-two or sixty-two or even ninety-two given his taste for Tom Jones' early hits.

It's also possible he could be some age that doesn't have a two in it at all.

'. . . BBC Radio 4 News.'

There is one new message in my Inbox.

Lydia. Don't put off a promising career . . .

It's spam, so how did they get hold of my name?

And if they know so much, why don't they also know that I have a perfectly respectable 2.2 Honours degree, so I don't need to buy a dodgy-sounding Diploma from them, thank you very much. I delete decisively.

Click on COMPOSE.

How old are you, by the way? L

No reply.

Andy 42 is not online. Silly of me, really, to expect he'll always be there.

He's probably working.

I wonder what he does?

If he's ninety-two, he'll be retired, of course.

I'm at a bit of a loose end.

I have done my preparation for tomorrow at school.

Andy is visiting Fiordiligi, who's in hospital on a drip.

I ring Michelle.

'Do you fancy a movie?'

'Sorry. I'm doing friendsreunited.'

'You're always doing friendsreunited. I'm a friend. Reunite with me.'

'You should join,' she says. 'Do you remember Patricia Hewitt?'

'Yes.'

'Apparently, she now Secretary of State for Trade and Industry.'

'It's not the same one.'

'How do you know?'

'Pat Hewitt went into her dad's undertaking business.'

'Cheeky cow!' says Michelle.

I can hear her keyboard tapping away in the background.

There are twins on *Millionaire*. They take the money at £64,000, when I would have won £125,000 by myself. I should dedicate the evening to ringing the *Millionaire* number, to get us on Newly Weds, although I'd rather do it on Andy's phone. I read in *Heat*, or was it *G2*, that one of the people who won a million invested £1,000 in phone calls in order to get through. You have to have a professional approach.

The deadline for applications for the senior teacher's post is looming.

I should take advantage of my free evening and update my CV.

My CV does not need much updating because I haven't actually done anything different since getting this job, ten, no it can't be ten, yes it is, years ago.

★ ★ ★

I know! I will make a list of Things to Do for my wedding.

Really, I need Andy here to do this properly, and he can't concentrate until *Così*'s out of the way.

Probably sensible to get an early night.

There is one new message in my Inbox!

Guess? A

42? L

Almost correct. I was when I set up this e-mail address, but I've recently had a birthday. A

Do you have a different age that automatically pops into your head when someone asks you? Mine's 22. L

43, at the moment. A

Oh dear. L

By the way, I do like Kurosawa's films, but prefer **Godfathers I** and **II**, if honest. What's your favourite film? A

I always say **Les Enfants du Paradis** by

Claude someone French, but then I'm terrified that someone will ask me questions about it, and I've only seen it once. Which doesn't necessarily mean anything, actually, because there are some films I don't really like at all but could answer any question in the world about. I know practically every frame of **No Way Out** starring Kevin Costner, for instance, because it often seems to be on late at night if I've dozed off during **Newsnight**. Stupid plot, but he does look nice in that white uniform.

Probably **Sleepless in Seattle** if I'm totally honest, which is weird because I don't fancy Tom Hanks.

Do you do this often, by the way? Writing to total strangers? L

Never before. You popped into my Inbox like a woman in a cake. Weird and wonderful things don't happen very often. Do you? A

No! Am I a weird and wonderful thing? I'm not the sort of woman you'd put in a cake, by the way. L

What sort of woman are you? A

I've just had a great idea. Why don't we do

twenty questions? Much cheaper than Casino Games, and cheaper even than **Millionaire** online because you don't win anything unless you pay to play. L

Do you mean like animal, mineral, vegetable? A

I'll give you a starter for free. I'm animal. L

Grrr! A

I meant in a defining sense.

Rules are: we each have twenty questions. Yes/No answers only. The person whose turn it is keeps going until they get a No, then the other takes over. The one who finds out the most about the other one wins. L

But how will we tell? A

Good point. Let's limit it to jobs, then. The one who finds out the other one's job wins. No lying, otherwise there's no point. Agreed? L

You're very keen on rules. Is this something to do with your job? A

Yes. 19. L

Do you wear a uniform? A

No. 18. But I admire the question. Slightly fetishistic, but you've knocked out several professions with the loss of just one point. Do you wear a uniform? L

Not usually. 19. A

Not usually. What's that supposed to mean? L

Look. I've got to run. Work. I'll come back to you. AX

Clearly, I am getting warm.
   But what sort of work could he be doing at this time of night?

CHAPTER 26

'Miss, Jesus died at Easter, didn't he?'
Suitably sad and serious face.
'Yes, Robbie, I'm afraid he did.'
'So he's dead, right?'
'Yes, he is.'
'No he's not, cos he rose again!'
He grins his gappy grin.
I hadn't realized it was a trick question.
'What's Chees-us?' says Nikita, making Him sound a bit like a savoury snack you dip a breadstick into.
'Jesus is the son of Bob,' says Geri, authoritatively.
'Not Bob, Gob,' says Gwyneth.
'God,' I say.
'It's rude to swear, Miss,' says Dean.

Easter is a difficult one with a multi-ethnic class of five and six year olds. We get through Christmas because Santa and presents kind of work for everyone.

After some discussion, Mrs Vane and I have decided on a Spring, Eggs and Renewal approach rather than anything too in-your-face Christian. They're just about young enough not to start asking too many birds-and-bees questions, especially if we keep away from 'All Things Bright and Beautiful'.

Miss Goodman thoroughly disapproves but even she lost her enthusiasm for the crucifixion last year when one of her class started trying to bang nails into his hands.

How to make an Easter bonnet:

1. Measure the circumference of child's head.
2. Take a broad strip of coloured paper cut it slightly longer than the circumference of head.
3. Glue ends together to make a tubular shape.
4. Sellotape ends together when the glue pops open. Ask classroom assistant why glue never sticks like it does on *Blue Peter*.
5. Snip small cuts into the base of the tube of paper like a fringe, then flatten out.
6. Cut a broad circle of different coloured paper and stick the tube onto the circle using glue on the flaps you've made.
7. Cut several further circles out because they never fit even if you've measured extremely carefully.
8. Hand over to classroom assistant to repeat twenty-nine times.
9. Sponge hair of child you've been using as a model which is now covered in glue.

CHAPTER 27

The Suburban Martyrs have rejected tradition and gone for a very hands-on type of quiz, which they're calling interactive (technically wrong because the answers are not affected by our input, but not wise to be pedantic).

There are several rounds involving tasting.

In Carbonated Drinks we have mistaken Dr Pepper for Dandelion and Burdock and Babycham for real champagne.

'Four points lost,' says Andy.

'But we're SUCH cheap dates,' says Jasper.

Jasper is New Andy's new boyfriend and he's black. If they stay together and we continue to get on as famously as we are, I will soon be able to say that some of my best friends are gay and black and that is as it should be at my age.

What does that expression mean, by the way? Is it that famous people get on extremely well with other famous people, or that we are getting on so well we might become famous for the strength of our friendship?

Jasper's got no idea either.
We open another bottle of white.

Fern urges us to play our joker on Teas of the World because she's got a cupboard full of Celestial Seasonings. Andy objects because we didn't have full confidence in his Breakfast Cereals expertise where he scored full marks, including identifying Kellogg's Sultana Bran which the rest of the room had down as Fruit 'n Fibre.

'I didn't think you were still seeing Alfonso,' says Fern, when he's up at the front arguing for a bonus point for getting Alpen No Added Sugar, as opposed to Alpen Original.

'We never do see each other what with *Cosi*, but there'll be plenty of time when we're married,' I assure her, because she's got her worried face on.

Almond Sunset, Emperor's Choice, Bengal Spice, they all smell wonderful. I shall have to take a closer look at the Well Being section in Sainsbury's.

Surely there'll be one General Knowledge round?

'The next set of questions,' says the quizmaster, 'concerns shrubs.'

The Suburban Martyrs have predicted that none of our team is a budding Alan Titchmarsh and we have been presented with a bag full of cuttings. One point for a correct answer. Two if we get the Latin as well.

'How well do you know your bush, Lydia?' Jasper asks me.

'How well do you know Lydia's bush?' New Andy says to my Andy.

But he's not really in with the spirit of the occasion.

I think he's feeling a bit redundant this year because no-one requires the services of his thumbs. Also, it's his turn to drive.

Hebe, clematis, wisteria. Fern knows them all because she did a Gardening Summer School last year.

'You're brilliant!' Jasper tells her.

'You have to expand your personal horizons, don't you?' says Fern, blushing.

After five rounds we edge into the lead.

The tension is mounting.

It's all going to hang on the final round which is: Karaoke.

I have a brief sickening flashback to New Year.

I remember with relief that Andy never actually received my New Year's Resolutions! So, really, I never made any! All that self-control for nothing!

My suspicions that the Martyrs have tried to rig the quiz against us are confirmed when our team's random selection is 'Bohemian Rhapsody' when all the others have ABBA songs.

Fern is a surprisingly convincing Freddie Mercury. The rest of us are loud and enthusiastic, even without Andy, who has declined to join us on stage because he doesn't want to damage his vocal chords this near to performance.

We win!

Some of us cannot resist a brief chorus of 'We are the Champions'!

'So, what do you think?' I ask, as we come in the door.

'About what?' says Andy.

'The colour. I've painted this room turquoise.'

'What colour did it used to be?'

'Yellow. Really bright, lemon-curd yellow.'

'Is that right?'

Andy just does not notice things.

'Drink?' I ask.

'Why don't we take the bottle upstairs,' says Andy.

I know I should be happy lying next to my future husband and half a bottle of Rioja.

There are no new messages in my Inbox.

CHAPTER 28

'Welcome to our Easter parade!' I say into the mike.

'Welcome to our Easter parade!' This time it's switched on.

Fern presses PLAY on the tape deck.

The children all walk onto the stage trying to balance their hats on their heads and looking very serious about their performance.

There is a collective 'Ahhh!' from the parents followed by the whirr of video cameras and some flash photography.

All credit to Fern, the children do look wonderful. Even though my class have all opted for the top-hat shape which I demonstrated, whereas Mrs Vane's have a mixture of bonnets, boaters and Chinese, they've each managed to get their personality into it. Dean's has bats for decoration. Ethan's has an owl perched on the brim. Not very Eastery, but actually more attractive than the cross that Gwyneth has on hers. I think she must go to Sunday school.

★   ★   ★

It is a beautiful spring day. The sunshine bathes the dingy hall in light so bright it makes the miracles Miss Goodman is talking about easier to believe.

We sing the song we've been rehearsing all week.

'It's a beautiful day in springtime . . .'

I wonder how it is that children's voices are high and flat at the same time.

'. . . it's a wonderful feeling . . .'

Why does hearing children sing always bring tears to my eyes?

'It's a happy, hoppy, healthy springtime DAY . . .'

It is almost the Easter holidays.

I'm as happy and hoppy and as healthy as anyone could be expected to be after ten weeks in a methane chamber.

There is no reason at all for me to cry.

Especially not in front of the parents.

CHAPTER 29

'What are we going to do today?' Andy asks. One of the great advantages of Honey was that they used to go for long walks together on Saturday mornings leaving me to snooze in bed surrounded by the week's celebrity magazines.

I open one eye.

'It's the holidays,' I say groggily. 'We don't have to do anything.'

Andy draws back the curtains and sunlight floods into the room.

'I had a Creme Egg for breakfast,' he says, 'you've got enough.'

'They were reduced,' I say, yawning and turning over.

Andy picks up the tube of Rescue Me gel from my dressing table and reads the ingredients out loud, then he winds the musical box in the shape of a Swiss chalet which my dad brought me back from a school trip.

It's the theme tune from *Dr Zhivago*.

He's got that frisky look that says he's not going to leave me alone until I get up.

'Actually, I've got a party to go to,' I tell him.

'I'm sorry but there's no adults without children,' the girl at the entrance announces without looking up.

'I was invited.'

'I've got no names on the door.'

'Look, would you mind if I just nip in and have a look? I am a primary school teacher,' I say.

'Anyone could say that though, couldn't they?'

There's something unmistakably surly about her.

'Kylie? It is Kylie, isn't it?'

Robbie's older sister.

'Miss?'

She stands up straight.

'Ever so sorry, Miss, but I've got strict instructions.'

'That's all right, Kylie. You're doing a good job. Are you actually old enough to work here?'

'I'm part time,' she says hurriedly, and presses the device that unlocks the turnstyle. 'Tell you what, I'll let you in free.'

I'm probably too easily bought. But then she's probably better off working underage than anything else she might get up to.

No sign of Ethan's dad, but Ethan spots me immediately from inside the vast cage of netting and tunnels that is the Spider's Web Play Centre.

'Miss!'

His smile makes the slight smell of feet and the noise of a hundred small children shrieking easier to bear.

I am in a rope tunnel suspended twenty feet above the floor. I was heading for the slide, which now seems to be on the other side of the web. How do kids find their way round these places?

If I hadn't been wearing the stupid knapsack Michelle's Charlene gave me for Christmas, I wouldn't have got caught.

'You don't want to wear a handbag on your back,' my mother said, as soon as I had it out of the wrapping paper.

I should know better than to defy her in a pathetic attempt to look younger than my age.

'Are you imagining what it's like to be a fly?' Ethan asks.

He's crawled the wrong way up one of the tubular tunnels to keep me company.

What a rewarding child to apply his new-found knowledge of mini beasts to the present situation.

'It's rather uncomfortable being a fly. And hot,' I tell him. 'Why don't you go and get someone to help me out?'

Ethan does a fire-engine siren as he slides down for help. You'd think the plastic tube would deaden the noise, but it has more of a brass instrument effect.

★   ★   ★

'There is a notice prohibiting adults,' the manager shouts up at me.

'The vertical slide was unmanned and two toddlers were about to launch themselves to certain death,' I shout back.

It was manned, actually, but from the ground you couldn't see the boy behind the giant spider.

I was fine shimmying up the rope ladder, but then I got overconfident.

'It's not really designed to hold your weight,' the manager shouts up.

Eventually Kylie cuts the knapsack from my shoulders with my folding nail scissors. When the manager hears that I'm a teacher, he offers me a complimentary Diet Coke for my trouble. Or possibly because I mention the Youth Employment Act in passing.

'I admire you for going in,' says Ethan's dad. 'I just take a deep breath and let them get on with it.'

'I'm sure it's best to be relaxed,' I tell him.

'Oh, I'm not relaxed. Not at all. You never quite get over the shock of being a parent, do you?'

'So people tell me.'

'You don't have children of your own? I assumed . . . you're so good with them.' He smiles.

'Probably *because* I don't have any of my own,' I say.

It's my standard response.

There's a short pause as we stare at the group of

children eating their party tea. I can tell he's trying to think of something nice or comforting to say like, 'well, there's still time,' but he doesn't know me well enough, and maybe I'm a lesbian anyway. Not that it really matters these days.

'Can I offer you some jelly? Or a bag of crisps?' he says.

'Thanks but I really ought to be off,' I tell him. 'I'm afraid I haven't got Ethan a present, because if I bought one for him, I'd have to buy them all one, and, you know, teacher's salary!'

I did actually buy him a Super Soaker Water Pistol. They had just come in with the barbecue stuff at Sainsbury's, which they were putting in the Seasonal Section alongside the cut-price Easter eggs. I had second thoughts at the till, in case I was frowned on for giving guns, or trying to replace his mother, or something. But the check-out girl had already rung it through, so I gave it to Andy, who was eager to try it out in my garden.

'We're honoured you came,' says Ethan's dad.

'I provided some entertainment, anyway.'

'It was certainly different!' he says, but nicely.

'Perhaps I should hire myself out?'

If I ever lose my job, a new career awaits me.

Clown.

Not that teachers do lose their jobs, unless they do something really bad. It's one of the trade-offs for the low pay.

★   ★   ★

I have to tie the balloon to my handbrake because it keeps wandering off and getting in the sight of the rearview mirror.

My party bag contains a lollipop, a piece of birthday cake in a napkin, a furry spider which walks down by itself when you throw it at a wall, and a spider's web made out of pale green plastic that glows in the dark.

I lick the icing off the web, and go into my bathroom to test its fluorescence. It's the only room in the house without a window.

'I got three squirrels and a little boy on a micro-scooter,' says Andy.

I jump because I'd forgotten he was still here. Not keen on leaving him alone in my house, but I suppose I shall have to get used to it when we are married.

He refills his Super Soaker at the sink.

'Oh, and the Queen Mother died,' he says.

CHAPTER 30

April

Hi! I'm sitting in a dark little Internet café in Portugal with a cup of café com leite, and a little custard cake with burnt sugar on the top. The sun is so bright, I can't see when I go outside, and there are tiled pavements. I'm wearing a T-shirt that shows my tummy button. Holidays are great, aren't they? L

Not if you're working. A

Why are you online at this time of day? L

Recalled to England temporarily. 18. A

For work? L

Yes. 17. A

You're not normally in England? L

No. 16. A

Why didn't you say so before? I needn't worry about sitting opposite you on the Metropolitan Line. Not that I use it very often. Are you English? L

PS. Your English is very good, by the way, if not. L

Yes. 15. Are you an English teacher? A

Not exactly. 17. What brings you to England? L

No wonder you're keen on rules. You're a teacher, aren't you? That explains the unseasonal holiday. A

OK, don't show off. 16. You haven't answered my question. L

Queen Mother's funeral. 14. I thought this was supposed to be Yes/No questions. A

Diplomat? Foreign dignitary? Member of the armed services? L

No. 13. No. 12. No. 11. A

Do you work for the Government in any capacity? L

I suppose technically I do. 10. A

You're not actual royalty, are you? What with the uniform and everything? Oh my God, you're Prince Andrew? Trying to remember if he's 42. L

Is that a question?

Yes. L

No. 9. Are you disappointed? A

In a way, because it would have been nice to think that a member of the royal family could be so informal. I used to think he was a total prat, but now I think he's one of the better ones. I don't know if it's me that's changed or him. The disadvantage would be that our e-mails would be read by strangers and/or the Sun. L

We are strangers. A

Are you in the secret service? L

How do you think I would answer that if I were? A

No. L

Well then. A

Think that must mean he is. Especially since he has failed to deduct a point. Which is a bit spooky. Perhaps he was one of those people who searches e-mails for words like bomb and hijack. Although I've always thought it unlikely that terrorists would actually use the words bomb and hijack. No wonder they had no idea about September 11th.

Dinner by the beach beckons. L

Hasta luego! A

It's Portugal, not Spain. L

Whatever they say in Portugal then. AX

Can't be very high ranking if he doesn't know that.

'What kept you?' asks Michelle.
   'Shopping.'
   'What did you buy?'
   'A coffee and one of those little custard cakes.'
   'Before supper?'
   She looks at me very suspiciously as I sit down.
   We both look out over the harbour.
   'This is nice,' says Michelle.

We always eat in the same restaurant and we always say the same things. Every year. It's what we do at Easter. Easter means Michelle's timeshare apartment on the Algarve which she bought with the insurance money. Obviously, she didn't want to go back to the Canaries.

'Shame it has to end really,' says Michelle.

'We've got a whole week left.'

'I mean, this'll be our last holiday on the Algarve.'

'Why?'

'Because you'll be married this time next year. You'll say now that it won't change you, but it will.'

'No it won't.'

'It will.'

'It really won't.'

'That's what you say now.'

I'm not going to protest any more. Partly because I think we're both a bit entrenched in our positions, and partly because, well, in a way, I'm quite keen on the idea of marriage changing my life. Just not in this particular way.

'The only thing I don't like about Portugal is this,' says Michelle, picking up the portion of sardine paste.

'Well, don't eat it.'

'I do like it, but by the time I've finished stuffing my face with bread and paste, I've got no room left for the main course.'

'It reminds me of tea after school,' I tell her.

'We always used to have paste. Whatever happened to paste?'

'People got paté instead,' says Michelle looking out over the harbour.

'I wonder if the Queen Mum had paste in her sandwiches.'

'She liked a proper tea.'

'Paste's probably a bit common for her. Although Gentleman's Relish is really just anchovy paste.'

'She definitely had Gentlemen's Relish.'

Michelle suddenly smiles at the piece of bread she's about to shove in her mouth, as if she sees it differently now that it's got royal approval.

'It's brilliant Michaela being pregnant, isn't it?' Michelle says. 'I mean, for the babysitting.'

'You wouldn't call them babies if you'd seen Charlene with the bloke who does the banana ride.'

'Beg pardon?'

'He's got this great big banana and he takes people round the bay on it,' I tell her.

'That's new,' says Michelle.

Michelle hasn't been out much during the day. She says it's because the sun has a detrimental effect on the skin, but it's never stopped her before, and the first thing she did when we got to the apartment was switch on the television. The shutters have rarely been open since.

We've seen the Queen Mother's funeral on BBC and CNN, Sky, in French, Spanish, Portuguese and a language Michelle assumed was German, but I think was probably Dutch. Her coffin's now disappeared into Windsor Castle and you'd think that we'd know everything we ever wanted to know, but even in English, amazingly, there are still gaps, like what does being Knight of the Thistle actually involve?

Apparently she planned her own funeral.

Did she set aside a couple of hours a week?

Did her diary read:

Thursday:	Breakfast
	Open Chelsea Flower Show
	Lunch
	Funeral Planning Committee
	Proper Tea
	Thistle Duties
	Cocktails

'When do you think she started?' Michelle wonders. 'Seventy-five, or eighty-five, or ninety? She could have spent a quarter of her life planning, which must have been a bit depressing, but she always kept a smile on her face.'

'Do you think the plans changed over the years?'

'Must have done.'

'Were there times when she favoured a Brazilian carnival approach, with steel bands, flowers on the gun carriage and the Guards dressed as peacocks?'

Michelle gives me a disapproving look.

245

'Do you think that was the real Koh-i-noor diamond?' I ask.

'David Dimbleby said it was.'

'But he would, wouldn't he?'

'Meaning?'

'Well, they're probably all geared up for a terrorist attack. Probably secret service men mingling in the crowds,' I say.

'At the Queen Mother's funeral?' Michelle's visibly shocked.

She's very naïve at times.

'Do you think the Queen's hat was a real Philip Treacy?'

'It did look a bit cool . . .'

'For a funeral.'

We both sip our drinks thoughtfully.

We're drinking gin and Dubonnet as a mark of respect. Actually, gin and port because the bartender didn't have any Dubonnet, but I think Her Majesty would have approved.

'At least we're not in England for it,' says Michelle. 'People will be going on about nothing else.'

The sun is setting over the bay.

We both stare at it, as if there's a tacit agreement to observe a minute's silence before eating, and then the waiter clatters knives, forks and plates of fish in front of us, and normal life can resume, just like at a football match when the fans start cheering again. I never know how they know that the minute is up.

'Tell you what, let's go to the disco?' Michelle says. 'What's to stop us? Michaela's babysitting.'

'Don't you think we're a bit old for it?'

Ironically, 'Murder on the Dancefloor' is what's playing when Michelle spots Charlene.

I volunteer to take her back to the apartment.

'She's old enough to look after herself,' says Michelle, scowling at her daughter.

'If she's not old enough to be here, then she's not old enough to walk back on her own.'

'Who are you, all of a sudden, her mother?' shouts Michelle.

It's a bit of a holiday low point.

'I did try to put her off,' I tell Charlene, as she kicks up a cloud of dust with every step. But we've never really got on, and she clearly thinks we only went into the disco because I told on her.

We were the oldest people there by about twenty years.

Michelle makes a great racket when she finally gets home.

'You'll never guess who I bumped into,' she says, not quite managing to step over my bed to hers.

We're sharing the double room. It's separate beds, but they're not very far apart.

'Ow!'

She's sitting on my leg.

'Declan,' she tells me. 'Now what do you make of that?'

She's forgetting I've had three hours for the gin and Dubonnet to wear off.

'I imagine you informed him where we were by e-mail and he got a cheap flight,' I say a bit humourlessly.

Now I understand why she went on about my marriage spoiling things. Michelle always likes to get an attack in before she has to defend herself.

```
Hi. Just saying hi really. I'm at a bit of a
loose end. My best friend has bumped into a
bloke from school and they're inseparable
even though she knows he's married. I'm
sharing a room with my heavily pregnant
goddaughter. The other's gone off with a
banana man, and the youngest hardly stirs
from Cartoon Network, which they don't have
at home. This afternoon, I am on chaperone
duty. L
```

Charlene must have been joking when she said this was the slow waterslide. Or trying to kill me.

Help!

I will do myself more harm by trying to slow down than by continuing.

Help!

Is this how they practise for the luge?

Help!

If I go any higher up the side on the next bend I'm going to flip over.

If I go any faster, I'll pass out.

Help!

If I go round one more corkscrew turn, my head will detach from my body.

Help!

The pool at the end is too small to stop me.

I'm going to crash into the wall and smash my legs into a thousand pieces.

HELP!!!!

It is amazing how little water you need to stop when you've been travelling at at least eighty miles per hour.

Oddly, the people coming down after me don't seem to be going nearly as fast as I did.

Perhaps my costume is especially aerodynamic? It's only Marks and Spencer.

I am still alive!

Wobbling a bit when I stand up.

Alive!

'All right, Aunt Lyd?' asks Charlene, all concerned.

'Fantastic! I'm going up again.'

That wipes the teenage smirk off her face.

Guess what? I've discovered the secret of human happiness. Waterslides! It must be the speed, or the proximity to death, or something. Have you ever tried? L

Hi. I've cracked two ribs. Nothing they can do about it apparently, although we'll see what they say when we get back to England. It was silly to come down face forwards, and specifically banned by pictures of people in red circles, which I thought meant No Diving. The insurance may pick up on that. How are you? L

Still immobile, but at least I'm not supposed to be captaining for England in the World Cup. I feel for David Beckham, even though I'm one of the few who doesn't fancy him. Still, it does mean the nation can move on from the Queen Mother. Funnily enough, I sustained a similar injury to my metatarsal a while back. It's not uncommon amongst people with jobs which involve a lot of standing. They can't put it in plaster. You just have to suffer. Declan, Michelle and I all put our hands on the photo of Becks' foot for a laugh. Then realized we were a day late, because they don't get the papers here until the afternoon! L

Bloody hell! If you're David bloody Beckham, they can put your foot in plaster! I may seek a second opinion for my ribs. Which are fine if I just sit. Which is why I'm spending so much time in the Internet café. Isn't it strange how people express pain in different languages? In England we say Ow! In Portugal they say Ay! But we're all human beings and since it's more of a reaction than a word you would have expected it to be more onomatopoeic. I wonder what they say in Japan and Korea? Weather is lovely. Wish you were here. In an online kind of way. L

Haven't heard from you and beginning to wonder if it's because you guessed that I'm a teacher. It doesn't have to be the end of the game. L

I'm not the sort who moans on about SATS, and although I do think we're poorly paid, generally I really love my job. But I won't talk about it, if you find it boring. L

If it's about your job, I haven't told anyone. L

You've still got lots of questions left! 16 in fact. You could ask me about anything. L

What I can't stand is not knowing if I'm going to hear from you again. OK? So just tell me. Yes or No. I won't even deduct a point. L

If I haven't heard from you by midnight on Sunday, I will assume that you are no longer interested in further communication. L

Fine. I'll take that as a No then. L

'What's wrong with you?' asks Michelle.

'Nothing.'

'Where have you been?'

'Shopping.'

'Again?'

'Where's Declan?'

'Had to get his flight.'

'Oh. Well, never mind,' I say. 'He's only down the road at home.'

'It's not the same.'

'I know.'

Michelle looks at me.

Lent's over now, so technically I can start confiding in her again.

'I've been having a bit of a thing with someone,' I confess. 'Actually, not really a thing.'

'I did wonder about all that shopping.'

'Nothing happened. It was purely epistolary.'

Michelle raises her eyebrows. She always thinks words with more than three syllables are rude.

'That's holiday romances,' she says, with a sigh.

'Nothing ever happens in my life,' I say, with a small stamp of my foot. 'If my life were a television series, it wouldn't get past the pilot.'

Michelle looks at me sympathetically.

'At least you've got a tan,' she says.

CHAPTER 31

Am I happy?

I'm getting married at the end of this term. I have a house which has doubled in value since I bought it, a job I love and, for the first time in my life, a proper tan. This morning I posted off my letter of application for the Senior Teacher's job.

The roadworks have been completed and there is only a small queue at the junction.

I'm through the lights first time.

What sort of person am I?

I am a grown-up person with a proper career trajectory, a fiancé, a house and a tan.

Michelle was right. It is all in the exfoliation, and the one benefit of cracked ribs is that you can't move around a lot. Normally I don't have the patience.

I am lovable, brown and altogether not bad at all.

'Somebody's been in the sun,' says Mrs Wates.

'You can get away with a lot with a tan,' says Mrs Vane, looking at my lime-green sundress.

Perhaps it is a bit skimpy. Always takes a while to adjust back to proper clothes after a holiday. I'd never wear halter-necks in England normally.

'Apparently, there's an exponential incidence of melanomas in Australia,' says Miss Goodman.

I shall ignore them because they are jealous of my tan and because I will not have to listen to them ever again after this term if I get the Senior Teacher job. And why shouldn't I? My Ofsted ratings are as good as anyone else's. Not Richard Batty's obviously. With a tan, I can easily pass as a grown-up person.

'Are you having a baby, Miss?' asks Geri.

'No.'

'You've got a fat tummy.'

Those bloody little custard cakes. Which wouldn't have mattered, actually, if I had been able to do some exercise.

'I think it's just the way I'm standing. I have broken some bones in my chest.'

Geri looks sceptical. Children of six are not generally very sympathetic to other people's injuries.

'Or maybe it's this dress. You're not used to seeing me in a dress, are you?'

Not the most practical garment for doing PE in, but I shall stick to standing-up exercises.

'Miss, you've got fat and you've gone all brown!' says Robbie.

'So?'

That stops him in his tracks.

'I think you look like a beautiful flower in your pretty dress,' Ethan says.

'Thank you, Ethan. At least there is one child with good manners in my class. Now, who remembers our palm tree exercise?'

'Miss?'

'Yes, Robbie?'

'I think you look like a beautiful tree in your dress.'

'Thank you. AYYY!'

Mistake to stretch my arms above my head.

Should have remembered after the incident with the overhead locker. Still, at least it was Charlene who got hit on the head with the *vinho verde* and not Michaela.

'Can I be godfather?' says New Andy, pointing at my stomach.

'I've cracked two ribs.'

'Have you got bandaging on under there?'

'No, it's just the way I'm sitting. And I haven't been able to go to the gym, obviously.'

Now I wish I'd had the baked potato with cottage cheese and asked them to hold the butter.

'I just thought what with you getting married . . .'

I'll just have the salad bit, avoid the coleslaw, and maybe just a tiny bit of chilli for protein.

'People get married for all sorts of reasons, actually.'

I snap the ring right off my can of Coke. Diet, fortunately, but the hole's so small it would take about a month to suck out the contents.

'So, what's yours?' asks New Andy.

Richard Batty's pretending very hard to concentrate on his food. There's a limit to the number of times you can prod the crust of your pie without it all collapsing into the gravy.

'What's my what?'

'Reason for getting married,' says New Andy.

'You don't have to have a reason for getting married.'

'You just said you did.'

'I'm in quite a lot of pain, actually,' I say.

'I'm going to get you another can.' Richard finally comes to my aid.

'Thank you.'

'You've got great legs. You should show them more often,' says New Andy.

I know he's gay, but babies, weight and reasons for getting married in the space of about thirty seconds for a woman of my age is going some. And it's actually a sexist remark concerning my legs.

However, I shall forgive him instantly.

'You know, you remind me of someone now your hair's gone a bit blond,' he says.

I brace myself and prepare a response in case he says Miss Piggy, which happened once when I let Michelle do my highlights.

'I think I know who you mean,' says Richard, opening a new can for me.

They're both peering at me with slightly screwed-up eyes, like you do at those pictures which are all dots, but turn out to be an eagle or something if you stare long enough. I always pretend I know what they're talking about, but I've never actually identified anything except lots of dots.

'I think I'm thinking of the one in *Bob and Rose*.'

Huge relief, because, 'You're hardly Kermit yourself?' makes no sense at all.

I put my fork down. I don't want to spoil the effect by chewing.

'The actress is called Lesley Sharp. She's much prettier than me.'

'You could be her older sister,' says New Andy.

'So, if my life were a television series, you reckon Lesley Sharp could play me?'

Silly to push it. Now they're both looking at me as if I'm delusional.

'Because, I have a wonderful idea for a detective series featuring a school teacher,' I improvise.

How to grow a sunflower:

1. Put seed in a plastic container.
2. Cover with earth.
3. Water thoroughly, but not so much that all the earth foams up and flows over the top onto the window sill and then drips into teacher's tote bag.
4. Wait.

The waiting bit is always a battle of nerves. I never quite trust that nature is going to do what it's supposed to, and the children don't understand why the shoots never appear when they're looking.

'When will it get a flower?' asks Gwyneth, staring sadly at her little yoghurt pot of soil.

'Not for a long time yet. First they get shoots and leaves, and when they're strong enough and big enough, we can plant them by the fence and then, if we're really lucky we'll get some flowers.'

'Why can't we do runner beans? Mrs Vane's class is doing runner beans in plastic bottles and you can see the roots and everything . . .'

'Miss?'

'Yes, Robbie?'

'I think you look like a runner bean in your green dress.'

I love the six year old's idea of what is rude.

What with runner beans and Lesley Sharp, the omens are looking very good for this term.

Beep Beep Beep Beep Beep Beeeeep!

'BBC Radio 4. The News at Five o'clock.'

I am not going to look up my Inbox when I get home.

I must forget about Andy 42.

I am certainly not going to write to him again.

In fact, I shall delete our entire correspondence.

There is the remote possibility that Andy 42's

computer has a virus which means he never received my e-mails.

Or he could have been cut off. If you forget to pay your server bill, even accidentally, they're on to you straightaway. It happened to me when I got a new Visa card.

He could, of course, have been run over and I will never know.

Or kidnapped.

It happens all the time in dramas featuring lone female detectives on television.

Actually, primary teacher turns amateur detective is a good idea for a series. You learn a lot of grown-up secrets from the things the children tell you.

I should write to the head of ITV.

'. . . BBC Radio 4 News.'

CHAPTER 32

'**B**asically we've got three options,' I tell Andy, after thoroughly studying the relevant magazines. 'They are:

1. Have a nice lunch in a nice restaurant with our families and closest friends.
2. Invite everyone we know, including distant cousins and schoolfriends we didn't really like but want to show off to, in which case we'll have to hire the cricket pavilion, cheap caterers and a disco.
3. Put a limit on it, like forty, and have a wedding buffet package at a hotel, with free honeymoon suite for the night. Apparently, some people find that whittling down the lists gives you a surprising insight into who's really important in their life.'

'Do we know forty people?' asks Andy.
  'Or we could elope and not tell anyone.'
  'So, in fact there are four options,' he says.
  'Correct.'

'But we've already told some people,' he argues.

'Look, we're meant to have decided all this about a year ago, at least.'

'Says who?'

One of the things I do like about Andy is his logic.

What we do for our wedding is up to us, and that's easy to forget when my mother and every single publication says that we're leaving it till the last minute, even though there are almost three months to go which is longer than I've ever had to organize a party.

If I had to choose between pure logic or pure spontaneity for the rest of my life, I'd definitely go for logic.

Unless, on a whim, I suddenly decided to go for spontaneity.

The publican is tapping his microphone preparing to start the quiz.

'How did *Cosi* go, by the way?' I ask Andy.

I have to look as if I'm interested, but don't want to risk a blow-by-blow account. I know that it was awful because I saw the review in the *Gazette* which I forgot to cancel when I was on holiday. The word they used was brave. They couldn't be too unkind because of Fiordiligi singing from a wheelchair.

'Are we ready?' says the publican very loudly with a little scream of feedback.

'We learned a lot from the experience,' Andy says.

'The first round is called Islands.'

I couldn't have timed it better.

'Question one: Is Auckland on the North or South Island of New Zealand?'

Andy just smiles and writes down the answer.

'I've always fancied New Zealand,' he says, in the general murmur between questions. 'How about it for the honeymoon?'

'You wouldn't go on a shopping day in Boulogne when they had that offer on the ferries, and now you want to go to New Zealand?'

'Question number two. On which island did Rupert Brooke die?'

'Skyros,' I say.

'Are you sure?' says Andy.

Differences between men and women:

5. Not knowing how you know things.

I often find answers pop into my head without me knowing where they come from. In fact, if asked whether I knew the answers before we started the quiz, I would probably say no. But then they just appear. I call it intuition. Andy calls it luck.

Andy could always tell you why he knows something and where he learned it.

It may of course be that he just has a better memory in some respects.

'It couldn't be the Isle of Wight?' says Andy.

'There's some corner of a *foreign* field that is for ever England.'

Don't know where that came from either.

'Question number three. What is the capital of Sri Lanka?'

Andy writes down Colombo.

'You never confer,' I say.

'Did you know it?'

'That's not the point.'

'The Lake District, then,' Andy suggests.

'What?'

'For our honeymoon.'

'I'm not going to the Lake District again.'

I'm still in disbelief about New Zealand. After three consecutive summer breaks in the rainiest bits of England, being told that he fancies New Zealand is like being told that he likes to wear dresses. I don't just mean for Hogmanay and the *Mikado*.

'Well, where do you want to go?' Andy asks.

'Not the Lake District or New Zealand.'

'You decide then. As long as it's nowhere hot.'

'It's meant to be you who decides, organizes, pays and makes it a surprise.'

'But you just said you didn't want New Zealand,' he says, as if it's me who's being unreasonable.

'Question number four. Bikini Atoll is part of which island group?'

Andy sucks the top of his Bic.

'The Bahamas?' I venture. 'Isn't Bermuda in the Bahamas?'

'It's not Bermuda, it's Bikini Atoll.'

'They've both got summer clothing named after them.'

'They're hardly likely to explode a nuclear bomb that close to the US coast,' says Andy.

I knew the name was familiar.

'Wait a minute,' says Andy.

He writes down The Marshall Islands, which I've never even heard of.

'How did you know that?'

'I did American History O level. Is there something wrong?'

'No.' I sigh.

We win, of course. The Marshall Islands clinched it.

'Remember my ribs!' I say, as Andy kisses me.

'Just about,' he says.

Which is quite a sweet way of saying he's missed me.

He hasn't mentioned my tan, but then he hasn't mentioned my extra pounds either. Andy simply doesn't notice things. And that works both ways.

It's terribly difficult to find a comfortable sleeping position.

Andy's snoring.

I could do some marking.

I could prepare my graphs showing time against sunflower height and print out thirty copies so that I didn't have to hog the photocopier on Monday morning.

My mouse glides over:

Royal Marines hunt Taliban

and clicks on:

Sexy Swedes: Sven and Ulrika Latest

She has made a statement saying it's over, which, technically, means it must have begun.

You'd never think it to look at him.

I will not look in my Inbox.

I will save myself the disappointment.

There's never anything but spam anyway.

Although, come to think of it, I did put my e-mail address on my senior teacher application and it would be a shame to miss a call for interview, especially after making so much of my IT expertise.

There is one new message in my Inbox.

Lose Weight While You Sleep!

I delete immediately.

'There's a letter for you,' says Andy, putting a cup of tea down on my bedside table and flapping a brown envelope in front my determinedly closed eyes.

I usually leave brown envelopes until the end of the week.

It is the end of the week.

'Aren't you going to open it?'

It's bad enough, frankly, having someone else wander around your house when you're fast asleep, let alone pick up your post from the mat, let alone expect to know what's in it.

The tea only goes some way to compensating.

If it's a parking fine I shall own up.

If it's a speeding offence, I shall deny it.

It may, of course, just be the reminder that my tax disc is about to run out.

Have I really had that car a whole year?

It's an interview for the senior teacher's job!

'Good news?' Andy asks, watching my smile.

'I suppose so.'

Haven't actually told Andy about going for the job. I think it's a superstition thing.

'Well?'

I am going to have to get used to sharing things.

'My smear was negative,' I tell him.

'Congratulations,' says Andy, looking awkward.

CHAPTER 33

Fern has booked herself a holistic holiday on a Greek island where you live in a hut and learn some sort of alternative skill like yoga or creative writing. It's a community so you all have to muck in, and it's ecologically friendly, which means that you can't flush the toilet too much. Sounds a bit too much like guide camp to me, but I pretend to be enthusiastic for her sake.

We're eating the detoxifying salads she's brought in for lunch sitting at the bus stop. It's the only place there's a bench, apart from the recreation ground which is littered with dog poo and syringes, and you can't walk and eat alfalfa at the same time. Desperate measures are called for to lose the extra pounds. Bad enough to be a size 14 in Monsoon without it creasing up round my thighs.

My mother's suggestion is that we try Jaeger, where the sizing is more generous. Or forget about the fish tail hem.

'You could get something specially made,' she says, staring at my hips where the red-on-red devoré velvet dress is meant to hang straight down. At the moment, it clings to my bum like something J Lo might wear if she was determined to appear in another Worst Dressed list.

'You can expand your personal horizons by learning new skills, like pottery or windsurfing, explore your problems in drama therapy, or simply get back in touch with yourself,' Fern tells me.

A bus pulls to a stop and we wave it on. The driver revs a cloud of exhaust in our faces which probably negates the cleansing effect of the fresh herbs.

'When you get back in touch with yourself, are you getting back in touch with the person you were before you got rid of all the personality problems or somebody else, in which case, how do you know you're going to get on?'

'Try saying this,' says Fern. 'I accept myself and cherish every wonderful aspect of myself.'

'But I don't accept my hip measurement at the moment.'

Munch, munch, munch. This constant chewing is doing nothing for my ribs.

'I think I may have a problem with sharing,' I tell Fern.

'Do you want to share it?'

'Not really.'

The island looks pretty in the brochure.

I wonder about Greece for our honeymoon. Trouble is, I once had a wonderful holiday in

Greece, and it's never the same when you go back, especially with someone who burns easily.

We should probably go somewhere grown up and educational like Florence or Prague, but if I try to picture us wandering around narrow dark streets pointing out interesting old buildings, Andy's always looking at the map and saying he thinks we've gone the wrong way.

If I see us sitting in a café which smells deliciously of coffee and warm pastries, he's got his Palm out and is searching the Net for the current sterling/Euro exchange rate.

If the Government ever wants a hand with the campaign to promote the Euro, I have a great idea for an advert: a couple are sitting at a pavement café somewhere recognizably foreign like Venice or Salamanca. She's got a load of designer carrier bags on the ground around her feet and has her face tilted towards the sunshine. He's crouched over the menu and a calculator with a frown.

The slogan is: 'Imagine a holiday where he doesn't say "How much is that in real money?"'

You'd certainly win the female vote.

Another one might be the same table, but with more shopping bags and two women with cocktails. 'Imagine a holiday without the credit-card bill for £3,000 afterwards.'

It happened when Michelle and I went to Milan for the weekend.

Trouble with lire is (was, I suppose. Can the

Italians really have got it together to convert?) there are just too many noughts, especially if you've been drinking aperitifs. We thought the shoes were such a bargain for Gucci that we both bought three pairs each and matching handbags.

I should write to Tony Blair. or Gordon Brown. I'm never sure which one is in favour of the Euro and which isn't.

That's before they start on the economic tests. Whatever they are. Does anyone know? Or is it just me?

Another bus stops. The doors hiss open.

'It's tempting, isn't it,' I say to Fern. 'To just get on and see where it takes us.'

'I think it's Harlesden,' says Fern.

CHAPTER 34

'It's a long and arduous climb for the Marines. First they have to find the caves and then they have to put them . . .' cue footage of a bit of mountain exploding, '. . . beyond use.'

The nice reporter is standing in a remote and unidentifiable spot, wearing a flak jacket. There's an explosion behind him. He ducks. I wonder if they fired that one especially for the camera?

What is the point of him being there, putting his life at risk to tell us what we already know, which is that the Marines are clearing some caves somewhere secret in Afghanistan?

And how on earth does he manage to shave in those conditions?

Also, does he carry his own rucksack like the Marines do, or is there a Sherpa type of person out of sight of the camera who lugs all the equipment around? And what is a satellite phone? They suddenly appeared when Afghanistan became news and then everyone was using them. Terrorists, journalists, the Army, as if there's always been satellite phones and everyone knew what they were.

Perhaps everyone does, and it's only me. Too late to ask now anyway. I can see the advantage if there aren't many masts around. The reception in part of North London is bad enough, but how do you charge them? Especially if you're living in a cave?

Cy and Ry are making exploding noises from inside their custom-made Thunderbird wardrobes.

'We're Al Quaeda, and we're hiding in the caves. Come and blow us up.'

'No.'

'You be Al Quaeda then.'

I switch the News off.

'What do I have to do?'

The boys are wearing Action Man pyjamas.

'Get yourself a beard and a machine-gun!' says Cy.

I find an umbrella and a dishcloth in the utility room.

'Will this do?' I ask.

'Have you got a beard under there?' Cy pulls at my headdress.

'Watch it,' says Ry, 'she could be a suicide bomber.'

'What's a suicide bomber?'

'It's when they strap bombs to their bodies and blow themselves up.'

If they were my children I would let them have toy guns, but no television in the bedroom. Joanna says she doesn't want to encourage violence, and apparently you have to be a parent to understand the benefits of Japanese cartoons in the mornings at weekends.

'But we're going to blow her up first,' Ry reasons.

'Bedtime,' I say firmly.

'Do we have to go to school tomorrow?'

'You do.'

'I hate school,' says Cy.

'I hate it more than you,' says Ry.

I wonder if the children I teach say this every evening, or whether it's just the independent sector.

'What story do you want?'

'Can we have *We're Going on a Bear Hunt?*' asks Cy.

They must be tired. It's one of the books they had before they knew about guns and bombs and terrorism. They just want the rhythm of a story to lull them off to sleep.

Cy and Ry have two modes.

Full Volume and Off.

I kiss their heads, breathing the wonderful smell of innocence and L'Oreal for Kids shampoo.

'Linda!' says the bald Canadian neighbour who's standing at the door, holding out a glossy magazine called *Beautiful British Columbia*.

'Working tonight?'

'In a manner of speaking,' I whisper.

'I brought this round for Joanna.'

'I'll give it to her when she gets back,' I put my index finger to my lips.

He actually tiptoes back down the steps.

'Asleep?' says Joanna, when she comes in from work.

She looks tired.

'Yes. And as sweet as the day they were born.'

'The day they came out of the special unit, you mean,' she corrects me. 'The day they were born they looked like two pieces of tandoori chicken.'

She takes off her mac, drapes it over the back of the sofa, and sighs.

'Heavy day?' I ask, like a solicitous wife in a headache pill advert.

'It was just bloody meetings all day long and then I had to get my eyebrows done.'

'You have someone to pluck your eyebrows?'

'Not pluck, thread. She's a wonderful Indian woman called Min. You should have her. Lasts so much longer, and it's only thirty quid!'

I'm glad I'm not beautiful. It's cheaper.

'Why have you got a dishcloth on your head?' Joanna asks.

I remove it.

'Shall we have a bottle of champagne?' she asks.

'I'm driving.'

'Oh go on! Vlad's in South Africa. We haven't had a girls' night for ages!'

I know that I shouldn't because I'm certain there's something important going on tomorrow that I need to be on top form for.

It can't be very important if I've forgotten.

Actually, I've never found that an entirely reliable rule.

Oh to hell with it. It won't be the first time I've been to work with a hangover!

'What happened to Conchita?' I say.

'Don't ask,' says Joanna. 'That's definitely the last from South America. Mimi's got a boy from the Czech Republic. It may be the solution. Do you think Cy and Ry would like a man about the house?'

'What would Vlad think?'

I try to remain neutral on the subject of child care.

'Vlad would not like it one little bit,' says Joanna, firing the cork off the champagne bottle, which sounds like a gun.

'What were you watching?' Joanna peers at the television.

'It's a look-alikes competition. The bloke just said that some of them are getting so famous they'll soon have look-alikes of their own, which I thought was rather funny.'

'Who's that one supposed to look like?' Joanna goes closer to the telly. She's always been a bit short sighted but she won't wear specs.

'Chris Tarrant.'

'Doesn't look a bit like him.'

'Perhaps they should have a programme about how they came to think they did look like someone. Was it looking in the mirror, or did people keep asking them for autographs? You could interview their mates from work. Call it *Before they were Look-alikes*. I might write to the head of ITV,' I tell her.

We drain our champagne glasses.

'Wasn't it meant to be the end of trivia?' says Joanna.

'What?'

'September 11th. Everyone said it was the day that trivia died. But I think there's more trivia now.'

On serious consideration, I think she's right.

'Terrorist nuclear attacks and biological warfare are probably too frightening for the human psyche to contemplate,' says Joanna.

'So we glide over War on Terrorism and click on Beckham's foot?'

'Exactly.'

I'm glad to know there's a proper psychological explanation for it all.

'Where were you on September 11th?' I ask Joanna, halfway down the bottle.

'Work. It came up on the screen. Where were you?'

'In the car. You know how it is? BBC Radio 4. There has been a terrorist attack on New York . . . you're like, yes, and I wonder what the sell-by date is on that Ocean Pie I seem to remember at the back of the fridge. Then it's like, terrorist attack? I stopped the car. Man in the car behind only just missed me. He's shouting at me as he overtakes, and I'm like, "Don't you know there's been a terrorist attack on New York?' When I turned on the television, I was so frightened. I think it was the people jumping out of the window. Do you think you would have jumped or stayed?'

'Jumped,' says Joanna.

I have a sudden image of her jumping off the top diving board at the open-air swimming pool in the days before the boy from Wealdstone fractured his skull and they put a rope across with a No Entry sign. I only ever got as far as standing on the edge and losing my nerve. But I was four years younger.

'Do you remember having cocktails in the Windows on the World?' I ask her.

'Don't,' says Joanna.

She pours more champagne. It feels really decadent to be drinking champagne and talking about September 11th at the same time.

'Apparently everyone in New York had sex,' she says.

'I can understand that,' I say. 'I didn't think about sex but I did think about giving it all up and going on holiday. But, if I'd gone on holiday, where would I be now? Broke, and without a job. Six months down the line and everything's the same.'

'Except it's not somehow, is it?' says Joanna.

'No. Everything changed. But I'm not sure how.'

Joanna opens another bottle.

'I took a black cab to the boys' school and brought them home,' she says. 'I sat here holding them, thinking, if we survive this, I'll take them to the villa in Tuscany and we'll just live. We've got enough money to last for as long as we like, if we're careful. We'll be safe there. I'll grow vegetables and make bread.'

I like the image of Joanna huddled up on her sofa imagining a better life. I didn't realize she ever had doubts. I lean over and give her a big hug.

'So when are you off?' I ask.

'Where?'

'Tuscany?'

'August, as usual. Not to live, obviously. Once the boys got fed up with seeing the planes crash into the towers, they were furious for making them miss after-school football, and the actual business of looking after them drives me crazy. After a very short time, I find I'm just saying yes and no randomly and not even listening. Vlad pointed out that I'd never even managed to keep a pot of basil alive without the services of a container gardener.'

We're chatting just like we used to in our bedroom when Joanna came home from Oxford in the holidays and told me about losing her virginity or becoming President of the Union.

'I had a terrible thought when I saw the first tower collapse,' I confess.

'What?'

'You won't tell?'

'I won't tell.'

'I thought, I wonder if this means I still have

278

to get married? Do you think I'm an appallingly shallow person?'

Joanna just looks at me.

'Maybe everyone had one really awful selfish thought,' she says.

I hate my sister.

'Did you?' I suddenly ask.

She nods.

'Come on!'

'I thought, I wonder if this means I can start smoking again?'

'I think that's worse than mine.'

'Not as bad as Vlad's, though,' says Joanna, waspishly.

'Tell me!'

'What he actually said was, "The house in the Hamptons has just doubled in value."'

'That's obscene,' I say, feeling suddenly much better.

Joanna absently strokes the glossy lake landscape on the front of *Beautiful British Columbia*.

'Your neighbour brought it round,' I tell her, nodding my head in the direction of next door.

'He's very keen to get to know you better,' says Joanna.

'He's Canadian,' I say.

'You can't take against a whole nation because of one guy,' says Joanna.

When I think about BerNARD, which I don't

often, these days, I think of staying up talking all night. And doing all that how-many-children-will-we-have stuff. And being so in love that when he talked about having a dog and a cabin up in Whistler, I pictured us all running through a meadow together, rather like the family in *We're Going on a Bear Hunt*, with the dog actually jumping up to lick my hand.

Bernard used to talk about the bears in Canada actually. Although I didn't know the book then, obviously.

'Bastard!' I say.
   'BasTARD!' says Joanna.
   I love my sister.

We're getting towards the end of the second bottle.
   'Do you find it easy to share with Vlad?' I ask.
   'Share? What exactly?'
   'Living space. Secrets?'
   'We've got quite a lot of living space, so that helps, as does having a good secretary.'
   'So that's your recipe for a successful marriage.'
   'If it is successful.'
   'Everything you do is successful.'
   There's a pivotal moment with alcohol when clarity turns to melancholy and there's no return.
   'Oh Lord, not this again,' says Joanna.
   Alcohol never has the same effect on her because she only really wets her lips.
   'And you're pretty . . .'

'It's what's inside that counts,' she says, patiently.

'Not if you want to be a newsreader. Name one female newsreader who's not pretty. There, you see, you can't. Or reporter? Not one. Even Orla Guerin is beautiful, in a haunted kind of way.'

'Would you want to be a newsreader though?'

'That's not the point.'

Joanna looks bewildered.

'And you've got a proper career,' I say sulkily.

'You've got a career.'

'I've got a job. You've got a proper career.'

'Would you want to be doing what I do?' Joanna asks.

'I don't even know what you do! That is my whole point. You know things . . .'

'Things?'

'The three economic tests for the Euro—'

'I think it's five, isn't it?' says Joanna.

'You see, you ARE a proper person, and I'm . . . shit!'

'What?'

'The senior teacher's interview!'

'What?'

'I've got an interview for a proper career tomorrow. That's why I'm not drinking, except I am and now I'm drunk and I can't even drive home!'

'I'll get you a taxi.'

'You can't solve my life with taxis!' I'm shouting now.

'I know. I know,' says Joanna, she puts her

arms around me. She's been dealing with me for a long time.

'The point is that I make an attempt to be a proper person and it goes wrong before I've even started.' I blub against the shoulder of her suit. It's extremely fine wool, probably Armani.

'Why do you want to be a senior teacher anyway?' she asks gently.

'Because it's the sort of thing that a proper person of my age does.'

'But it's bound to be all admin, isn't it?'

'Now you're the expert on teaching as well?'

I sniff.

'Have some water and go to bed. I'll wake you up early and you'll be fine.'

CHAPTER 35

'You are a proper person and you will be a wonderful senior teacher,' says Joanna, slamming my lime-green door and blowing me a kiss. 'Drive carefully!'

I am a proper person who will be a wonderful senior teacher.

It sounds a bit like one of Fern's mantras, but designed especially for me by someone who actually knows me.

I'm feeling surprisingly calm.

I am a calm proper person who is perfect for a responsible job.

I've got plenty of time.

It's actually quite nice driving up the A40 at this time in the morning.

Slight sharpness in the air.

Talking to Joanna really cleared my mind and I do not have a hangover.

Cy and Ry jumping on my bed at 5.30 reminded me why I wouldn't want children and I now understand about the Japanese cartoons.

★   ★   ★

I am a calm person stepping into my shower at home.

I am a smart person with an aubergine trouser suit from the Per Una range, size 14, that fits perfectly.

If I breathe in.

I am a calm person who has two recently recovered ribs, don't forget, so shouldn't punish herself, and who might find it easier to put on shoes lying back on bed with leg in the air.

Can't reach feet.

I am an unflappable person who has realized that she must take off trousers, put shoes on, then put trousers on again.

Yes!

I am a proper person in a bit of a hurry now, who's caught the hem of the left trouser leg on the heel of her shoe. But only at the back, so no-one will notice if I don't trip on it.

Still masses of time.

I am a slightly vain person who should have worn flat shoes for driving but didn't want to risk forgetting the proper pair like she once did to a wedding, although scuffed brown suede flatties wouldn't look so weird with aubergine trouser suit as they did with floaty dress and lilac straw hat.

I am such a calm person, I didn't see the new set of temporary lights and braking distance is much harder to judge with sling-backs.

Oh F off your F-ing self!

I am a calm, grown-up, apologetic person who smiles when she gets out of the car to exchange numbers with the driver in front.

'What the hell are you smiling about?' shouts the man in the navy-blue pinstripe suit. It's one of those double-breasted things and he's got a handkerchief in his pocket.

'I'm not smiling.'

'Yes you are!'

'Not consciously. Probably an involuntary reaction because I'm nervous.'

'Do you even know the word sorry?'

'I was going to get on to that, but you started in on the smiling.'

'Were you asleep?'

'Look, this obviously isn't getting us anywhere. Why don't we start again and try to be civilized.'

'Are you accusing me of being uncivilized?'

'Oh for God's sake, it's only a bloody Toyota.'

'Don't you swear at me, young lady.'

I know it's not the right time, but it's rather nice to know I'm not past the age of being 'young lady'.

'Don't you start smiling again. If I weren't already late, I'd call the police.'

'As far as I know, smiling is not a crime.'

He sniffs the air suspiciously.

'Have you been drinking?'

I summon my extremely unamused face, and offer to furnish him with my details.

I am a calm, mature person who knows how to behave with dignity in a minor traffic accident.

Surely six hours is long enough for a half a bottle of champagne to wear off? Even a whole bottle?

I am a clever person who, even though she's lost a bit of time, parks a couple of streets away from the school where she's being interviewed so no-one will see her trying to reverse into a space.

I am late, but it doesn't matter because I am third on the list to be interviewed, and the first one has only just gone in.

The other candidate is a very petite woman. So short that I mistook her for a pupil standing by the notice-board reading the fire drill, until I noticed she was wearing a red suit and tiny high black patent leather pumps.

What on earth made her want to be a teacher when she must have known the sort of remarks people would make? She's wearing a wedding ring. I wonder if her husband is short too, or whether he's one of those hugely tall men who fancy petite women because they've got an inferiority complex, or a problem with willy length.

Did she wear white? She's so tiny, she could probably have got away with a First Communion dress, which would have been cheaper because there's no VAT on children's clothes.

She has the unfortunate affect, although I don't think she intends it, of making me feel gargantuan.

I move as far away as the room will allow, but I'm still taller than her.

Even sitting down, the ceiling is closer to my head than hers standing.

I inadvertently pick up *OK!* magazine rather than the *G2 Education* bit, and then I don't know whether to put it down quickly, or keep reading it as if there's no shame involved in case there's a hidden camera and it's some sort of trick psychological test.

I can hear murmurings of laughter in the interview room. Obviously getting on very well in there.

Then there's silence, and I realize I'm bracing myself for the whizz of a high-speed drill.

I remind myself that I am not in a dentist's waiting room.

The door opens.

The tiny woman is called. She has a French name. She glances at me as she goes in. Tiny little steps.

'Lydia?' says a voice above me.

'Richard! What are you doing here?'

He looks reassuringly huge, and as guilty as sin.

Bloody Hell!

'How did it go?' I ask, as if I've come to pick him up after some nasty root canal work.

'Not too bad.'

'Right.'

'Good luck, then!' he says, walking out of the

room sort of sideways, as if he's afraid to turn his back on me.

I might as well leave now. Unless they have some reason for particularly wanting a woman, in which case, I must have an advantage over a French pixie.
   I try to think of some of the considered and articulate answers I have prepared, but the only words I can remember after thirty-six years on this planet, are the lyrics of 'Thumbelina'.

'Thumbelina, what's the difference if you're very small?'

I go over on my heel as I walk past my rival on her way out.

I am a calm and sensible person who has suddenly become Dick Emery.

'When your heart is full of love, you're nine feet tall!'

I am a shivering sweaty person whose hand is so clammy on the doorknob she can't actually twist it without getting a tissue out of her handbag except she doesn't have any tissues so she has to use her sleeve.

I am a silent person whose heart has suddenly jumped from her chest into the cavity in her head where her brain used to be before it dissolved.

I am a panicky person whose eyes swim around the interview panel, pulling to focus on a navy-blue double-breasted pinstripe suit which says, 'We've already met,' as the headteacher introduces him as chairman of the governors.

The good news is that I didn't tell anyone about going for the job.

'Never mind,' says New Andy.
'About what?'
He looks me up and down.
'You've been for an interview because of the suit. You didn't get it because you would have taken the rest of the day off.'
'My dear Watson, you're in the wrong profession,' I snap at him. 'So am I, apparently.'
'I was hoping you'd get it because I'm in for you.'
'It was stupid of me to put theatre on my CV when the only production I've seen in the last year was the Year One *Ugly Duckling* assembly.'
'It had some memorable performances,' says New Andy. 'Anyway, everyone puts theatre on their CV.'
'Do you?'
'Yes, but I'm an actor.'
Always seems to lose his sense of humour when he mentions it.
'Did Richard get it?'
'Yes. They just called him.'
'I knew he would,' I smile brightly. 'Excuse me.'

I cry a lot in the ladies' loo, because I didn't get the job and because my only real friend is a traitor who is leaving me to face the witches on my own.

New Andy is waiting for me outside.

He hands me a tissue.

'I didn't want the job anyway,' I say. 'Why would I want to do all that admin? What I really like is the kids.'

'You are such a great teacher, you know,' he says. 'Your class has been clamouring for you all morning.'

'Have they really?'

I do a loud and unfeminine sniff.

'Of course they have,' says New Andy, giving me a little squeeze round the waist. Doesn't hurt. Like David Beckham's foot, my ribs are making encouraging progress, and that's without all the tabloid interest.

'Where's the nice man gone?' says Nikita.

'Men are better at teaching than women, aren't they?' says Robbie.

'It has nothing to do with whether you're a man or a woman,' I tell him.

'Why are you wearing a man's clothes then?' asks Geri.

'Some of our sunflowers started to grow when the man was teaching us,' says Dean.

Sure enough, there are lots of little shoots peeping through the soil.

Which is an encouraging sign.

CHAPTER 36

May

'How are you getting on, teachers?' sneers Anne Robinson.

Everyone in the studio laughs.

Teachers are doing poorly.

'That's just typical of the anti-intellectual attitude of this country, isn't it?' I say. 'They're supposed to be testing the nation's intelligence, and all the presenter wants to do is make fun of teachers.'

'Sssh,' says Andy.

He's doing the National IQ test out loud and checking his answers on the computer at the same time.

I am hopeless at sequences. I'd be all right given enough time, but I've just about worked out what they're asking when there's an ear-piercing electronic bleep and that puts me right off.

'Think I got all of those,' says Andy.

I am hopeless at fitting a shape into a lot of mixed-up shapes.

'Think I got all those,' says Andy.

'Maybe next time you'll be able to pack the boot of the car when we go away?'

A bit mean, I know, but last time he made me take my stuff in plastic bags because he couldn't find a way of getting my suitcase in.

I think this test has been set by a man because there's nothing intuitive in it.

I'm slightly better on the verbal stuff.

As achromatic is to neutral, salutary is to wholesome.

Easy. And actually a lot more useful than those stupid shapes.

As miser is to save, refuge is to shelter.

Andy gets it right.

I thinks it's as friend is to support.

Actually, I don't see why I'm wrong. But there's no debate allowed, even though an ability to discuss something rationally is part of intelligence, in my humble opinion.

I'm only a teacher after all.

And a teacher's role in this particular show is to be vilified by a red-haired quiz mistress who's labouring under the illusion that reading out the answers in a strict voice is the same as knowing them.

'I am a genius,' says Andy, when he's totted up his final score.

'Well done.'

He has only missed two correct answers, and he claims that I put him off one of them swearing at the television.

'What did you get?' he asks.

'I didn't bother to add them up,' I tell him.

Really, it's beneath my intelligence.

As a group, teachers came out top, despite Anne Robinson's best efforts, and I am happy to count myself among their number.

I work in the most intelligent profession in the country.

I am wearing a huge white wedding dress that takes up most of the back garden. Behind me, my mother is saying, 'Come on now, you're going to be late.'

I'm staring at the flower bed. It's a pile of freshly dug earth.

'I planted some sunflowers, but they haven't come up,' I tell her.

'Sunflowers?' says my mother. 'For a wedding?'

I wake up, seething. Why shouldn't I have sunflowers?

I must make a note in my Wedding Book (actually an exercise book with the coloured paper letters I cut out and pasted on spelling Wedding) to ask the florist about the feasibility of having sunflowers on the tables, or even a sunflower bouquet, although not, obviously, if I am having the red dress.

Actually, I could grow them myself.

Anyway, I doubt that the dream was really about sunflowers at all.

Andy is snoring so loudly I cannot get back to sleep.

My mouse glides over:
   No Al Quaeda found. Operation 'a success'
   and clicks on:
   The right lingerie for your wedding dress

Lucky this. I didn't even know I had to have special underwear!

It's not just bra and panties, either. There's a whole language of lingerie I don't know. Backless basques, seamfree moulded cups, waspies, thongs with tummy-control panels (can't possibly work, can they?), bottom-lifting briefs. Some of them sound like quite a good idea even if you're not getting married.

And don't forget hosiery!

As if.

Apparently I have to choose between lace-topped stockings, which I think might slightly ruin the lump-free silhouette that the seamfree G-string will provide, or hold-ups, which in my experience don't. If they're loose enough to be comfortable, they end up in a concertina of wrinkles round your ankles, if they're tight enough to stay, you're asking for deep-vein thrombosis.

I'm sure there will be no new messages in my Inbox. There never are.

There are 4 new messages in my Inbox!

I'm sure they'll all be spam. They always are.

There are 4 new messages in my Inbox and they're all from Andy 42!

Internet access can be limited for reasons I will explain when more time. You're the best thing that's happened to me for ages. Please keep writing! AX

Oh dear! Surely you didn't mean it about not writing any more. I miss you. AX

I am so sorry. I promise to try to give you some notice in future if I'm going to be unreachable, would that help? AX

This may be really out of order, but I'm wondering if you may be under the illusion that I am in the secret service. If you want, I will tell you what I really do. Ax

Click on REPLY.

Are you crazy? I'm not giving in when I've still got 9 questions. Sorry I haven't writ-ten recently but I've been so busy trying to organize my wedding. L

Should show I'm not bothered.
Almost instantly a new message appears.

Wedding? Not the kilt, I trust? A

How weird that he's also up at this time of night!

As a matter of fact he's a genius. It's
official. L

I suppose I should say congratulations, but
I'm not a big fan of marriage. A

Me neither. I mean the whole organization
thing, obviously. There's a load of people
I don't know and don't particularly like
who've somehow become involved: the assist-
ants in the dress shop, the cake baker, the
photographer, the florist and the woman who
will give me false nails with pearls stuck
on them which I think look like growths, but
are apparently what everyone is having this
year. They've all got these slightly whiny
voices, half cajoling, half patronizing
and when I decide on something wrong – like
balloons instead of flowers at the reception – they sort of sigh and say 'Well, it is
Your Big Day,' as if I'm making a terrible
mistake which I will regret for the rest of
my life. Probably OK now that I've decided
to have sunflowers. But still the issue of

the cake. I don't even like wedding cake. If it were up to me, I would go for a mountain of profiteroles. L

Surely it is up to you? A

Ask my mother. The more she says, 'it's up to you', the more I know I should just go along with what the 'professionals' are telling me. L

Have you done The List yet? That's the worst. The sheer greed of it. I think I fell out of love with my wife on the day she said, of the Royal Doulton dinner service under consideration, 'We're spending about £50 a head, why shouldn't they pay £24 for a dinner plate?' I hadn't seen that side of her before. A

You're married? L

Was. 8. A

Are you divorced? L

Separated. 7. A

You can't deduct points for personal questions. I would have won long ago on that reckoning. Why? L

The official reason is because of my work. I am away a lot, in quite dangerous places. She couldn't handle it. A

What's the unofficial reason? L

She knew what I was like when she married me, but she thought I'd change. I thought I knew what she was like, but she did change. She became all wifey and materialistic. Or maybe I didn't know her very well. A

Did you divide the dinner service when you split up? L

No. I was delighted for her to have it, soup tureen, gravy boat, the lot. A

I'd better go to bed. Good night. L

Good night. I'm glad we're talking again. AX

Yes. L

Night then. AX

Night. L

Night. AXX

Oh, for heaven's sake! Did you go to a public
school or something? L

Yes. Good night AXXX

I pretend to sleep through Andy rising, Andy turning on the radio in the kitchen while he eats his
cereal, Andy practising his scales in the shower.
    I admit defeat only when he starts prodding
me.
    'What are we going to do today?'
    I yawn.
    'I think we'd better have another look at china.'
    'China?' he says, as if I'm talking about another
expensive honeymoon destination.
    'Apparently, we're meant to have a gravy boat.'

CHAPTER 37

'**M**iss, what's a nuclear war?' asks Nikita.
'Where did you hear it?'
'My father said there's going to be one.'

'Really? It's a big war. Big and not very nice, actually.'

'Is it the same as a custard war?' asks Ethan.

'A custard war,' I repeat.

'What is a custard war?'

'Do you mean a custard-pie fight, when two clowns throw custard pies at each other? No, it's not the same as that.' I laugh.

'My father said there's going to be one with my mum.'

'He means a custody battle, Miss,' says Nicole, wearily.

'Yes,' says Ethan smiling. 'That's it!'

'It just means you never see your dad again,' Nicole informs him with the experience of one who's been there.

Ethan's face falls.

'That's not necessarily true,' I tell him. 'It's a bit

of an argument between grown-ups. Is your father picking you up today?'

'He's in the air.'

'In the air?'

'Flying.'

Do parents not realize how traumatic it is for the children when they split up?

I am going to have to have a word with Ethan's dad.

There's a meeting in the staffroom at lunch to decide how the school should celebrate the Queen's Golden Jubilee.

'If we run off several hundred outlines of the Union Jack, the children could colour them and use them as flags,' says Richard. He's always got an educational agenda.

I can see the room is going to divide into those who think we should try and teach the children something, and those who think we should have a good old patriotic knees-up. The Party People Party needs a leader and I am prepared to take it on. Not as a matter of principle, because if we could get beyond the prospect of Tony Blair as Queen, or, worse, Richard Branson, then I would be a Republican, but out of sheer bloody-mindedness.

'They won't flap,' I say.

The witches' heads swivel in my direction, relishing the first hit of the campaign.

'Flags made of normal paper don't flap. I may

not have had quite as many years' teaching experience as you have, but I do know about flapping,' I tell him. I can feel support for me mounting. 'Anyway, think of the expense of the crayons.'

'Good point,' says Richard.

Trust him to back off instantly. Coward!

My supporters are looking to me for leadership.

'My suggestion is a garden party,' I'm thinking on my feet, even though I'm actually sitting down. 'A proper garden party like the Queen has, with cucumber sandwiches. The kids could all bring cakes and dress up as posh people, and we can hang some bunting up.'

'It's simple,' says Mrs Vane.

'But effective,' says Miss Goodman.

I just knew that she'd have a pastel hat left over from a niece's wedding that she's been dying to wear again.

So that's that.

Which of us is wondering if we really are senior teacher material now?

'And since it's a mufti day, the children could all bring 50p for a charity,' I add, which clinches it.

There isn't even a vote, although I anticipate differences of opinion about which charity, but we will leave that for another day.

'Daddy!'

Ethan screams past me. His father stands out in the playground because he's wearing a crisp white short-sleeved shirt and white trousers and looks not dissimilar to Kevin Costner in *No Way Out*.

Michelle thinks that Sven Goran Eriksson looks a bit like Kevin Costner, but I think it's just her way of understanding why all those attractive younger women are after him.

I wonder if Ethan's dad is in the US Navy? I suppose there might be an intelligence unit. Odd, because this part of North London is one of the farthest points in England from the sea and strange to put staff in uniform if it's secret.

He could be a dentist, of course, or an osteopath.

'You look well,' he says, as I approach.

It's a bit of a familiar comment, but we have seen each other outside school. It's often difficult to adjust.

'Ethan needs a name label in his sweatshirt,' I say, trying to reassert the professional boundaries.

'I'm sorry,' he says, giving my body a frankly in-appropriate once over.

I shiver, even though it's quite a summery day.

'I've been away quite a bit,' he says.

'Yes, I've been meaning to have—'

'Dad, guess what?'

'What?' his father and I say in unison.

'I'm going to be someone famous.'

'I'm sure you will be,' says his dad, putting his arm around him.

I like it when parents encourage their children's ambition. There are quite a few not a million paces from where I'm standing who would say something like, 'Not if you spend all your time watching television.'

But I've missed the moment for a quiet word.

It's coming up to the news on Radio 4, but first the presenter tells us, with exactly the same calm mixture of enthusiasm and sang-froid as she would have if she was announcing the end of the world, there is a series of programmes about food preserving beginning later in the week.

Beep Beep Beep Beep Beep Beeeeep!

'BBC Radio 4. The News at Four o'clock.'

'The Foreign Office has advised all British citizens to leave India . . .'

How on earth can they get a whole series out of preserving food? Even Radio 4, where they stretched the history of one lifeboat out for weeks. I mean there's freezing and there's canning, isn't there? End of story.

And drying, I suppose.

There's pickling and bottling (but they could get those into the same programme), and preserving itself, like jams and chutneys and things. But that's it.

Oh, there's salting. Curing. And smoking. Bound to get a whole programme out of an Orkney smokery where you can't understand a word the smoker is saying, but there's lots of sloshing around in fish tanks.

When we went to that Korean restaurant, I'm sure Andy told me that they used to bury cabbage in pots underground. It tasted like it, frankly. And in France you sometimes get paté and bits of duck embalmed in fat. There's a name for it. Is that what confit means? Or is it potting? Like potted shrimps?

God, I love potted shrimps. How could I have forgotten them until this minute? Trying to remember the last time I had them.

We could have potted shrimps on the wedding buffet table. Got to have something other than poached salmon and coronation chicken and Mum won't tolerate Thai.

'Thai?' she says, as if I'm being somehow disrespectful.

Potted shrimps are English and traditional. They'll no doubt appear in the Radio 4 series, which she is bound to listen to, and she'll be OK if Gary Rhodes gives them the thumbs up. Of all the celebrity chefs you could follow, fancy choosing Gary Rhodes!

Vladimir gets a rash with seafood, but there will be other things.

'. . . BBC Radio 4 News.'

CHAPTER 38

Differences between men and women:
6. Astronomy.
'What we need is a western horizon with no street lights,' says Andy.

We're speeding up the M40.

He's read in the paper that all the planets are in a line which won't happen again for seventy years. So, we're driving out of London to look at the sky.

Even though he's planned it, it feels like a really spontaneous thing to do.

'We've missed Mercury because it sets at around seven o'clock, but we should get Venus, Saturn and Jupiter, if we're lucky.'

'But it's still light at seven o'clock, so you wouldn't be able to see Mercury anyway,' I reason.

'Exactly,' says Andy, taking his eyes off the road for a second to smile his approval of my logic.

At Thame we turn off the motorway, and park in a suitably lonely lay-by.

It is certainly dark in the countryside.

And smelly.

And cold.

The sky is so starry, hundreds more stars seem to appear each second as my eyes adjust.

'I think that must be Venus,' says Andy, pointing.

'Which?'

'The bright one.'

'That one?'

'No! That one! And that one must be Saturn.'

He points again.

'Amazing.'

When he said we would be able to see the planets really clearly, I admit I was expecting rings and moons and pretty colours like the pictures of the planets in the Encyclopedia of Astronomy.

What we've actually got is a few celestial bodies shining a little bit brighter than the rest.

I've trodden in something squelchy.

'Or it may be the Space Station,' says Andy.

I had the same feeling of disappointment the Christmas my dad bought me my Atlas of the Stars and we went out into the garden together when everyone else was watching *Morecambe and Wise*.

I was expecting lines joining the constellations up.

'Look, three in a row, up there,' said my dad, trying to help me see the patterns.

307

'Follow the North Star up. There! No there! There!'

In those days, I didn't know about pretending. When I finally did spot Orion's Belt, it was like, great, three stars in a row, so now can we go in and have a warm mince pie?

Why is the hunter's belt so important anyway? And where's his head, arms, legs and bow and arrow?

That before we start on Great and Little Bears. Doesn't anyone else find it weird that the alternative name is the Frying Pan? I can't think of a single feature bears have in common with that particular utensil, but at least I can see it does look like one.

It's not that I don't like looking at stars. It's just that if I'm going to stand around in the dark and chilly places gazing at the heavens, I'm more inclined to be wondering about infinity, eternity and the human condition. That sort of thing.

I wonder if Andy 42 can see the planets lined up where he is?

I am on the panel for *Through the Keyhole*. It's a much nicer house than usual, with a knocked-through downstairs room, but there's no furniture. The camera zooms in to close up on a picture frame on the marble fireplace. It's the one from the awful photo session Michelle got me as a birthday present. You get a make-over too. I went into the studio looking like myself and came out three hours later wearing a mud pack of foundation and clutching a soft-focus portrait of someone who might almost have been a relative of mine, but who'd been embalmed with a fixed simper on her face.

'You should get this chap to do your wedding photos,' said my mother, when she saw it.

'Who lives here?' asks David Frost. 'And who is the woman in the photo?'

I wake up, shivering because Andy's got the duvet round him like a caterpillar in a cocoon.

I wonder why I keep having such weird dreams?

My mouse glides over:

2 million troops mobilize on Kashmir border

and:

Free Jubilee Ring Tone download!

There is one new message in my Inbox.

Dream Home. Find the right house for you!

I delete immediately.

Click on COMPOSE.

Are you happy? L

Difficult one. I suppose it depends on how you define happiness. I'm incredibly privileged compared to most people in the world. But I don't know if it's really possible to be happy given all the injustice. The worst thing is that it doesn't seem to shock me any more. I am neither happy, nor sad, nor outraged. It's like, another day, another famine, another war. Is this just middle age, or is it that I'm so overwhelmed by the enormity of human suffering I can no longer feel? I don't know. Are you happy? A

No. You've just made me feel really depressed. L

Sorry. A

It's not that I'm unhappy. It's just that I feel I should be doing something with my life. L

Snap. A

Really? L

Think it's called a mid-life crisis. A

Mine can't be that, because I'm still young,

and I haven't done the marriage thing yet and failed like you have. L

Thanks. A

Sorry. I just meant that I haven't even got to my mid life yet. I look like a woman in her mid thirties, but inside, I don't really feel grown up. L

I thought that is what a mid-life crisis was. A

Oh. That's one more thing to worry about then. L

What else worries you? A

I'm not a deep person. L

Hoorah! A

No, I meant, that's one of the things that worries me. If I had to watch Samuel Becket or **The Bill** for the rest of my life, I would choose **The Bill** without hesitation. L

But why would you ever have to make such a choice? A

True. But don't you find it useful to give

yourself alternative universe scenarios to determine how you really feel? L

No. A

I think it's a girl's thing. Did you have an awful selfish thought after September 11th? L

When I saw the towers collapse, I do remember thinking, I wonder if this means I can give up my job? Will this do? A

Not really. What is it you dislike about your job? L

I think I'm only doing it to prove that I'm brave. It's a boy's thing. A

You're clearly weird, but not as awful and selfish as I hoped. L

Have you ever been truly happy? A

I sometimes think about this, and the image I come up with is a day on holiday in Greece once. We hired motorbikes. We didn't have driving licences or anything, but the man didn't care as long as we left a deposit. It was really hot and there we were flying along this dusty road with the wind in our hair, overtaking each other, yelling and laughing. I remember thinking, oh to hell with it, if I die, I don't care! That's the moment I think of. L

Who's we? A

Canadian ex-boyfriend. L

Bastard! A

The waterslide in Portugal was a similar experience, but shorter, obviously. Maybe it's something to do with confronting my fears, or being forced to lose control, or whatever. There used to be flumes at Watford Springs, but Michelle says they've knocked it down to build flats. Perhaps a rollercoaster? Or the luge? Although realistically, I am a bit old and anyway there's only been snow here once in the last five years. L

Do you think happiness is just about moments, then? Maybe I'm wrong to see it as some sort of continuum. A

No, you're right. Real happiness would be a kind of glorious freedom from anxiety. I don't just mean weapons of mass destruction and what George W. Bush might do next (are weapons of mass destruction safe in the hands of a man who can't aim a pretzel into his own mouth?). There's all sorts of other things too, like what's the Euro all about, and how can I live my life thinking that the world is going to end tomorrow when I have to earn my living today in case it doesn't? My sister thinks I try to block it all out with trivia. The really alarming thing is that I think I may just like trivia. L

Does trivia make you happy? A

It makes you good at quizzes, which brings happiness of sorts. L

Maybe the question we should ask ourselves is not Am I happy? But, How can I be a better person? A

It's late. I'm going to sleep on that one. L

Good night. A

You didn't X. L

Good nightXXXXXXXXXXXXXA

Sorry to be so needy. L

CHAPTER 39

'D o you think you can have secrets from the man you're going to marry?' I ask Michelle. It's a nice evening for a change.

We're rocking gently backwards and forwards on the swings in the park just like we used to do in the hour after school before *Crossroads*.

'You're asking the wrong person,' she says.

Kirsty is hanging upside down from the monkey bars in her pink Britney Spears T-shirt and hipster jeans.

'Seems like only yesterday she was a baby,' says Michelle. 'And now she's into her first teen bra.'

'She's only nine.'

'They grow up younger these days.'

'There are secrets, aren't there?' I persist. 'And then there's things that you just haven't discussed for one reason or another.'

'Because they're secret,' says Michelle, as if she's lighted on the solution to a crossword clue.

'Do you think it's possible to fancy someone you haven't met?' I ask.

'This isn't about Robert Redford again?' says Michelle.

'It hasn't been about Robert Redford for years,' I say. 'I'm talking about someone you really don't know. Don't even know what he looks like.'

'Internet dating?'

'Not exactly.'

'Like me and Declan!' says Michelle, enthusiastically, as if I've just joined some cult she's got herself involved in.

'You two do know each other, I point out.

'But it's different when it's just you and him meeting somewhere up in the sky, isn't it?' says Michelle.

'Yes,' I say. 'It *is* different, isn't it?'

Swing. Swing.

We've both got dreamy smiles on our faces now.

'What's he like?' Michelle wants to know.

'He's funny and a bit troubled and I feel I can talk to him about anything.'

'Everything?' asks Michelle.

'Almost everything.'

'Sounds perfect! Who is he?'

'That's the weird thing. I don't know who he is or what he does or where he is. Part of me is desperate to know, and part of me doesn't really want to find out. You can be more honest,' I say.

'Or you can lie more easily.'

'There's no point in lying with someone you don't know, is there? If you're not going to be honest, you might as well not bother.'

'Like a priest,' says Michelle.

'Sort of. He's always up really late at night. He gets me through the small hours when I can't sleep.'

'Like a radio phone-in?'

'Sort of.'

'Maybe he's in a different time zone?'

'Maybe.'

Hadn't thought of that. Michelle's had more experience of Internet dating.

Not that we are dating. We're just talking all night.

I look across the park. The view hasn't changed much since we used to sit here in our navy uniforms, our long white socks around our ankles, debating the merits of roll-on versus spray deodorant, and giving the boys who passed on their way to the soccer pitches marks out of ten for skin quality and snoggability.

I feel an involuntary smile come to my face.

'He's made me think about being a better person,' I say.

Michelle just looks at me.

'You're like *The Thorn Birds*,' she says.

'What?'

'She fell in love with a priest. Ralph Bric-à-brac or something?'

'De Bricassart,' I correct her. 'He's not a priest. And anyway, I'm not in love. You can't possibly *fall in love* with someone you've never met,' I assure her.

'Better be getting back,' says Michelle. 'We don't want to miss the Beckhams' party.'

My mouse glides over:

Kashmir: Pakistan refuses to rule out nuclear option

and:
The Stars Are Out. Beckhams' World Cup Party
Click on COMPOSE.

I've decided to get people to give to charity instead of a wedding list. L

Good idea. A

You're not a priest, are you? L

No. 7. A

NSPCC, because I work with children, not just because the Beckhams had it for their World Cup party. Is there anything more grotesque, by the way, than a celebrity auction? Why can't famous people just get pleasure from being good? Why do they have to have David Beckham's boots as well? I think the Beckhams should have charged £5,000 per ticket. Then they would have raised £2 million and still had his old boots to sell if they ever needed to. And who wouldn't pay £5,000 for an invite to that party? My suggested wedding contribution is £25. I'm going to get it printed on the invitations. L

Doesn't NSPCC get enough? How about Medecins sans Frontières? A

Interesting suggestion. Are you a doctor? L

I wish. But no. 6. A

I don't think my mother would like anything French. Are you in a different time zone? L

Yes. 5. A

That's why you can chat all night. Because it's not all night? L

Sort of. I'm about to be sent somewhere else. Won't be able to chat except early in the morning for you. A

Is it somewhere dangerous? L

Yes, it is rather. 4. A

Take care. XL

It's the first time you've Xed me! Good night. XXXXXXXXXXXXXXXXA

It really is ridiculous to be counting, because he probably just pressed the X key until the end of the line. But if he did do it deliberately, there are three more than last time.

CHAPTER 40

How can I be a better person?

I shall give money to the needy.

Not directly though. I recently bought a Brie and Bacon baguette for the homeless person who sits in the tube station forecourt with the sign saying 'Hungry'.

He said thank you and pointed out that I was getting a cold sore on my lower lip. The trouble with being plain is that people don't observe the rules like they do with an attractive person. When people greet Joanna, they say 'Darling, you look wonderful!'. (Not tramps obviously, but even they would probably manage something like, 'Gord bless you, pretty lady.) When people greet me, they say, 'Lydia! That's a nasty spot.'

I'd hardly got through the ticket barrier, when I noticed him trying to get a cash refund on the baguette.

Traffic's very bad this morning.

I shall be nicer to my mother. I'll ring her up more

often. I'll agree to lilies in my wedding bouquet if that's what she really wants. I may even suggest we look at sheltered housing together, if the moment seems right.

I shall trade in my car for a smaller, more ecological model. Or at least switch the engine off in the queue for the temporary lights.

Why don't they just make them permanent lights? They've been temporary so long, but the permanent ones still seem to know the traffic conditions better. It's a bit like supply teachers.

I shall start speaking to Richard Batty again.

I'll join the witches' Sponsored Jubilee Weight-Loss Relay, which will help me win friends, lose weight and do a little bit extra for charity, even though it is the Prince's Trust, which I object to in principle. Until he turns over all his profit from the Duchy of Cornwall, I don't see why people on public-sector salaries should donate a single penny. Or buy his Organic Lemon Biscuits, for that matter, which are twice the price of Sainsbury's Lemon Thins and don't taste all that different.

I will give up trivia. Or at least try to cut down.

New Andy's boyfriend Jasper is a producer on the local news bit that comes on after the main news, which I usually turn off, unless there's a film premiere in Leicester Square or Madonna in a West End play or something.

'So?' says Mrs Vane.

She can't abide show-offs.

'So he's coming along today with a crew,' says New Andy.

'You mean we're going to be on television?' Miss Goodman touches her hat, which is fine lemon straw with a white satin band, and looks at her feet. She's cursing herself for not wearing the lemon pumps that match the outfit, but heels can be a problem in the playground, especially when it's been raining.

'I think the headmaster might have something to say about this,' says Mrs Vane, who has on her usual taupe slacks and sweater with the simple addition of pointy ears, a tartan choker, and a stubby tail.

'Yes,' says New Andy.

'What?' She's rattled now. Usually, she's a stickler for 'I beg your pardon?' and her tail's waggling.

'That's what the headmaster said. Yes.'

Mrs Vane hurries out of the room.

'She wouldn't have come as a corgi if she'd known,' says Miss Goodman, patting her flounces.

'She does look a bit of a dog's dinner,' says Mrs Wates, who's a vision in aquamarine.

Witchy cackling.

'A saucer of milk for the ladies!' says New Andy, with a little theatrical, ooh-aren't-I-awful look. He tosses his head so violently his tiara slips, then minces towards the door in his white stilettos.

The witches smile at his neat little bum. They'll forgive anything from a man in drag.

'Who are you?' I ask him.

He looks at me from under heavily mascaraed lashes.

He has blond streaks in his floppy fringe.

'Have you forgotten me already?' he asks in a wounded little voice.

'When you're writing your stories, try to remember what you put at the beginning of the sentence. We put a capital letter, don't we? And a full stop at the end.'

'Miss, why is India fighting with Pakistan?' asks Nikita.

'What does your father say?' I ask her. He's Indian. I'll probably learn more from listening to his views than I ever would from Radio 4.

'He says they're on the brink. What is a brink?'

'It's when your telly's broken, dur brain.'

'No, that's on the blink, Robbie.'

'Why's England going up against Argentina?' asks Robbie.

'That's a football match.'

'Is India having a football match with Pakistan?' asks Nikita.

'It would be more sensible, wouldn't it? Why don't you write your name in the Happy Book?'

She looks startled.

'Can I write my name in the Happy Book?'

'No, Robbie. I'm afraid people who call other people dur brain are not allowed to write their name in the Happy Book.'

'Who are you, Miss?' says Geri.

She's wearing a white bikini top and leggings and carrying a yoga mat.

They're a bit too excited to concentrate on their stories.

'Princess Anne.'

Boring I know, but I found it difficult to think of any famous women who weren't much younger, or much older than me – there's Cilla and there's Atomic Kitten, but who's in between? – and I am one of the few people that jodhpurs flatter. I've always wanted a Ralph Lauren polo shirt with the proper logo and not just an M&S imitation. Choosing the colour was tough. I decided on cantaloupe finally, although they never look as great on their own as they do fanned out in a rainbow in the window.

'Why are you wearing that stupid hat?' asks Dean.

He's Buzz Lightyear again.

'It's a crash helmet for if you're on a horse.'

Vlad owns a polo pony.

'Where's your horse?'

'I left him on the playing field.'

The entire class rushes over to look out of the window.

'Joke!'

'You look really stupid,' says Dean.

Not as stupid as I would have looked if I had come in full hunting gear and a curly wig, as New Andy suggested. Did he know about the television when he suggested Camilla Parker Bowles? Was he trying to orchestrate a cat fight for the cameras? I'm not a monarchist by any means but a tranvestite ghost of Princess Diana is pushing it for a First and Middle. I suppose it's his acting background.

'Who are you?' I ask Richard, which is technically speaking to him again, although I've chosen the words to make him feel slightly uncomfortable.

He's stapled some tinsel on to his jacket and is wearing a pair of huge orange specs with windscreen wipers which he operates from a switch in his pocket.

'Elton John,' he says.

'The hair's far too natural,' I inform him.

There are a couple of children wearing large hats and their mothers' high-heeled shoes, but most of the girls have come in midriff-baring tops with gold shorts or miniskirts and glitter on their faces. Ethan has his cloak and wizard's hat, but nearly all the boys are wearing football strip.

'Pop stars and footballers, the new aristocracy,' says Miss Goodman, with a sniff.

I like it that way. It's more democratic. They're famous because they're talented. Or at least good looking.

★   ★   ★

When the television crew arrive I have the inspired idea of a look-alike competition, which doesn't have to be competitive, if you can think of enough categories.

'Every picture tells a story, darling,' says Jasper. 'You've got a natural gift for television.'

Nicole and Robbie win as Posh and Becks, in the Celebrity Couples Category. He's in full England strip, she has a crown on her head and a cushion shoved under her dress.

'Can we have a kiss?' the cameraman shouts.

'Certainly not,' says Nicole, regally. She's really taken to the role.

Robbie plants one on anyway.

'Robbie,' I warn.

'He told me to!'

Gwyneth, who is wearing a long pink dress and won the Oscar Winners category bursts into inconsolable tears.

Then three children throw up their fairy cakes and several others start whizzing around because of the food colouring.

It's all threatening to go wrong when a downpour arrives and we adjourn to the Hall.

Some of the Year Five girls do an a cappella rendition of 'Whole Again'.

I don't think we could have hoped for better.

And we have raised almost £200 for charity.

It's my first time in a car showroom and I'm not sure how to behave. Should I tap on the window of the glass office where a man in shirtsleeves seems to be very involved in a telephone conversation, or should I get myself a coffee from the machine and wait.

Are you actually allowed to have a coffee if you're just making an enquiry? I stare at the price card on a convertible and walk round its perimeter. I give a black car a tentative stroke.

'Can I help you?'

I jump like I've been caught doing something wrong. I look around the grey carpeted walls of the showroom for a door. Where did he come from, and how did he know I was here? Perhaps there is a secret camera?

He's wearing a shiny grey suit and he smells as if he has just put out a cigarette.

'I was wondering what my car was worth?' I say, pointing at my lime-green Beetle on the forecourt.

'People want new cars. It's as simple as that,' says the man in the garage.

'But it is almost new,' I tell him.

'Almost new is not the same. As soon as you drive a new car out of here, it halves in value. Why are you selling, by the way?'

'I want a smaller, more eco-friendly car, something more environmental. It doesn't have to be new actually.'

'Well, that's where new cars have the advantage. You won't find a much more environmentally friendly car than yours,' says the man.

'It's the colour, as well, though. I didn't choose it myself.'

What's going through his head is that he can't imagine a man buying it for me, which is why he's suddenly lost for chat.

'A gift from my sister.' I help him.

'Wish I had a sister like yours,' he says, back in salesman mode. 'How about a re-spray? For a few hundred, it'll feel like a new car.'

The black one does look a lot cooler than lime green. I'm tempted.

'I'm trying to reduce my outgoings,' I tell him firmly, reminding myself why I'm here.

'Second-hand market's completely flat,' he says with a sigh. 'Price promotions have killed it right off. Murdered it completely. Dead.'

'RIP.' I say.

'To be honest, your best option would be if someone stole it,' the salesman says.

I'm almost expecting him to add, '. . . which is part of our promotional package . . .'

But he just walks away. I'm not sure whether this is part of a negotiating tactic and he's coming back, or whether he's finished with me. I stand there for a few minutes and then, for the benefit of the secret camera, I look at my watch and make a surprised face as if I have an appointment to go to and I had no idea it was so late.

I feel quite protective of my garish Beetle as I climb into its luxury interior, but I wish I had put it into neutral before switching the engine off.

CHAPTER 41

'Have you got the telly on?' I ask, as Michelle opens the door.
'I thought it was your quiz night.'
'I'm trying to give them up.'
'It's only the news,' says Michelle.
'I may be on,' I tell her.

'At the moment, both Pakistan and India are saying they won't be the first to use nuclear weapons, but the situation is tense . . .' says the reporter.

'Do you think they draw lots?' I ask.
'Who?'
'The reporters. I mean how come some of them get Live from a Karaoke Bar in Tokyo with some Fat England Supporters Dressed as Geishas, and some of them get This Could be the End of the World as We Know It?'
'I think this one gets the war zones because he's got such a nice reassuring face,' says Michelle.

'. . . there's daily shelling.'
There's an explosion behind him.

'Perhaps he's not interested in football,' says Michelle.

'Everyone's interested in the World Cup.'

'. . . some of the aid agencies are saying we're looking at a humanitarian crisis the scale of which the world has never seen before.'

'Do you think they help the aid workers when they're not filing a report?' I wonder. 'Or do they just ask questions and generally get in the way?'

'If they started helping, they'd never stop,' says Michelle.

The reporter's interviewing the man who's in charge of a refugee camp.

'Oh my God!' I say.

'What?' says Michelle.

'Who was at the Queen Mother's funeral, apart from the royal family?'

'Tony Blair?' Michelle looks at me like I've finally flipped.

'No. Apart from Tony Blair, other politicians, foreign dignitaries, the regiments she was in charge of . . . who else?'

'Representatives of the various charities she was involved with?' says Michelle.

'Exactly,' I say.

★   ★   ★

'. . . for the people here,' says the reporter, 'war has already begun.'

'I'll be back after this from your area,' says the news-reader.

There's the local news music.

'As Jubilee fever hits London, we'll show you some of the celebrations . . . But first, a gruesome discovery today as police were called to—'

'I thought there was supposed to be a watershed,' says Michelle. 'People don't want to hear about a headless corpse when they're having their tea.'

'Can you confirm that some of the body parts were cooked?' asks the local reporter.

I'm dying to use Michelle's computer, but I don't want her looking over my shoulder.

'. . . at one school, some very important people turned up at the Jubilee Garden Party—'

'Lyd! Watch!'

Film of Nicole and Robbie receiving the gold chocolate coins they got as medals from a woman in an orange top. They all smile and wave at the camera.

'There you are,' says Michelle.

'Where?'

'. . . in Lambeth they got a visit from a different sort of Queen . . .'

'There!' she says, pointing at the Pearly Queen waving a Union Jack who has taken my place on the screen.

'Was that really me?'

'Was there anyone else wearing a riding hat?'

I have made it to the screen, and I didn't even recognize myself.

Actually, I didn't look as bad as I thought.

My mobile rings.

'You're on the news,' says my mother.

'Hang on a minute, there's a call waiting!' I tell her.

'We saw you on telly!' shouts Cy.

'Hang on!'

I go back to my mother, but there's only the dialling tone.

I've never quite got the hang of the technology.

Michelle's phone rings.

'It's Michaela!'

I wonder how Andy Warhol knew that everyone except me watches the local bit that's on after the News!

'The contractions have started,' says Michelle.

There are no new messages in my Inbox.

Click on COMPOSE.

```
Hi! 4 questions still in hand, but I've got
it! Well done, by the way. I thought about VSO
myself after university. Talk soon. LX
```

I wait, but there's no reply.

It's a bit early in the day.

And he's got work to do. Important work.

CHAPTER 42

June

I am standing outside the toilets in the St Anne's Shopping Centre. My mother seems to be taking an inordinately long time, but she always does. I wonder how many hours of my life I have spent outside public lavatories waiting for my mother, and why it is that we never want to go at the same time. I wonder if she feels the same way when she's waiting for me? Does a quick wee seem quicker to the person who's doing it than the person who's waiting? Joanna always pops in with her, chattering away companionably, even when they can't get adjacent cubicles. Then, as they wash their hands, they swap tips on beauty products and make faces at themselves in the mirror, checking for mascara speckles and lipstick that's bled.

'Can you spare a couple of minutes?'

It's one of those charity people with neon bibs.

Normally, I avoid eye contact and walk on quickly, but I can hardly pretend I'm rushing somewhere when I've been standing here for at least five minutes, and, actually, I've been meaning to get round to signing up for a direct debit. It wouldn't be my charity of choice, but it's the principle that counts, and at least it's got nothing to do with dogs.

'What do I do?' I ask him.

'Nurse?' he guesses.

I laugh. I think they're trained to engage, but nobody's ever told me I look like a nurse before. For men, it usually denotes an attractive combination of caring and a bit dirty. He's got quite a nice smile.

'I meant, how can I help,' I say, pointing at his clipboard.

'It's only two pounds a month, but if everyone were prepared to make that commitment, we could reduce our overheads by eighty per cent . . .' he begins.

'All right, where do I sign?'

'What does two pounds a month buy you these days? A cappuccino maybe . . .'

'OK, I'm convinced.'

'A cappuccino can pick you up, yes, but think how much better you'd feel if you knew that—'

'Stop!'

I hadn't even thought of a cappuccino until he mentioned it, and now I'm gagging for one.

I think he's surprised. It must be quite refreshing after hours of spieling to people like my mother, who are longing to talk because they're old and lonely, but adamantly opposed to parting with a single digit of their debit card number.

'You put your details here,' says the man, pointing. 'And sign here.'

'It is a registered charity?' I say.

'You're right to check,' he says.

I sign with a flourish.

'That's my good deed for the day!'

Not quite true, actually, because I consider shopping with Mum a good deed as well. I really am a much better person!

My mother eventually appears, smelling of face powder and looking less tense than she was when she went in.

'Why don't we have a coffee?' I ask her.

'Can I interest you . . . ?' says the charity man.

'No you can't,' says my mother.

'They'd get more money with a collecting tin and stickers,' she says, as we make our way to the Food Court. 'Who'd be stupid enough to hand over their bank details to a complete stranger?'

'There must be safeguards. Data protection, and all that,' I say.

Never quite understood what data protection is. I always tick the box that says I don't want unsolicited mail, but I still receive half a bin liner each week. Only this morning there was a catalogue featuring things to make life easier, like a hot-water bottle you can heat up in the microwave and a pack of three bra extenders.

'We guarantee you will be happy!' it said on the front, but I think it may take more than a plastic egg that absorbs unpleasant fridge odours, and some soft silicone toecaps to guard against chafing sandals. Not that they're not both excellent ideas.

'I may look old and vulnerable,' my mother is saying, 'but I play bridge three times a week.'

'You don't look old and vulnerable,' I say, which seems to please her.

Certainly not vulnerable anyway. Not in the piercing royal blue suit she's bought for the Jubilee and the new perm.

'How about a pizza for lunch?' I say. 'Or there's baguettes . . .'

'Impossible with my teeth.'

'Indian?'

There are so many choices in the Food Court.

But none of them suits my mother.

'Tell you what, why don't we drive out to the Harvester?' I suggest.

It only takes a little effort to be a better person.

And I'm rewarded for my selfless gesture, by the sound of 'Land of Hope and Glory' from my mobile.

CHAPTER 43

There are so many staircases, up and down, and corridors to get to the delivery room, by the time I reach the entrance I am not sure whether it's on the top floor, or underground.

In fact, it's on the ground floor, which is probably an advantage from the ambulance point of view.

'It's for security,' says the nurse in charge.

She's one of those women who makes me feel as if I've no right to be here. The receptionist at the health club is another. I always make the mistake of trying to befriend them.

'I suppose I do look exactly like the sort of person who would steal a baby,' I say. 'Mid to late thirties, single, desperate!'

The nurse doesn't laugh.

'In fact, I'm engaged, and not sure I'd want children anyway,' I explain, but it only feels like I'm digging myself in deeper.

There's a horrible shriek close by.

'I'm a teacher. I see enough of them all day!'

'You're here for?' says the nurse.

I give Michaela's full name.

'I am her birth partner.'

She closes the door and comes back with a file.

'You're not on the plan.'

'Not on the written plan, no, but she has just called me on her mobile, because her real birth partner couldn't handle it.'

Whatever is the matter with Michelle?

Another eardrum-piercing cry for help.

'Mobiles should be switched off,' says the nurse.

'I know,' I say, trying to meet her halfway, 'but her mother has let her down. Frankly, I would have liked to arrive after the baby myself, but here I am, godmother in waiting, presenting myself for duty.'

'You're for the one with the mother?' says the nurse. 'All right, you'd better come through,' she says.

Giving birth is absolutely appalling, and nothing like it is on television.

It's not sweat and a brave smile through a tear-streaked face.

It's horrible contortions of death-throes pain with lots of blood and poo.

I didn't know about the poo. I haven't seen Michaela's poo since I changed her nappies.

Now I know why she called me, because there are friends, and there are people who you're so close to you don't mind them seeing everything.

'Aunt Lyd!' screams Michaela.

'I'm here now,' I say, as if that will solve anything.

I wonder if Michelle knew about the poo. She had three caesarians, so it's possible she didn't. That's possibly why she collapsed. Or she couldn't bear all the attention being on someone else.

The agony goes on for hours, although it's always difficult to tell in hospitals, with the blinds down so that people passing can't gawp. Which is one of the disadvantages of being on the ground floor.

'Push!' shouts the midwife.

'Don't fucking shout at me,' says Michaela.

I didn't mention the swearing. Lots of it. Very unlike Michaela, who's always had lovely manners.

'Don't fucking shout at her!' I shout too. 'Now, Michaela, breathe and let's have a big push.'

Michaela pushes really hard.

'I got her through her GCSEs,' I say to the astonished midwife.

'Good girl. Come on, I can see the head,' says the midwife.

'Come on, Michaela, you can do it. Just one more. Push!'

Suddenly, all of a slither, a little creature, with a great ugly rope of gore attached, slides out into the midwife's hands.

And then it cries.

And before my eyes it changes from something raw and animal into something tiny and recognizably human.

'It's a little boy,' says the midwife, putting him on Michaela's chest.

The screaming, blaspheming torture victim that was Michaela is suddenly a serene mother.

'Hello,' she says to the baby. 'That wasn't very nice, was it? Never mind. You're here now.'

Adam, the father, arrives at the same time as the placenta. He's white with shock until he realizes that the paediatrician has got the baby on the scales.

'Have I missed it?' he asks.

'Only just,' I say.

'I was playing five-a-side,' he tells me, while they're stitching Michaela's perineum. 'They said it might go on for hours.'

It is so not the time for recrimination.

It is time for me to go.

No amount of getting warm or cold drinks, or checking Apgar scores will make me useful now.

I leave the three of them to it.

Standing in the hospital porch on a soft underlay of cigarette butts, I breathe the cool air of the early hours of a summer morning. The grey concrete buildings behind me hum with the timeless activity of human ends and beginnings.

I have cried like this, in this same spot, for life's

340

unfairness and cruelty. And now I cry, with equal ferocity, for the miracle of pure human happiness created within the unlikely walls of Northwick Park Hospital.

Then, I pull myself together and walk across the almost empty car park to A&E.

'I feel such a fool,' says Michelle, once she's got over the shock of it being a boy.

She's sitting on a trolly with a bandage round her head.

'It's different when it's your own child. I couldn't deal with seeing her in pain.'

'The gas and air were meant to be for her,' I say.

'It made me a bit giddy,' says Michelle. 'That's all I can remember.'

'You hit your head on the monitor,' I tell her.

'They want to keep me under observation before discharging me,' she says.

'You never faint except when you're pregnant,' I say.

'You've been crying,' she tells me.

CHAPTER 44

Are you there? I can't sleep. I saw a baby being born tonight and my heart is full. I never understood what that meant before. It means it's full of joy and wonder, and I think it must have more oxygen in it, or something chemical, because I can't sleep, even though I'm exhausted. I feel like it's the night before Christmas, or one of those times at college when you stay up all night talking to someone you've just met and suddenly realize you're in love. I always thought that Jesus was born in a stable because there really were no rooms at the Inn, but now I realize that the Nativity is a symbol of human potential in the midst of adversity. You'd understand if you'd been in Northwick Park Maternity Unit tonight.

When I held him (I was the second person in the whole world!), I had this wonderful feeling that I would do anything to make him happy. His vulnerability made me strong.

I think maybe I got an insight into what

your work is like. Isn't happiness in the end something to do with a willingness to sacrifice yourself on behalf of someone else?

Or am I just quoting Elton John? I inadvertently do that sometimes when I think I'm having a profound thought. L

Click SEND.

I wait a little while online, but there is no reply.

I suddenly feel completely alone in the world.

CHAPTER 45

The whole room is bobbing with balloons. Blue balloons and pink balloons tied to baskets of blue flowers or pink flowers and to the paws of blue or pink teddy bears.

Michaela is sitting up in bed. Next to her, in a little Perspex pod is a little yellow creature fast asleep.

'It's a touch of jaundice,' whispers Michaela.

'He's golden for the Jubilee,' I say.

'He's small,' Andy points out.

I wish I'd left him in the car park.

'He's a baby, dur brain,' I hiss.

Seem to be hissing quite a lot these days.

'He's smaller than that one,' says Andy, pointing at the next pod.

'If he were any smaller they'd have had to put him in the special unit,' says Michaela. 'But he's just on five pounds, so they're monitoring him.'

She's been a mother less than twelve hours, but already she's become an expert, talking as if she's been dealing with babies all her life.

If Andy doesn't say something like Well Done! or

344

Congratulations in the next thirty seconds, I shall kick him.

'You look like a film star, Aunt Lyd,' says Michaela.

I am rather proud of the dress I bought in the Oxfam shop. It is a 1950s frock with a full skirt and tight bodice and a pattern of yellow cabbage roses on white background. There are a few rust stains on the skirt and the bodice is a bit too tight, but you can't have everything. It's fine if I squash my breasts in the right direction and hold my breath when I sit down. It's gold, it's approximately fifty years old and a charity benefited.

'Ouch!' says Andy, rubbing his shin.

I hand over the little blue outfit I swapped this morning in Mothercare for the little pink outfit I had bought before. I'll have to have a rethink about the locket I was getting engraved.

'So sweet!' says Michaela, and gives me a kiss.

'Are you managing OK with the feeding?' I say, pointing at her swollen chest. I know that's what you're meant to say because it's sometimes difficult at first.

'I'm feeding for England,' she says.

'So you won't be calling it Lydia then,' says Andy.

'Chandler,' says Michaela. 'Chandler Joe.'

'Nice,' I say. 'Sounds like an American restaurant. You know, Chandler Joe's Rib Shack.'

'What are you like!' says Michaela.

Andy's staring at the baby.

'Perhaps you'd like to be godfather,' says Michaela, trying to make him feel part of it.

I feel really proud of her immaculate manners even though she's just given birth. She has been well brought up, and I am partly responsible for that.

If Andy doesn't say thank you or something appropriate in the next thirty seconds, I will call off our engagement.

'Can I pick him up?' I say.

'Of course.'

Chandler Joe's little head fits almost exactly into the cup of my palm. His little lips open and close, like men's mouths sometimes do when they're thirsty in their sleep. He is a little person who has grown from a cell in my goddaughter's tummy and whose life is now in front of him. I cannot brush away my tears because even though he is very light, he is so precious I need both my hands to hold him.

'I don't believe in God, unfortunately,' says Andy.

I put Chandler Joe back in his pod.

'I'll come and see you properly tomorrow,' I give Michaela a kiss.

'Happy Jubilee!' she says.

'Isn't he beautiful?' I say, as Andy pulls out of the car park.

'They all look the same to me.'

Andy twiddles the radio to Classic FM.

I hate it when he does that because I like Capital in the mornings and he invariably forgets to twiddle it back. It's a bit like some people get annoyed about the toilet seat.

I hate it when he sings along with the duet from the Pearl Fishers.

By the time we turn on to the A40 I'm so furious, I scream.

'Don't you think we ought to at least talk about having children?'

'Is anything wrong?' asks Andy, turning the volume down.

I must just have been screaming in my head.

Is this the right time for this conversation?

'We've decided on *The Barber of Seville*, by the way,' says Andy.

There's been trouble at the Metropolitan Opera since the director quit in order to concentrate on more lucrative Gilbert and Sullivan theme nights at the local mock Tudor hotel. I hear all about it from Fern. Despite the resounding failure of *Cosi*, some of the senior members headed by Andy and Fiordiligi, whose real name is Daphne, are in favour of pursuing a classical repertoire with a bid for Arts Council funding. Others want a self-financing Christmas production of *Grease!*. Fern is sitting on the fence. It's early days for her and she's not expecting anything more than a role in the chorus, however it pans out.

'Will you be the Barber?' I ask.

What an idiotic question for a grown-up person who's a computer expert.

'I shall have to audition like everyone else,' says Andy, a touch smugly. 'It is quite a good role for Daphne because she can sit on the balcony for the first act.'

'How did her operation go?' I ask in my concerned voice.

'Not as successful as they'd hoped.'

We're nearly at Joanna's now, but it usually takes at least half an hour to find a parking space near her.

I take a deep breath.

'I've been meaning—' I say.

'That's lucky,' says Andy, with lightning response on the indicator. 'One right outside.'

CHAPTER 46

Joanna has gone for gold rather than Union Jacks. There's very clever lighting that makes it look as if the house is swathed in gold silk curtains, and the balustrade on the roof terrace has become a giant crown.

Inside, minimalist is out and palace kitsch is in. Red carpet, gold banisters, sculpture on pedestals and panelled walls with *trompe l'oeil* portraits. There are liveried waiters, carrying platters of canapés with little curls of gold leaf on top, and flutes of champagne.

The dress code was Gold, but all the other females I can see are wearing black. Joanna herself has a little sleeveless shift and some heavy gold Chanel jewellery. Being the perfect hostess she's gone almost as soon as she's greeted us, leaving only a fleeting trace of her perfume.

'Linda!'

Greg pops out from behind a sculpture.

'I don't think you've met my fiancé? Greg this is Andy.'

It's at times like this when a fiancé comes in very useful.

'Greg,' says Andy, holding out his hand.

'I used to be known as Andy myself,' says Greg.

If he weren't Canadian, I would think he was taking the piss.

'Why?' I ask.

'There were four Gregs in my class at school, and my surname is Andrews.'

'Well, Andy is his first name,' I say, taking my second glass of champagne, 'So you will have to be Greg for tonight.'

'Whatever you say, Linda,' says Greg. 'You're a lucky man, Andy.'

'Thank you, Andy,' says Andy.

'Are you a performer too?' says Greg.

'I dabble,' says Andy, with due modesty.

'Excuse me, I must say hello to the children,' I attempt to float off like Joanna does, but I'm wearing a small heel.

Cy and Ry and their friends are in the garden throwing red, white and blue jelly at each other across the trestles table that's been set out for their tea.

'Totty's done such a beautiful Buckingham Palace cake,' says Joanna, pausing for a moment beside me. 'Seems a shame to cut it.'

Joanna never really liked getting toys out of their original wrapping when we were little.

She gazes at her offspring in a kind of bewildered disbelief.

'Totty?' I ask.

'The children's caterer.'

'Do you have an adult caterer as well?'

'Eddie did all the sub-contracting.'

'Eddie?'

'My party organizer. Darling, how lovely!'

She air kisses another woman in black and they waft off together.

A couple of men are discussing England's prospects against Argentina.

'I don't think Batistuta is the force he was,' I say. 'I'm Lydia, Joanna's sister, by the way.'

They look at me like, yes, and what is the reason for your interrupting our conversation?

Parties always used to be about meeting new people, but I think it must change when you're successful or married. Or perhaps it's my dress.

If I stand nearer the children I will look as if I have a role.

'Are you the entertainer?' asks one little girl, who has jelly in her hair.

'No. I'm just a helper. What's your name?'

'Matilda,' says the girl.

'She's our aunt,' says Cy.

'You look like my gran's armchair,' says the girl.

'I don't want this!' Ry hands me his plate.

'When is the entertainer coming?' says the girl.

'I don't know if there is an entertainer coming,' I say.

'When can I go home?'

★   ★   ★

'Doesn't three thousand pounds a term buy you kindness and respect for other people as part of the syllabus?' I ask Joanna on her next waft.

'I know, I know,' she says both bored and impatient at the same time. 'But you should see the state schools round here.'

'Did you actually see them?'

'It's different when you're a parent,' says Joanna. 'Mimi! You made it!'

More air kisses.

'Whose idea was it to have a Jubilee party?' I ask.

'Vlad's of course. So American of him!'

Is it just the mood I'm in, or is Joanna particularly sparkling tonight? I mean, if I'm honest, a little over-sparkling. Her eyes have a gleam. It may of course just be the flaming torches, which are a bit dangerous when there are children throwing things, but they do make my silhouette look very slim against the back wall of the garden.

'Lydia,' says Vlad behind me, 'will you move your car? It's blocking the projection on the front of the house.'

'Tell Andy. He's driving,' I polish off another flute of champagne.

Vlad shoots a glance from my glass to Joanna. It's something he often does when he thinks I'm about to embarrass him, even though it's only happened once.

It was a mistake to do corporate entertaining on

a pool terrace if he didn't want anyone to go in. I didn't actually need rescuing, anyway, because I'm quite a good swimmer, even in an evening dress, as it turns out. Like a mermaid, was the way one of Vlad's nicer colleagues put it.

Joanna just stares at him. Vlad is the first to look away.

I feel as if I've been caught eavesdropping on an intimate conversation, although nothing was said. Joanna's gleaming eyes stare at his back as he walks away, leaving a whiff of menace behind him.

I wonder if all is well between them.

'I'm thinking of selling my car, actually,' I tell her. 'If you've no objection.'

'Why?'

'I'm trying to be a bit more aware of the environment.'

I like the way that sounds. Rather grown up.

'Why don't I get you one of those sweet little Smart cars,' Joanna suggests, beaming with the prospect of a new purchase. 'I saw one the other day painted like a ladybird.'

'No, thanks.'

'But they only use about one tank of petrol per year!'

'I wouldn't be able to get the children in the back,' I say.

'But you don't have any children,' she says.

I hate my sister.

'Your children,' I say.

'Oh, that's a point,' she says.

'I saw my new godson being born last night.'

'Where?' she says.

'Northwick Park Hospital.'

'How ghastly!'

'It was rather beautiful, actually.'

'Oh Lyd, don't.'

Champagne does sometimes make me weepy, and I was up most of the night.

Joanna puts her arm briefly on my waist.

We must look a rather odd pair, one effortlessly chic, cool and pallid, one who's raided the dressing-up box, with heaving shoulders and a red face.

And mascara everywhere.

Think I have had enough champagne as I took a moment to realize that the person sitting on the opposite loo in the chintz dress is actually me.

'What you have to remember about Rossini . . .' Andy is saying to Greg in the hall where I left them.

The cake's got candles that spit and fizz like fireworks lit on top. There are a couple of Wows before it's destroyed in a frenzy that brings to mind the French Revolution.

And then the children depart with their nannies.

I take Cy and Ry up to bed.

★   ★   ★

'We're lucky in British Columbia . . .' Greg is saying to Andy as I pass them on the way down.

A giant television screen has been erected in the garden so nobody has to miss the Party at the Palace.

'Have you said hello to Greg?' says Joanna.

'He and Andy are taking it in turns to bore each other,' I tell her.

'I read an article about your relationship with that man the other day . . .' says Joanna.

'Is there no limit to my fame?'

'. . . in the *Observer*, or was it the *Guardian*? Apparently it's called downsizing. You've achieved everything you want in life without a man. Except for a man. So when Mr Spectacular doesn't come along, you choose someone reliable for sex and support.'

Being a good hostess, Joanna is speaking just a little bit louder than normal conversation thereby inviting any spare people into the conversation.

'Apparently, all the supermodels are doing it. Kate Winslet . . .' she adds.

'She dumped him for Sam Mendes,' I say.

Actually, there are so many things wrong with this analysis of my relationship with Andy, there's no point in starting.

And I think I preferred it when Joanna couldn't understand why I was marrying him.

'Forget sex and support,' says an American woman in black Donna Karan who is living proof

355

that you can be too thin, and too tanned. 'I just need someone to do something about mould in my bathroom.'

'I must give you Vaughan's number,' Joanna tells her. 'He came with the conservatory. Damp is his speciality!'

'In Vancouver, you can swim in the sea in the morning, and ski in the afternoon,' Greg is saying.

'I'm really more of a walker,' Andy replies.

I hurry past in search of a waiter.

'Do you think Canadians actually have to sign a contract with the Tourist Board as part of their passport application?' I ask Joanna.

'Actually, he's not officially Canadian. His parents moved there when he was fifteen.' Joanna replies. 'He's terribly rich, you know. And rather sweet.'

We both look at the giant screen.

'Whatever has happened to Paul McCartney?' says Joanna. 'I used to dream about him. I used to think he was singing "When I'm Sixty-Four" just to me, and now he is almost sixty-four and honestly, I don't think I'd even want to have him over to dinner.'

'Not much of an advert for being rock stars, were they, the Beatles?' I say. 'One murdered, one dies of a smoking-related illness, one does the voice over for *Thomas the Tank Engine*, and one, well . . .'

'All that winking was fine when he was a cheeky lad in a suit, but now he's like an uncle who thinks he's a bit of a character, and you have to laugh at his jokes because otherwise he won't slip you a tenner when he goes home,' says Joanna.

Just sometimes I get a glimpse of what it must be like to sit across a negotiating table from her.

'Plenty of walking in beautiful British Columbia,' says Greg. 'And a fair few nightclubs for Linda.'

'It's Lydia,' says Andy.

Quite forcefully, as a matter of fact. I suddenly feel enormously affectionate towards him.

'Shall we go now, darling?' I say, like proper people in grown-up couples do.

'Darling?' says Andy, as if it's the first time I've called him that.

Actually, it may well be.

'I've been trying to persuade Andy to come to Vancouver,' says Greg, the moment we're alone together. 'You can swim in the sea in the morning, and ski in the afternoon.'

'But who would want to, unless they were training for a triathlon?' I challenge him.

That wipes the orthodontic grin off his face.

'I have actually been to Vancouver,' I tell him. 'And to me, a much more attractive feature was the number of good sushi restaurants, but nobody ever mentions those. In fact, I had no idea how good the food would be, because it's always this skiing and swimming stuff. You ought to take it up with the Tourist Board.'

★   ★   ★

'Are you trying to be a better person?' I ask Andy in the car on the way home.

'I think you've had a bit too much champagne.'

He switches on Classic FM.

I reach forward and switch it off.

'Better than what?' he says, seeing I mean to have a conversation.

'Do you have a monthly direct debit to charity, for instance?'

'No. Do you?'

'Of course.'

'I pay my taxes. I reckon that's my debt to society paid in full.'

'So, are you actually in the forty per cent bracket?'

Couldn't stop myself. He looks a bit taken aback. Which certainly means he is. Or he isn't, and he's embarrassed because anyone who works in computers should be.

'It's not just about money, is it?' I say.

'What?'

'Being a good person.'

'You tell me.'

He's very guarded. Almost as if he has something to hide.

'It's about reaching out and touching somebody else. It's about trying to make this world a better place,' I say.

Am I quoting Tony Blair? Or Nelson Mandela. I can't remember.

'Let's have a CD,' says Andy.

The one that's in the player is *The Greatest Juke Box Hits in the World* compilation.

The words are actually Diana Ross's. But no less wise.

'Shall I come in?' Andy asks, when we reach my place.

'I'm really tired,' I tell him. 'And I'm going to the hospital first thing.'

'We haven't had sex since May 3rd,' says Andy.

'What happened on May 3rd?' I ask.

'We had sex.'

'I meant why do you remember the exact day? Do you make a note in your diary?'

It's a joke, but he doesn't laugh.

'I don't believe it! You do, don't you? What do you use? A star?'

'You've had too much wine,' says Andy.

'But is it a star?'

'If you must know, I just put a B,' he says.

'B?'

'For bonk,' he says.

CHAPTER 47

My mouse glides over:

   US Envoy in bid to reduce Kashmir tension
   and:
   Police estimate 2 million to celebrate Jubilee

There is one new message in my Inbox.

Re: sacrifice

Who is this fortunate baby? By the way, I think you have me down as something more noble than I am, but I have been having similar thoughts myself. Although, possibly a bit more Bob Dylan. A

My godson. It's probably the age difference. For me, profound means full orchestra, wall of sound, words you don't really understand, but seem really meaningful, which you can belt out in the car with the windows closed. Motown also very good.

You're more protest poetry and the sim-ple chords of an acoustic guitar, aren't you? L

I suppose so. A

Do you have a campfire? L

Where? A

Where you are. L

I'm in a hotel at the moment, so wouldn't be very practical. A

Blimey! No wonder you need my £2 per month. L

Are you talking about the licence? A

I'm talking about overheads. Monthly direct debits. It may not be your specific charity, but the principle applies. L

I am not a charity worker. 3. A

Sorry. I know they're called aid agencies now. L

No. I'm not an aid worker either. 2. A

Oh. But you do something important? L

I used to think so. Now I'm not sure whether it is or not, or whether I'm actually making any difference. You've got 2 questions left. A

I think I've probably drunk a bit too much champagne. I shall go to bed now. L

Hope you're not disappointed. A

Good night. L

Good night. A XXXXXXXXX

CHAPTER 48

Wun sopon a time thair wos a prinses in a tawr watin for prins he wos lat sudenly monster giv her a frite and ate prinses the end.

It's short, but Nicole has remembered to put a capital at the beginning and a full stop at the end, even though her sentence structure has got a bit lost in the middle. She's also used some of the joining words I wrote on the whiteboard. Best of all are the illustrations. I especially like the fact that the princess is wearing a great big watch which she seems to be looking at impatiently, and the violence is implicit rather than stated, since in the second picture, the monster has got blood dripping from his smiling teeth.

I don't know what a child psychologist would make of it, but I write, 'Well done! What a scary monster!'

I do love my job, even though it's half term and marking their stories is technically work.

★   ★   ★

One of the children I have taught may win the Booker Prize one day. I don't think Nicole, actually, but who knows? In the interview afterwards, when the presenter asks them what made them start writing, they'll think of me, even if they don't realize they are, even if they don't actually mention me on air.

In a deep dark toom in anshunt eegit lived the mummy. People tried to steel his trezer so he kill them. Then he turn into sand then flyed away. The End.

This one hasn't got a name on it, but it has to be Dean's. It's actually a well-constructed story with an atmospheric beginning, a pacy plot and a conclusion of sorts.

I write 'Excellent. Some very good punctuation.' I put a Well Done sticker on too.

We need to do a little more work on endings.

On my television screen, a carriage so ornate and golden it could only have been magicked from a pumpkin, is trundling down the Mall.

Two million subjects are waving flags at the Queen.

I had expected the Jubilee to be more Emperor's New Clothes than Cinderella, but I have misjudged the mood. There are so many people in the Mall, I almost wish I had gone down myself to be part of history being made.

My mouse glides over:

Cometh the Hour. England v Argentina
and:
US Envoy 'optimistic'

There are no new messages in my Inbox.

Click on REPLY.

I know what you mean about making a difference, doing something meaningful, sort of
thing. I was all for Cycling Cuba for the
Deaf last year until Michelle pointed out
that my bike hadn't been out of my mother's lean-to since I got a puncture in the
fifth form.
   Do you ever feel that you're living in
history? Like right now, we're at a turning point. It's almost like there's these
scales, and on one side there's Really Serious Things, and on the other there's Trivia.
The End of the World in Nuclear Conflict
kind of balanced against the Jubilee, but
now there's the World Cup too and it's
tipping towards Trivia. Is this what news-
papers mean when they talk about The End of
History? L

I thought you weren't deep. A

I'm on half term. Lots of time to think. L

Not so aware of the Jubilee here, but I know what you're saying. At least your job is important. A

Nice of you to say so. Teachers don't get a very good press. L

I would have loved a teacher like you. A

A lot of people say that to me, but I only got one 'good' in my Ofsted. The others were all 'average'. L

But the children must love you. How is the baby, by the way? A

He's fine. Chandler Joe. I wasn't keen on the name at first, but now I can't imagine him called anything else. What I like best is the way he sleeps with his arms above his head, like he's stretching out after having been curled up all that time. L

Bet you can't wait to have one of your own. A

Who in their right mind would want to bring a child into this world? L

I know what you're saying, but I thought, well, never mind. A

I have to go, actually. It's the match. Aren't you watching? L

Can't get the match here. A

Where on earth are you? L

Endings

CHAPTER 49

Am I happy?
I have an England flag attached to the aerial of my car, a house with a widescreen television, and England beat Argentina!

Of course I'm happy. Everyone's happy!

I think I am in love with David Beckham.

His smile when he converted that penalty just looked like pure happiness.

Feel slightly disloyal to Gary, but still always watch BBC when there's a choice. The late-night highlights and pundits show on ITV is actually rather addictive too.

And the immediate threat of nuclear annihilation seems to have receded.

The car behind is beeping me.

Oh F off your F-ing . . . Here we go, here we go, here we go!

He's got an England flag too!

'Did anyone do anything interesting over half term they'd like to tell us about? Yes, Robbie?'

'Watched the World Cup, Miss.'

'Did anyone else watch it?'

It's the first time I have seen the whole class with their hands in the air.

'Wasn't it great? When Beckham ran up to take that penalty were you all really scared? God, I was, my heart was really thumping and then it was like YES!'

We all cheer.

'Everything all right, Miss Blane?'

'Yes, thank you, Miss Goodman.'

Probably not the best time to ask her whether we can watch England v Nigeria during the literacy hour tomorrow morning.

'Did anyone watch the Jubilee? Geri?'

'I saw S Club, but my mum made me go to bed after that.'

'Did anyone see the golden carriage with all the horses?'

Blank faces.

I can't have made it up, can I? Or dreamt it?

'There was something I enjoyed even more than the football. Can anyone guess what it was?'

'Sex, Miss?' says Dean.

He's heard his older brothers saying it, and he doesn't really know what it means.

'It was reading your stories.'

Beaming smiles all round.

'Good half term?' asks Richard Batty, selecting a prawn salad.

'Very.'

'Anything special?'

'Apart from England beating Argentina and the world pulling back from nuclear war? Is New Andy in today?'

'Don't think so.'

'I thought I saw him at break. Wearing a suit.'

'New Andy wearing a suit? I don't think so.'

I take a bite of my Mexican Chicken Wrap. Is it just me, or do wraps always taste as if they haven't been cooked?

'As a matter of fact, I have a new godson,' I tell Richard.

'Congratulations!'

'Chandler Joe.'

'Chandler Joe?'

'Yes, that's what I thought at first, but it grows on you.'

'Both well?'

'Yes, thank you. Well, Chandler has a touch of jaundice, but sunshine helps. I've found a sunny spot on a fire escape where I'm not in anyone's way. Michaela says she can only relax when I'm around because Adam wakes her up every time Chandler even blinks, and Michelle would just as easily forget she's meant to be looking after him the mood she's in. She thinks he likes me better than her, but she absolutely freezes when Michaela calls her Granny, and I think Chandler's picked up on that. He's a very intelligent little boy . . .'

Richard's nodding, but his usually patient eyes are beginning to glaze.

'I bet you're looking forward to having one of your own,' he says.

'I'm so not. "The Prime of Miss Jean Brodie",' I say.

'What does that mean?' he asks.

'Just because I'm in my mid thirties, and I'm a teacher, doesn't mean I'm hankering after children, OK?'

'I just assumed, what with you getting married . . .' he stutters.

'Well, you assumed wrong. And I'm not eating this. It's raw,' I add, as if it's his fault.

'Who would like to read out their story? Thank you, Ethan.'

He takes a huge breath and says, all in one go: '*One morning a baby owl woke up in his tree and his mummy and daddy had flied away. He ate some flies for his breakfast and then a cat come up the tree and he jumped off the branch and he couldn't fly and then he woke up and it was all a dream.*'

He breathes again.

Must have a word with his father.

'That's a very good story, Ethan. And it has a very good ending too. What was Ethan's ending, Robbie?'

'Can't remember.'

'It was all a dream. Ethan, you can write your name in the Happy Book. Who can think of some other good endings for stories? Gwyneth?'

'They lived happily ever after?'

She smiles at Robbie, who actually blushes.

'Very good. Anyone else?'

'It was all a nightmare.'

'Excellent. Can you tell us what a nightmare is?'

'It's a scary dream.'

'Very good. So that would be a good ending for a scary story.'

Several of the boys make ghost noises.

Ethan's father is standing on his own, smiling at me.

'That colour suits you,' he says.

If I didn't already have bare arms, I would say he was undressing me with his eyes. Since I do, I suppose technically he's dressing me.

If he's an osteopath, he could just be noticing my posture, of course.

In any case, what I was going to say to him comes out all wrong.

'I've been wanting to get you on your own.'

'I've been having similar thoughts,' he says with one of his adult smiles.

He's very confident, but if he were my dentist, I don't think I'd be able to lie still enough.

'Have you signed up for your parent interview?' I ask, as primly as I can. 'There's a timetable blu-tacked to the door. Slots are going fast.'

'I bet they are,' says Ethan's dad.

'Guess what?' says Ethan, rushing up.

'What?' his father asks, bending down to take his

lunch box, his sweatshirt and his baseball cap, and giving him a kiss on the top of his head.

'I've got a very good ending,' Ethan tells him as they walk off together hand in hand.

CHAPTER 50

'Have you voted yet?' says Michelle.

'No. I don't like any of this lot.'

'You are still watching, though,' says Michelle.

'Just the highlights.'

'What do you want to drink?'

'White wine.'

She pours me a large glass.

'Aren't you having any?'

She looks at me.

I look at her.

'I did a test after you mentioned it,' she says.

'Mentioned what?'

'Me being pregnant.'

I sit down.

'Bloody hell!' I say. 'Is it Declan's?'

'Who else's would it be?' Michelle says hotly, like I'm casting aspersions on her fidelity.

'What does he think?'

'Do you think I'd tell him before I told you?'

Like I'm casting aspersions on our friendship. She always gets like this. I think it must be the hormones.

'Anyway,' she says, 'there's something I want to discuss with you first.'

Michelle has to call me a minicab home. It is the Chinese driver again. He keeps smiling at me in the rear-view mirror, as if he's open to another conversation, but I've got things whirling round my mind.

My mouse glides over:
Big Brother: Who will be the next to go?
and:
Can England win the World Cup?

There is one new message in my Inbox.

I'm in Kashmir. 1. But on my way home soon as things seem to have quietened down. A

Kashmir? I can't believe it. You're the US special envoy? On behalf of ordinary people throughout the world, thank you very much for your efforts. L

I am not the US special envoy. And you've just run out of questions. A

Does that mean it's over between us? L

Do you want it to be? A

No. Sorry I jumped down your Inbox the other day. L

That's OK. A

The reason was, I can't have children. Not of my own, anyway. Bit sensitive on the subject. Michelle made me promise never to click on send when I'm drunk, but fuck it, what have I got to lose? L

I don't know what to say. A

Nobody does. I never talk about it. Grisly operation when I was 22. You don't want to go there. Yes, that is when I decided to become a teacher if that's what you're thinking, but that was more to do with Dad. He was a teacher and it was something I knew he'd be happy about. And I do love kids. I'm only crying, actually, because I've had a bottle of Chardonnay on my own and I never got to say goodbye to Dad. L

I'm really sorry. A

It's my own fault. I could have stopped, but Michelle said I might as well because she didn't want Charlene getting hold of it again. L

I meant about children. And your dad. A

I read the other day that the more successful you are, the less you're likely to have
children, if you're a woman. In the **Guardian**, so it's official. Which means I must be
very successful, doesn't it? And I can sleep
as long as I want on Sunday mornings, and
there's enough to worry about, isn't there? L

True. A

I'm not a broody old maid, am I? L

No. A

Yes I am, actually. Michelle just offered
to let me adopt her baby. How sad is that?

That's secret by the way, because she hasn't
told the father yet. L

Declan? A

How did you know? He doesn't even know yet. L

You mentioned him in Portugal. A

That's where it happened. Even Michelle
can't get pregnant over the Internet, which
is the only time they meet in England. L

What does the kilt think? A

Haven't mentioned it yet. So might be odd to talk about adoption first. He's not keen on Michelle anyway. L

You haven't told him about you not being able to have children? A

Trouble is, it's never the right time. You can't really put it in your Soul Mate ad, and if you mention it too early in the relationship, it looks like you're getting ideas. By the time you are serious enough, it's too late. It's become a question of trust, as in 'I don't understand why you didn't trust me enough to tell me before!' but that's usually a smoke-screen so that they can bail out blamelessly. L

No! A

Take my word for it, there's nothing less attractive than a barren woman. You'd think men would relish the opportunity for limitless condom-free sex without responsibility, but it's cool to be a dad. I blame David Beckham, actually, even though I think I love him.
Anyway, my most attractive feature is

that I would make a wonderful mother. I know this because the love of my life told me so before he finished with me after my operation. Being Canadian, he wanted to be totally honest. To be fair, he did leave it until after my dad's funeral. L

Bastard! A

What do you think about Michelle's baby? Should I, or not? L

I think you ought to talk to the kilt. A

You're right. Thanks, by the way. I feel much better after a good cry. L

You're welcome. AXXXXXXXXOOOOOOOOOOOO

What's OOOOOOOOOOOO? L

Hugs. AX

CHAPTER 51

I have to go to the bank to sort out the fraud on my current account which was £2,000 overdrawn by the time they alerted me to the fact I'd gone over my agreed limit, and is now £3,000 overdrawn because I didn't open the white envelope with the bank manager's letter in it until the end of the week because it looked a bit serious.

Someone is on a spending spree with my card, which is peculiar because I haven't actually lost it, but the manageress says that it's easy enough to make a new one if you've got all the details and an imprint of the signature. Perhaps I let my card out of my sight when paying in a restaurant, she suggests.

I sign the declaration that the statements I have made are true. I did not think it absolutely necessary to tell her about the monthly direct debit to charity, which I notice has not yet been claimed against my account. Their admin side probably isn't what it might be.

The bank manager snips my card into four pieces in a slightly vengeful way and tells me she will

call me when my new card is ready for collec-
tion.

I don't much like using the lifts in the car park,
because my mother has read in the local paper
that there have been muggings, but it's late-night
shopping and I had to go right up to the tenth floor
to find a space.

At least, I think it was the tenth floor.

A car very similar to mine is parked in the space
where I remember parking it, but there are two lads
about to get in through the broken window.

'I think that one's mine,' I say.

The one on the driver's side has a rabbit-caught-
in-headlights look of terror on his face that is
slightly familiar. The other one has snatched the
key from my hand and is holding the point of a
knife to the spot where I visualize my right kidney
is situated before I've properly registered what's
going on.

My first thought is that the chances of the same
person being the victim of a fraud and a mugging
in the same week must be so slim I should probably
buy a lottery ticket. But since my card's just been
cut up, I'll only be able to do that if my assailants
leave me with enough cash.

My second thought is that the youth on the
driver's side is actually Wayne, Dean's brother.
And I think he recognizes me too, because he says
to his associate, 'Don't hurt her. She taught me
to read.'

The grip on my arm relaxes.

It's actually one of the prouder moments in my teaching career.

None of us seem to know what to do next.

I'm sure Wayne just wants to run away.

I'm not so sure about his friend, who's fidgeting a bit beside me.

If I don't make an on-the-spot decision, I think I will lose the advantage.

'Look,' I suggest, 'there's something I've forgotten to get in M and S. So I'm going back down now, and when I come back up, you'll be gone, right?'

I speak nice and slowly for Wayne's benefit.

He looks at his mate.

'Fair enough?' he asks.

'Fair enough,' the mate agrees grudgingly.

I run.

It's only when I step out of the lift in the Food Court that I realize how much I'm shaking.

I know I should call the police, but I've always had a bit of a soft spot for Wayne. We've both suffered at the hands of his brothers. He's not really a bad lad, just easily led. I'd hate to see him in prison because he would fall in with terrible people who'd use him. Anyway, they've probably learned their lesson, and no harm done. Don't really fancy going back to my car on my own, though.

I call Andy on my mobile.

He has sung the message on his answerphone to

that 'Figaro, Figaro' song they used to have on the Fiat advert.

Strangely, I feel compelled to sing my message back.

Must be the shock.

I call Richard Batty, who is with me in less time than it takes to queue for a cappuccino.

'Why didn't you call the police?' he asks.

'I just ran,' I said.

'We'll drive straight to the police station now,' he says, slowly and loudly, like he's talking to a deaf old person, which he's probably used to with his mother.

We take the lift to the tenth floor.

'Can You Remember Where You Left The Car?'

'Over there!' I point to the empty space.

We check the other floors just in case.

The police sergeant on the desk is particularly obtuse about understanding what happened.

Of course, I didn't *give* my attackers the key to my car.

I am the victim of a mugging, for Heaven's sake!

'Will you be all right?' Richard Batty asks as we turn into my street.

'I'll be fine,' I say bravely.

'I don't like the idea of you being on your own,' says Richard.

Really, you can't give him the slightest encouragement.

'Well, I won't be,' I say.

Because oddly enough, Joanna and the twins are sitting on my doorstep.

She happened to call me on my mobile when I was at the police station, but I couldn't really talk.

'You didn't need to come,' I say, giving her a hug. 'But I'm glad you did.'

'Are you in trouble?' Joanna asks.

'It's a long story,' I say, ushering them inside.

'Turquoise!' says Joanna, looking around.

'You hate it, don't you?'

'No, it's very . . . very refreshing for summer,' she says.

'You make it sound like some ghastly cocktail.'

Actually, now that I look at it properly, it is the exact colour of a daiquiri made with blue Curaçao. A trip to Homebase will be my top summer-holiday priority.

'Is it all right if we stay for a few days?' Joanna asks.

'There's no need,' I tell her. 'It's really not as bad as it sounds. My car's been stolen. End of story.'

She gives me a there's-something-we-have-to-discuss-but-not-in-front-of-the-children look. We retreat to the kitchen leaving Cy and Ry to fight with the scatter cushions.

'Vlad and I have split up,' says Joanna. 'And he's threatening to take the children to America.'

'Why?'

'Because he caught me smoking.'

'Cannabis?'

'Marlboro Lights.'

'Bloody Americans!' I say. 'They're all for a pre-emptive nuclear strike on Baghdad, but light up a low-tar cigarette and you're an unfit mother.'

'We've been having a few other problems,' says Joanna. 'I turned a blind eye to the affairs—'

'Vlad's been having affairs?'

How dare anyone treat my sister like that!

'*Entre nous,*' says Joanna, 'I didn't mind when it was people at work. He's so . . .' she thinks carefully about her choice of words, 'athletic . . . to be honest it was a bit of a relief to hand over the experimental stuff.'

Joanna is so good at delegating, she even sub-contracts out the sex part of her marriage.

'But when he started on the au pairs, and then Totty, actually during the Jubilee party—'

'I thought there might be something going on,' I say sagely.

'That's what Mum said.'

'Oh, she always sees the worst side of everything. Why did you tell her first?'

'I thought we could stay there, but apparently she's got the house on the market,' says Joanna.

'On the market? She never told me.'

'She says whenever she tries to talk to you about the future, you clam up.'

I shall have to have words with my mother. Or not speak to her again. Depending on how I feel.

'Why has she got her house on the market?' I ask.

'She's planning to get a little sheltered place, and spend the rest on a round-the-world cruise.'

'Round-the-world cruise?'

'Why shouldn't she take advantage of the property boom?'

I can't think of an answer to that. Except I think I'll be a bit lonely without her round the corner.

'Why can't you stay in one of your own houses?' I ask Joanna.

'Norfolk's too far to commute, and the children still have two weeks school. Ditto Tuscany. Vlad will obviously keep the Hamptons.'

'Don't you want us to stay?'

Cy and Ry are standing in the arch that leads from my kitchen to my living room.

'Of course I want you to stay!' I say, bending down and hugging them with one arm each.

Over their heads, I give Joanna an I'm-not-at-all-happy-with-the-situation-but-we'll-talk-about-it-when-the-children-are-asleep sort of look.

'Where's our tent?' says Ry.

'Tent?'

'Mum said it would be like camping,' says Cy.

Joanna is conveniently hunting in one of my high cupboards for the proper coffee she bought me last Christmas.

'I haven't got a tent, but the sofa is magic,' I improvise.

'Does it fly?' asks Ry.

God, they're so spoilt!

'No, but it becomes a bed if you tell it to, so you can camp down here,' I say.

Cy looks doubtful.

'Sofarus bedibus!' he says, pointing at it.

We all watch it as if something's going to happen.

'You have to have the magic wand,' I say. 'But I've forgotten where I put it. I'll try to remember when you're in your bath.'

They're clearly not convinced.

'You'll be in the same room as the television,' I say in desperation.

I know I should be pleased, flattered even, that my successful older sister chooses to land on me when she is in trouble, as opposed to, say, getting herself a suite in a five-star hotel. It's just that the *Big Brother* highlights have become a bit of a habit, and the language is far too strong for seven year olds.

CHAPTER 52

July

'Are you coming to the wedding?'

There's great excitement in my classroom.

'Who's getting married?' I ask.

'Gwyneth and Robbie!' says Nikita.

She runs outside.

Usually, I go straight to the staffroom at morning break, but I can't miss this ceremony.

In the far corner of the playground, Gwyneth and Robbie are standing in the shade of an oak tree facing each other holding hands.

'You have to promise to love me for ever,' Gwyneth prompts.

'Yes,' says Robbie.

'You've got to say, I do.'

'I do,' says Robbie.

'I promise to love you for ever,' says Gwyneth.

'You didn't say I do.'

'I do. Then you say, till death us do part.'

'Till death us do part.'

'Till death us do part,' Gwyneth echoes.

A respectful silence has fallen on the whole class.

I look at these children whose lives have coincided with mine in the second year of the twenty-first century and I wonder how long we've got until death parts us all. Strange to be living in an era where the technology will soon exist to prolong our life expectancy almost indefinitely (I think that's what I heard on Radio 4), or eradicate us in minutes.

I always feel a bit gloomy at weddings.

I think it's the rites of passage element.

'The science of hope over experiment, that's what my mum always says,' Nicole tells me wearily.

'Oh, I made you a ring,' Robbie remembers, taking what looks like a blob of Blu-Tack out of his pocket. 'It's got a bit squashed.'

It could be the most valuable diamond in the world as far as Gwyneth's concerned.

The solemnity of the occasion is curtailed by a chorus of 'Snog Time Snog Time Snog Time!' from the rest of the class.

As Robbie kisses her, Gwyneth closes her eyes.

I always cry at weddings.

'Hay fever?' Richard asks.

'End-of-year blues,' I tell him. 'I don't know if it's the perilous state of the world that's depressing me, or the end of the World Cup.'

'At least it was Brazil,' he says.

'I mean, what have we got to look forward to?' I ask.

'Henman could win Wimbledon,' he says.

'Dream on,' I say, opening my Diet Coke.

It foams all over my hands.

It's that sort of day.

I stare at the clothing section of the supermarket. They've got a three-for-two on bikinis, but I never wear a bikini because of my scar, so I certainly don't need three.

'It's not the same without New Andy, is it?' I say to Richard. 'It's like the *Big Brother* house now Spencer's gone. It's just no Fun any more.'

It's not that I mind Cy and Ry using my bed as a trampoline so much as the fact that I keep having to hoover up light falls of plaster dust from my Jeff Banks-At-Allied-Carpets sisal-effect floor covering.

'Stop it!' I call up the spiral staircase.

'Stop what?'

'Jumping.'

There's a few moments of silence, which is always a bad sign, then renewed banging, and another dusting of turquoise'n'pink.

'I said Stop Jumping!' I call up.

'We're not jumping. We're hopping!'

Joanna, whose powers of concentration are such that she can ignore her children completely, looks up from the legal papers she has out on my pine table, and says, with a nice helpful smile, 'Why don't you get a cleaner? You don't want to spend your life cleaning.'

I snarl at the top of her head as she goes back to her work.

'Aren't children supposed to have some sort of bed time?' I ask.

'You'd know more about that than me,' she says.

It's the penultimate round and it's time to vote off the Weakest Link.

We all hold up our cards on which we've all scribbled the word ANDY.

'Lydia!' sneers Anne Robinson, 'which Andy?'

I look at my two fellow contestants. Andy who I am going to marry and a man I don't know.

'That one,' I point, but they're standing next to each other and the cameraman goes to the wrong one.

'Well,' says Anne, 'we've had some competitive people on the programme, but never one yet who's prepared to vote off her fiancé . . . Andy, why Andy?'

I can't hear his answer. I'm trying to get Anne's attention, but my mike's switched off.

'Well, Andy,' says Anne, 'with no incorrect answers, statistically you were the strongest link, but your fiancée has decided to get rid of you. You are the weakest link. Goodbye.'

He gives me a filthy look as he does the walk of shame.

'I thought I knew Lydia,' he says to the interviewer,

as we regroup for the head to head. 'But this is a side I have never seen.'

I wake up, sweating.
   Joanna is sleeping peacefully beside me.

My mouse glides over:
   Arise Sir Mick Jagger!
   and:
   Big Brother – under cover sex?

There are two messages in my Inbox.

Time to move? Free valuation!!!

I'm back in London.

Any chance of us meeting? A

My hands hover over the keyboard for quite a long time before I click on REPLY.

Not sure that's a good idea. L

I wait, but he's clearly out, or in bed, like most normal people are at this time of night. Perhaps he's with his ex-wife? Or a new girlfriend?
   Ridiculous to feel even the slightest bit jealous.
   I don't know anything about him.
   I go back to bed.
   Joanna doesn't snore. Of course not.

CHAPTER 53

'What comes next?' asks the publican.

'We're usually good at these,' says Andy.

He's smiling, biro in hand, looking at the publican like the cleverest boy in the class.

I wonder for a moment whether this is really a suitable way for two intelligent people to be spending an evening. I take a swig of my Stella Artois.

Andy looks at me slightly resentfully because it's officially my turn to drive, but it's his own fault since he hasn't got round to putting me on his insurance.

'Alec Douglas-Home, Harold Wilson, Edward Heath . . . ?' says the publican.

I write down James Callaghan. Quite pleased with myself for getting a politics one, until I see that Andy has written Harold Wilson again, which I imagine is the correct answer.

'Seoul, Barcelona, Atlanta . . . ?'

I write down Sydney. Andy doesn't write anything.

'Mercury, Venus, Earth . . . ?'

I put the Moon. Andy puts Mars.

'Taurus, Gemini, Cancer . . . ?'

I write Leo. Andy writes nothing.

Serious and trivial. There is no getting away from the fact that we complement each other perfectly.

Emboldened by this thought, I whisper, 'What comes next: Meeting, engagement, marriage . . . ?'

If my life were a film, this would be the point at which the Andy I am going to marry says something which makes me suddenly realize that he is in fact Andy 42 who I have been talking to in the middle of the night for months.

And there is absolutely no need to have the conversation I am dreading.

Luckily, I've never said anything derogatory about him in my e-mails except calling him the kilt and – quick thinking here – since he is in fact Andy 42, he started it anyway.

'I've told you I can't do anything about the honeymoon until the *Barber*'s sorted,' says Andy irritably.

'Portland, Plymouth, Biscay . . . ?' says the publican.

'It's the shipping forecast,' I say, which surely comes under geography.

'You're the one who listens to Radio 4,' says Andy, throwing back the responsibility.

'I'm usually in the car.'

'So?'

'Not on a ship.'

'But you still hear it.'

'Not consciously.'

'Come on then, let's work it out,' says Andy, with a significant sigh.

On the edge of a beer mat, he draws a rough map of the coastline of Western Europe.

It hadn't occurred to me before that the names in the shipping forecast correspond to actual places. I had in mind currents or isobars or some boaty type of thing.

'I think it might be Finisterre,' says Andy, sucking the top of his biro.

I've actually been to Finisterre. It's in the cold bit of Spain. Sounds exciting when they call it the Most Westerly Point of Continental Europe in the guide book, but it's just cliffs with sea round it. I think Land's End in Cornwall is actually further west. For me the ultimate Nothing-but-Ocean-between-Here-and-New-York experience is the Aran Islands off the West Coast of Ireland, where you can also buy a handmade jumper.

'Finisterre sounds right to me,' I say.

'C. Day Lewis, John Betjemen, Ted Hughes . . . ?' says the publican.

I write down Andrew Motion.

You see what I mean about everyone of a certain age being called Andrew? You only have to look at the telly. There's Andrew Neil on *Despatch Box*. Jonathan Ross's sidekick Andy. Andy Townsend the ex-Ireland footballer with a cockney accent who gave another dimension to the ITV World

398

Cup Commentary team, Andrew Marr with the ears . . .

'I wasn't actually talking about the honeymoon,' I whisper.

'Meeting, engagement, marriage . . . ?' Andy repeats. He's concentrating hard.

'Not sex, is it?' he asks.

'No, that comes between meeting and engagement.'

'Doesn't it continue after?'

This is a conversation we can have at another time.

I can see I am going to have to spell it out. Unless he's avoiding it for some deep psychological reason, the obvious progression from marriage to children simply hasn't occurred to a mind with a genius IQ. That's how interested Andy is in children.

So, really, I have my answer before I've asked the question.

But I've started so I'll finish.

'Children,' I whisper.

'Genesis, Exodus, Leviticus . . . ?' says the publican.

Andy writes Deuteronomy.

'Isn't it Numbers?' I say to him.

A vicar used to come to our primary school and ask us what the first five books of the Bible were. It's all the religious education I can remember. Much better now with the National Curriculum. I've had to learn all about Judaism and Christianity, although I'm not sure how much I've managed to transmit to the children. Dean told me he wanted to be a Jew the other day because they go to the cinema every Saturday.

'I think you're right,' says Andy, with another impressed smile.

'Children,' I say, in a slightly louder whisper. 'Would you like to have children?'

'If it happens, it happens,' says Andy.

'But what if it doesn't happen?'

I'm starting to hiss again.

'It doesn't happen,' he says.

'But what if we found out we couldn't? Lots of people can't, especially at our age,' I say, exasperated.

'Especially if they don't have sex,' says Andy.

'Assuming they do have lots, all unprotected,' I say.

It's a difficult enough conversation without him trying to divert it all the time.

'One, one, two, three, five, eight . . . ?' says the publican.

Andy smiles at me.

'We could always adopt,' he says.

At least, that's what I think he says. There's a scream of feedback from the mike.

He writes down thirteen.

Wow! It's a great feeling when you find out that you've underestimated the person you're about to marry.

I smile at my fiancé.

He does have hidden depths, even though he's not Andy 42.

Maybe this is what loving someone feels like.

'Much less trouble,' he says. 'And expense.'

'What?'

'A dog,' he says, 'We could always get a dog.'

'Edgar, Foxtrot, Golf . . . ?' says the publican.

Andy writes down Hotel.

Am I the only person who thinks there should be an alternative alphabet for initials, like A as in Arse, B as in Bugger, F as in oh Fuck?

We lose.

The correct answer was Fitzroy, not Finisterre, and there's a very good team from our nearest rival pub with a man who owns a yacht.

'Shall I come in?' Andy asks when we draw up outside my house.

'It might be a bit crowded with you and Joanna in the bed,' I say.

There's just a flicker of excitement before his face goes back to normal.

Rain is pelting on the roof of the car.

I have my hand on the door, but I am thinking that sometimes it's easier to say things in cars. No one else can hear you. And the other person can't walk away or hide his expression very easily. I know it's silly to start a conversation like this after three pints of Stella, but . . .

'There's been something I've been wanting to talk to you about,' I say.

The windscreen wipers swish backwards and forwards.

'Me too,' says Andy.

'After you, then,' I say.

'No, after you.'

'Shall we toss a coin?' I suggest.

Andy always keeps change for car parks in his ashtray.

It's heads, I win.

'So?' says Andy.

'No, I won. Therefore I choose. You go first.'

Andy sighs.

'I don't suppose it will come as much of a surprise to you that Daphne and I have become close,' he says.

Actually, it is a surprise. Which, in itself, is a surprise.

'Close in what sense?' I ask.

'How many senses are there?'

'Well, there's very, which is platonic, or there's quite, which isn't,' I explain.

'Quite close,' he says, pretending to look in his sideview mirror, but the windows have steamed up.

'What about her foot?' I ask.

'I think it's only since the talk of amputation that I've realized the strength of my feelings,' says Andy.

I'm thinking a number of unsayable things, one of which includes Paul McCartney, but we don't want to go there.

'It's terrible weather for July, isn't it?' says Andy.

He's not going to get away with that.

'So, that's it?' I say.

'That seems to be it,' he says. 'Sorry.'

'When were you going to tell me?'

'I've just told you.'

'But I started it.'

'No you didn't. You made me go first.'

I think I may be too drunk to win this one.

'If Joanna and the boys hadn't been staying, would you have had sex with me before telling me?' I demand to know.

The wipers are still furiously wiping the fogged-up windscreen.

If anyone's watching the car, they're probably thinking we are having a passionate snog.

I shall take the silence as affirmative.

Don't know whether to be flattered or not.

I open the door.

'What were you going to tell me?' asks Andy.

'Doesn't matter now,' I say, slamming it.

Differences between men and women:

7. Endings.

Women finish relationships when they don't love someone any more.

Men finish relationships when they have another woman to go on to.

With BerNARD, it was his best friend Mary Beth, in whom he confided during holidays back in Vancouver.

They still send me a Christmas card every year, as if I'm a grown-up person who couldn't possibly bear a grudge for all this time.

I think they're up to five children now, all smiling mouthfuls of metal at the camera.

It's nice having people to come home to. Sometimes the house itself seems to be breathing slowly and evenly as I quietly open the front door and tiptoe upstairs.

My mouse glides over:
Henman out
and:
Kylie's cellulite shocker

There are two new messages in my Inbox.

Dreammate. Still single?

Re: Meeting

Why isn't it a good idea? A

I click on REPLY.

I've just split up with the kilt. L

Sorry. A

You don't sound very sorry. L

Sometimes difficult to get the right tone on the screen. A

So much for your idea about telling him. L

You split up because of that? A

I was about to tell him that I couldn't have children, but to be honest, I could just as easily have been going to say that you can't marry someone you don't love. Even six year olds know that. L

Difficult enough when you do love someone. Can we meet? I've got so many things I want to talk to you about. A

Actually, I think I prefer it this way. It's much easier talking to someone you've never seen. L

You may have seen me. Even though you may not have realized it's me. Intrigued? A

Not really. Goodbye. L

Clearly a stalker after all. Which is what I suspected all along.

CHAPTER 54

'How about stories on the corkboard and boats on that table?'

'How about boats hanging from the ceiling?' Fern asks.

'Great idea!'

I love stuff hanging from the ceiling on Open Evening. It gives the impression that you've done so much work, there's not enough room to display it all. It makes parents say 'Wow, it's like Aladdin's cave!' as they come in.

'What about the mini beast games?'

'We could laminate the mini beast games so they don't get torn, then put them out on the tables so that parents can play.'

'Like a casino?' I say, getting slightly carried away.

My classroom is going to turn into a gaming grotto, and Mrs Vane's will still look like a classroom.

'Sunflower graphs over there, with the sunflowers that haven't died,' Fern suggests.

'Goodness, haven't we done a lot of work this year?' I say. 'Cup of tea before the hordes arrive?'

'I've got to get going,' says Fern. 'Audition night.'

'I've got Red Zinger,' I say, temptingly.

'Just a quick one then,' she says.

We're such a good team in the classroom, I sometimes forget that whenever Fern and I try to venture further into the realms of friendship, we have very little in common. And the trouble with herbal tea is it takes so long to cool down. You can't just slap in some cold milk, and make a quick getaway.

'How are you feeling about Andy?' says Fern, eventually.

'Andy and Daphne?' I say, with studied bright-and-breeziness.

'Yes,' says Fern.

'The irony is that if I hadn't made her do Sandie Shaw properly, she wouldn't have cut her foot and they never would have become close at all,' I say, blowing on the surface as regularly as politeness allows.

'Sandie Shaw?' says Fern.

'Hasn't anyone told you about the New Year's Eve party?'

'No.'

Perhaps if I re-live it just one more time, the dreadful shame will go away?

'The scene is a church hall,' I tell her. 'A mostly teetotal crowd of amateur singers has gathered around a piano. A significant percentage of the men are wearing kilts. Enter Pissed Woman, who, in vain search for more alcohol, discovers in the adjoining kitchen, a karaoke machine which the WI have forgotten to return after their Christmas party. After a word-perfect rendition of "Tie a Yellow Ribbon", she hands the mike to a fat lady . . .'

God, I didn't say, 'It won't be over until you sing!' did I?

Yes I did.

'When Fat lady starts singing "Puppet on a String" in a ridiculously pretentious soprano, Pissed Woman boos and insists she takes off her shoes for authenticity. You can guess the rest.'

'It's an ingrowing toenail,' says Fern.

'What?'

'Daphne has an ingrowing toenail so bad they had to operate, and then she contracted one of those superbugs. Denise is the one who cut her foot, but it soon cleared up after an aromatherapy foot bowl.'

'Denise was the fat one at your party?'

'She's comfortably covered,' says Fern, who never likes to criticize.

'She wasn't Fiordiligi?'

'No, she was Despina.'

'*Cosi fan fucking tutte!*' I say. 'You mean I've been feeling guilty all this time for nothing?'

'Anyway,' says Fern, 'I hope it goes well tonight!'

She hurries down the corridor.

'You too!' I shout after her. 'Break a leg!'

That's what you say to people about to go on stage, isn't it?

Robbie's dad is the dad from Hell. His tattoo says so.

I'm trying to explain tactfully the need to help Robbie with his maths, when he snaps the workbook shut.

'So, he's all right with his sums. But what about his behaviour?' he asks, leaning forwards on his elbows.

The table shudders. I'm surprised that the little children's chair he's sitting on doesn't buckle under his weight. It's not a particularly hot evening, but his biceps are glistening. Call me old-fashioned, call me middle class, but is a black vest really suitable attire for a parents' evening?

'His behaviour is usually fine,' I say.

'Usually?'

I think he must take anabolic steroids because nobody's arms could be that size just from working out.

'He's a boy!' I say, laughing a bit nervously. 'And sometimes boys will be boys.'

He joins in with the last three words like a chorus.

I was going to have a word about the bullying, but I can't bring myself to now. And the swearing's much improved since he's been married.

'And you're not allowed to hit him!' his dad growls.

'No, of course not,' I stammer.

'I'm going to give you something,' says his father, slamming his great hand down on the table so hard that the pile of workbooks beside me jumps into the air.

He rattles off a long number.

He points at the notepad I have in front of me. 'Got that?'

'Err, you couldn't just repeat it?'

This time, I write it down.

'That is my mobile,' says Robbie's dad. 'If you've any trouble with him, any trouble at all, you call me and I'll be down to give him a hiding. I'm only working up the road.'

'I'll make sure his new teacher is aware of that,' I say.

We stand. We shake hands. His grip is enthusiastic, to say the least. He claps me on the back with his hand. I wonder if it's meant to be a friendly gesture, or a demonstration of the punishment.

At the classroom door, he winks and says, 'Remember now!'

I wave weakly.

Only one more.

Ethan's father. His face appears above the row of children's self portraits that I've stuck on the half-glass wall which separates classroom and corridor. Robbie's dad shakes him by the hand. I see the wince. Then the head of the dad from Hell floats off above the smiling children's faces, and Ethan's dad appears in the doorframe. He's wearing white. White trousers, white shirt. The dad from Heaven.

'I'm sorry,' he says, 'I didn't have time to change.'

'Can take a lifetime,' I say.

Rather unprofessional I know, but we've seen each other outside school.

I wonder what it is he does. Perhaps I'm going down the wrong route with the medical profession?

He's a little too smooth. I'm wondering Minor Celebrity Chef, but don't they normally wear checked trousers?

Odd, really, that I don't know, because Ethan's one of the children who talks.

He sits down.

'Ethan's a pleasure to have in the class,' I begin. 'He's got good communication skills, and he always plays his full part in classroom discussions. He listens well and works hard. He's achieved the targets in maths we talked about last time. I think that was with your wife—'

'Ex-wife.'

'Number bonds to ten are fine. He needs to do a bit more work with money now . . .'

'Don't we all?' says Ethan's dad.

He's staring at my mouth as I speak. It's slightly disconcerting.

'His writing's coming along nicely. He's very imaginative.'

I look up. He's nodding his head, taking it all in.

'Actually, sometimes I wonder if he's a little too imaginative . . .'

'What do you mean?'

'I'm a bit concerned about him blurring the line between fact and fiction . . . Perhaps to be expected when there's been some problems at home.'

'What do you mean?'

'It's just that he's so keen on owls. I sometimes think that maybe he thinks he is an owl. He's most insistent that you can fly.'

'Me?' He laughs.

'Yes!' I laugh.

'I *can* fly,' says Ethan's dad.

Oh dear. Now I'm going to have to do a report for the social services.

'I wouldn't be much use if I couldn't,' he says, balancing on the back two legs of the chair.

'Be careful you're very likely to . . .'

Too late. He's over. Legs and arms in the air like an upturned tortoise. He managed to get his elbows down before his head, so probably no damage apart from the humiliation. I notice he's narrowly missed the spillage of Muller yoghurt that the dinner ladies should have wiped up after lunch.

He seems in no hurry to get up.

'I haven't got wings or anything like that . . .' he says, doing a little flappy demonstration with his hands. 'Well, only in a manner of speaking.'

I'm hovering between pretending he's normal, and smashing the glass over the fire alarm button.

'I am a pilot,' he says. 'Aren't you going to give me a hand up?'

I'm actually not sure whether I fall or he tugs me down on top of him.

'I've been wanting to do this for some time,' he says, as his lips come closer to mine.

'Everything all right, Lydia?' asks Mrs Vane at the door.

CHAPTER 55

'What is the matter with you?' asks Michelle as she opens the door.

'Nothing's the matter with me,' I hand over three bikinis I've bought for my god-daughters.

'Who is he then?'

'Who?'

'The new man.'

'How did you know?'

'You've got lipstick round your mouth and a white mark on the back of your trousers.'

'That's just yoghurt,' I say.

'Just yoghurt? On your dry-clean-only trousers? Must be love!'

'It's just a date,' I say, trying to play it down.

A date! It's been so long since I've been asked out on a date by someone who knows what I look like. And I didn't even have to advertise!

'What's his name?'

I'm sure Ethan told me once. I can see a picture of an owl beside the blackboard and me writing . . .

'Andy,' I say.

'Not—'

'Certainly not!'

'Sounds perfect,' says Michelle. 'So, what's he like?'

'You tell me.'

She appraises me for a moment or two, looking me up and down and walking right round me so she can see back and front.

'He's very good looking,' she says.

'How do you know?'

'You're pulling your tummy in, and you keep doing that thing with your hand to get your fringe out of your eyes,' she says.

'He's way above me in the league tables,' I tell her. 'I've no idea what he sees in me.'

'Don't be silly.'

'He is on the rebound, so maybe he thinks I'm safe?' It's the only plausible reason I can think of.

'He sounds brilliant,' says Michelle. 'What does he do?'

'He's a pilot.'

'Terrible womanizers, pilots,' says Michelle.

Funny how best friends will make any suitor into a potential life partner and then almost immediately start finding reasons you need protecting from him.

'How many pilots do you know?'

'I do three air hostesses' nails. There's a lot of them live round here because of the symmetry to Heathrow.'

She means proximity, but now is not the time.

'All of us wanted to be air hostesses at school,' I remember.

'Then we all wanted to be hairdressers,' says Michelle.

'And then we got a social conscience and wanted to be nurses.'

'Some of us kept wanting to be hairdressers,' says Michelle.

'Nobody wanted to be a teacher.'

'What did you want to do?' asks Michelle.

'Travel and help people. But I wasn't pretty enough to be an air hostess.'

'And you can't walk in heels,' Michelle adds unnecessarily. 'Still, he's bound to get air miles, isn't he?'

'It's early days. I don't really know him. He's a parent.'

I slip that in to get an objective reaction. I still haven't quite decided what the ethics of the situation are.

'You won't be wanting my baby, then?' says Michelle.

I could see she was anxious about something when she opened the door.

'It was a lovely offer,' I tell her.

'Thing is, Declan's quite into the idea,' says Michelle.

'I'm pleased for you, really I am.' I must not cry.

'I did mean it,' says Michelle. 'At the time.'

'I know you did,' I say, giving her a hug. 'But it wouldn't have worked, would it? You'd always be trying to buy her face glitter and stuff.'

'What's wrong with face glitter?' Michelle wants to know.

Best not start.

The clock on the mantelpiece chimes ten.

'News or *Big Brother*?' asks Michelle.

We should watch the News.

'Doesn't seem to be much going on at the moment, does there?' I say.

'Four of them are up for eviction!'

'In the world, I mean. All these big American corporations with fraudulent accounts. But what does it all mean? Does it actually make any difference?'

Michelle looks at me like I'm crazy, then points the remote at the television like it's a gun and presses Channel 4 decisively.

'Have you voted yet?'

'I've decided not to,' I tell her. 'As a matter of principle, actually. I didn't like the way they split them into rich and poor. Isn't there enough poverty in the world without people playing at being poor for the benefit of a television audience?'

We sit watching seven people we do not know or like doing nothing much.

If you see *Big Brother* as an experiment with controlled variables about what human beings will do when they have nothing to do, the results are a bit dispiriting.

The only answer in the *Big Brother* house to the question 'why are we here?' is 'to win £70,000' (although some disingenuously employ the expression 'to have a good time'). The question 'is human happiness possible?' doesn't ever arise in the *Big Brother* house, but if it did, the answer would almost certainly be 'yes, as long as there are adequate supplies of alcohol and cigarettes'.

I'm not saying that if I were a housemate I would want a continuous Socratic dialogue, but talking about that sort of stuff might pass the time.

Perhaps they do, and they edit it out of the high-lights?

'Do you think we're all just waiting for something to happen?' I ask.

'They've done their weekly task,' says Michelle.

'Not *Big Brother*. The world. Is the world holding its breath?'

'Why are you suddenly so interested in the world?' says Michelle.

'I've always been interested in the world,' I tell her. 'That's why I wanted to be an air hostess.'

'You know the really weird thing,' says Michelle, flicking idly through the channels.

'No.' I say.

'They don't have a telly,' she says. 'At least it would give them something to do.'

'Stop!'

Michelle stops on BBC 2. It's *Newsnight*.

There's a round-the-table chat in the studio.

'I think she's the one I saw at Mr Kong,' I say pointing. 'She looks a lot thinner in real life.'

'According to a comprehensive analysis of last year's programming,' says the blonde presenter, 'the British are becoming increasingly ignorant of how eighty per cent of the world lives, thinks and acts because television has abandoned serious examinations . . .'

'Look, it's that nice reporter,' says Michelle, pointing at one of the studio guests.

'. . . Andy, you've reported from some of the places mentioned in the report. Now you're poacher turned gamekeeper. Presumably you think we should be worried by this?' the presenter asks him.

'Yes, I do . . .' the nice one begins.

'So it is,' I say. 'I didn't recognize him in a T-shirt.'

'. . . sometimes it really does feel as if the balance between seriousness and trivia is tipping too far in the direction of trivia,' he continues.

'How come they let him wear a T-shirt in the studio, when it was smart casual in the Tora Bora?' Michelle wants to know.

'Ssssh!' I shout at her.

'. . . I'm afraid we're going to have to leave it there,' says the presenter. 'But thank you all for coming in, and, Andy, good luck in your new job.'

'What's his new job?' I ask.

The presenter turns towards a different camera.
    'Jeremy will be back tomorrow, but from all of us here . . .'

'I think she said gamekeeper,' says Michelle.

There are no new messages in my Inbox.

Click on COMPOSE.

Have I seen you on television? L

There is no reply.

He's probably given up on me.
    Who could blame him?
    Anyway. I have other fish to fry.
    Fish again!

CHAPTER 56

Am I happy?

I have a lovely little house and a job I love.

My car has been stolen, but as soon as the insurance claim is settled, I shall buy a newer, smaller, more eco-friendly model, and, in the meantime, I have virtually sole use of Joanna's 4-wheel drive after I've dropped the twins at their school.

The cars behind do not beep half as much at a big powerful car.

I have possibly been conducting a correspondence with a television reporter, which sounds very grown up.

I am not getting married, but I have the prospect of a date with a handsome man who already has a child, so probably won't care about having any more.

The car behind is beeping.

I've missed green.

Oh F off your F-ing self!

'Miss, what is a secret weapon?' Ethan asks.

He's last in the line-up and we walk in together.

'Where have you heard it?' I say.

I have great difficulty resisting the urge to give him a great big hug and kiss on the top of his head, but that can wait until I am no longer his teacher.

'You're one, Miss, and we're going to be seeing a lot more of you . . .'

'I'm a secret weapon?'

Must have been something he has heard his father say.

Secret Lover, perhaps? Or even bombshell?

Surely not.

Not on the basis of just one kiss.

Although it was a long one. Powerful urgency melting into questioning, exploratory tenderness, firing again into passionate, probing, intensity, yielding, quivering, helpless, oh my God, gorgeous, please don't stop . . .

'Miss?' says Geri.

'Yes?'

'Why are you smiling?'

'Because I'm happy.'

'Are you going to write your name in the Happy Book?'

'Yes, I think I am. In fact, since it's our last day in this class together, why don't we all write our names in the Happy Book?'

A cheer goes up.

I love my job. I love the innocence of children aged six.

And I am a secret weapon.

Which sounds exciting.

The omens are looking very good for the summer.

The three witches stare at me as I walk into the staffroom at break, and then simultaneously look away.

'Biscuit?' says Mrs Vane. 'It is the last day of term.'

'I need a bit of a pick-me-up after last night,' says Mrs Wates.

I've got my back to them, but I know they've all exchanged looks at her unintentional pun.

'I think the parents are more exhausting than the children,' says Miss Goodman.

Now they're all pulling very serious faces to stop themselves laughing.

I turn round quickly. They all look down.

'Are there rules about relationships with parents?' I ask Richard Batty, who's always good for a bit of protocol.

'There are no rules, but obviously there's a potential conflict of interest,' he says.

Splosh!

A wet sponge hits him full on in the face, which makes me laugh, although I know I shouldn't, partly because it's cruel, and partly because it means I've got my mouth open when the next wet sponge hits me.

I don't think either the water or the bucket the sponges are in is very clean.

I wonder what the chances are of suing the Local Education Authority if we catch Legionnaires' disease, or cholera?

'Why are we doing this?' asks New Andy.

The three of us are kneeling in a row, our heads and hands are peeping through a set of stocks one of the Suburban Martyrs' husbands who's keen on DIY rigged up out of hardboard a couple of years back. It's considered part of the younger teachers' duties to volunteer for half-hour shifts on the last afternoon of term. Actually, I'm probably old enough to get out of it now, but I think I'd rather suffer the indignity than admit that.

The kids have to donate 10p for each sponge thrown.

It's cheap revenge for the Year Six boys who bear a grudge and won't suffer the consequences next term, but a charity benefits.

'I'm doing it out of guilt for my negative feelings towards the people who work so tirelessly to make the Summer Fun Afternoon a success,' I tell New Andy. 'But I have no idea why you or Richard are.'

'I'm doing it because I'm a prat,' says Richard Batty. 'I forgot I didn't have to do it any more.'

He waggles his left wrist around in an attempt to show the Martyr in charge that our time's up, but she pretends not to see.

Splosh!

'I'm doing it because I am on the staff from next year,' says New Andy. 'I got Richard's job,' he says.

'Hooray!' I shout.

Splosh!

All the sponges seem to just miss New Andy. I think it's something to do with his great beauty.

'Has anyone seen Fern today?' I ask.

Splosh!

'She's broken her leg,' says Richard Batty. 'Fell off the stage at some audition or other. Rotten luck just before her holiday.'

The hall is filled with sunlight and the smell of the Year Six boys' feet. The headmaster has chosen the parable of the Good Samaritan to send the children home with for the summer.

'Can any of you think of someone who has unexpectedly helped you, or your friends, or family?' he says.

I hate it when the headmaster tries to elicit responses during assembly. Most of the kids sit there trying not to catch his eye, and he invariably fails to get the answer he wants from the ones who do put their hands up.

'Yes, Nikita?'

Silence.

'Have you forgotten?'

A nod.

'Luke?'

The head chooses a Year Six boy whose last day it is at the school.

Doesn't he have any idea?

'My girlfriend unexpectedly helped me wank—'

'Go and stand outside my office!'

There's a buzz of whispering. All the older ones want to know which girl it is, while the younger ones are learning a new word that's not strictly on the common words list for Key Stage 1 or 2.

'Would anyone like to make a sensible contribution?' says the headmaster.

You'd think he'd learn.

'Yes, Dean?'

'Miss Blane, sir.'

'A very good suggestion, Dean. Tell us what Miss Blane's done that makes her a good Samaritan?'

All eyes turn on me.

The witches can barely contain their envy that I have been singled out. I'm slightly embarrassed, but mostly really chuffed that it's me not them.

It's a bit like being the one who gets the Reading Prize (which I was two years running as a child when schools still gave prizes – now, you can't even win one for running on Sports Day unless the whole class gets one for taking part).

From Dean too! Of all people.

'Well, sir,' Dean begins.

He turns towards me and smiles in a nice way,

a grateful, genuine way that I've never really seen before.

'Well, sir, she gave my brother the keys to her car, sir, and he sold it for a shit load of money, sir, and I got all the new Star Wars toys!'

I have to wait outside the headmaster's office while he deals with Luke from Year Six.

The playground is deserted, except for a man dressed in white and a small boy.

I walk towards them.

'Dad, Miss doesn't know what a secret weapon is,' says Ethan, as I approach.

Ethan's father's perfect smile freezes for just a fraction of a second, but it tells me enough.

It tells me that Ethan has said something he shouldn't have said, something that I wasn't supposed to hear.

Ethan's dad tries to give me one of his out-of-the-mouths-of-babes adult smiles, but can't quite manage it today.

'Apparently, I'm a secret weapon,' I say, making him suffer a bit.

'In our Custard War!' shouts Ethan.

The penny finally drops.

I should have trusted the League Tables. We may not like them, but there's no doubt they have their uses.

Of course, he will have a far better chance of keeping Ethan if he has a nice sensible primary school teacher on board as his partner. Probably helps that I'm plain.

'I suppose you thought I'd be the ideal candidate to parade in front of the social services,' I say.

'It wasn't just that . . .' he begins.

It's a good effort. He employs an authoritative, calm voice, similar, I imagine, to the one he's trained to use on a planeload of passengers when he's going into an emergency landing.

But I'm always a complete wreck at the slightest judder of turbulence.

'I'm afraid you chose the wrong person,' I say. 'In a number of respects, actually.'

Beep Beep Beep Beep Beep Beeeeep.

'BBC Radio 4. The News at Six o'clock.'

I switch straight over to Capital.

CHAPTER 57

Joanna and the boys are waiting for me outside my house. She's gleaming slightly.

'Are you all right?' I ask, taking out my key.

'Fine,' says Joanna, stepping in front of me. 'Look, Lyd, I've had such a great idea, why don't we all go back to our place? The injunction's been lifted!'

'Great!' I say, putting my key in the lock.

'So what are we waiting for?' says Joanna, holding her arm across the door. 'Boys, get in the car!'

They do. Meekly. Which is when I realize there's something wrong.

'Let me just drop my stuff.'

'Bring it with you!'

'I need to change.'

'I've got plenty of clothes you can wear.'

'You're two sizes smaller than me.'

'I'm sure I have some left over from when I was pregnant.'

I open my front door. And close it again.

Must be the wrong house because inside, it's just a pile of rubble.

I look at Joanna.

'It can be rebuilt,' she says. 'I've already been on to Phil. He says you can have it just the same, or you could go back to his idea about glass—'

'I told you boys not to jump on my bed!' I shout.

'A ceiling shouldn't come down because of two six year olds jumping!' says Joanna.

'They're seven!' I scream at her.

I sit down on my doorstep.

'I don't believe this.'

'You should have got a proper builder,' says Joanna. 'If you're knocking through, you need an RSJ . . .'

'So it's my fault?' I say.

Frankly, I'm too weary for any more shouting.

'It's just a house,' says Joanna.

'That's easy enough for you to say with your two-million home in Notting Hill, your farmhouse in Norfolk and your villa in Tuscany.'

'I think it's more like five million,' says Joanna. 'And I only have the villa for half the year now.'

'I've had such a great idea,' says Joanna later.

'You're full of them today.'

We're sitting at her kitchen table with a bottle of champagne. Joanna only has champagne in the house.

'Why don't you come and live with us?'

'Permanently?' I ask.

'We could keep each other company, and the children would love it,' she presses on.

'You're not getting back together with Vlad then?' I ask.

'No way! I've been so much happier with you. What do you say?'

Typically, Joanna wants an answer straightaway. I'm tempted. We always used to think we'd share a house together when we were little. Before Joanna became a successful person.

'It would be much more convenient than having a different au pair every month or so,' I say.

'You'd be so much better for them,' says Joanna.

And then she realizes that I've tricked her.

Strange that just about everyone I know wants me to be mother to their children.

'Don't cry, Lyd. Look, I know things don't look so great at the moment, but—'

Fortuitously for her, the doorbell rings.

I hear her footsteps across the hall.

And then a familiar voice says, 'You're back! and Linda too!'

And she says, 'Not now, Greg.'

And closes the door.

'Don't turn away the bald Canadian,' I hear myself calling.

On a list of ten sentences I would bet my home against uttering, if I still had one, this would come pretty near the top.

'He's my sole admirer in the whole world,' I say, milking the self-pity a bit. 'Even if the only reason he likes me is because he thinks I'm a belly dancer.'

'That's not the only reason he likes you,' says Joanna.

'I'm afraid it is,' I tell her.

'No, he likes you, because he knows you're important to me,' she says, gleaming slightly.

I'm lost for words.

Which I shouldn't be, because it's the story of my life.

CHAPTER 58

My mouse glides over:
Who wins? You decide
and:
Becks appeal? Commonwealth Games Controversy

There are two new messages in my Inbox.

Don't put off a Career Opportunity!

Which I delete.
And:

Congratulations!

I was on television, but I'm not now. I'm now a press officer for an aid agency. No point in wasting your life wishing you'd trained as a doctor or a nurse, you have to use what talents you have. And I'm much happier. I've been wanting to do something useful for some time, and talking to you tipped the balance. Can I buy you a drink to thank you? There's loads of demand for teachers, by the way. A

No thanks. I don't think I could bear any more disappointment right now. L

Thanks! A

I meant yours in me. L

I'd love to meet you. A

No, you wouldn't. L

Why? A

It's all about the proper, grown-up-person league tables. L

You've lost me. A

Look, I'm the sort of person who spends the whole of the celebrity telethon after September 11th trying to work out what I would say to Jack Nicholson if he answered my call. Here's ten quid, Mr Nicholson, and can I just say that you were great in **As Good as it Gets**, but my absolute favourite was **Terms of Endearment**?
It just wouldn't work in real life. L

Not even if I found a waterpark with five giant slides? A

No. L

Got you tickets for Elton John Live? A

No. Thank you. L

A motorbike holiday in Greece? A

Actually I'm already going to a Greek Island to expand my personal horizons. If I manage to get back in touch with myself, I may be back in touch with you on return. OK? L

CHAPTER 59

Am I happy?

I am living in a hut. I have to walk a hundred yards to running water. I am surrounded by well-meaning people who want to hug me a lot.

I can't pinpoint exactly why I'm uncomfortable here.

The island is idyllic, the weather is beautiful, the food is delicious.

Perhaps I chose the wrong life-improving options?

Drama therapy is actually quite a lot like the stuff I do at school with the kids. Used to do, I should say, because I'm officially suspended until the insurance people and the police have completed their enquiries.

The yoga is a bit vigorous. I thought yoga was about stretching gently and getting toned, but I think this is the sort that Madonna does, and I haven't been able to move without hurting since the first session.

I think I should have gone for the creative writing.

At the time, I thought it would be more painful to sit listening to other people's stories.

There's a strange system that everyone except me seems to enjoy which involves mucking in with cleaning the site and cooking the food. The people in charge talk about it as being part of the community, but frankly, it must keep their costs down.

I can't get over the feeling that we're all just playing at being good people, trying to make ourselves feel better, and not really doing any good at all.

But it may just be that I'm lazy.

The drama therapy sessions take place in a rather beautiful gazebo type thing where you can see the sea stretching away for miles.

'Today,' our leader is saying, focusing specifically on me with the kind of expression alternative practitioners always seem to use. It's not exactly unfriendly, because there's an encouraging smile, but it brooks no dissent either. 'Today, you're not going to believe this . . . today, we are going to become one great big green wobbly jelly! Is there a problem, Lydia?'

I could share what I'm thinking.

It's probably very uptight of me not to.

Actually, I think the yoga must have had some beneficial effects because I feel rather calm.

I smile back at her.

'No. You carry on.'

I'm calm as I stand up and walk away.

I'm calm as I pack my belongings.

I'm calm as I wave goodbye to all the people who constantly, and rather oppressively, offered to share my problems, and let's be honest, didn't come up with any solutions when I did open up one evening after two bottles of retsina.

They're eating gado gado together.

Did I say the food is quite delicious? I could definitely recommend the food.

Probably not a good idea to set off in the middle of the day, with the sun blazing, but I'm very cool and collected as I start the long walk back to the village, from where I'll catch a bus to the ferry.

'What's to lose?' Michelle said, when I told her I was going to buy Fern's holiday as soon as the funds were back in my current account. It was the least I could do in the circumstances.

'You're in Greece, you've got your flights booked. If you don't find your inner self, you can always leave and have a holiday.'

Wish I'd had the foresight to ring for a taxi, but would have spoiled the symbolism.

I am walking away from my problems instead of embracing them.

I feel better already.

I wonder if there's motorbike hire in the village?

If there is, I shall take off and feel the wind in my hair.

Although, it may not be quite the same with a suitcase.

I now understand the point of rucksacks. Always thought they were just another way men with beards, prevented themselves from having a good time.

It may take me a week to walk to the village at this rate.

I should have worn in the new sandals as my mother advised. Or had the foresight to buy some of those silicone caps for my toes.

God, it's hot!

It didn't seem nearly this far on the coach that brought us here.

I think I'm getting dehydrated.

Mad dogs and Englishmen go out in the midday sun!

Possibly hallucinating because that's a motorbike I can hear.

Getting closer, getting closer.

Zooms past, spraying a cloud of dust all over me.

Oh F off your F-ing self, or whatever it is in Greek!

Help! He's turned round.
    English Tourist Butchered in Greek Island Road Rage!

The motorbike swishes to a halt beside me.

'Lydia?'

Must be hallucinating, because it's the nice BBC reporter.
    He's wearing a patterned shirt, and a funky long pair of shorts.

Must be the sun. Or a weird dream.
    Oh God, if they've sent him, it's bad news.

'It is Lydia?'
    'Yes.'
    Any minute I'm going to wake up.

'Hello, I'm Andy 42,' he says.
    'What are you doing here?' I ask.
    'I came to find you,' he says.

I close my eyes. But he's still there when I open them.

'How did you know where I was?' I ask him.

'You left clues in your last e-mail. I did the research.'

'But how did you know it was me?' I ask. 'Just now. When you went past?'

'Not many people with Steffi Graf's legs,' he says.

'I have one question,' I say, climbing on the back of the bike, putting my arms round his waist.

'Yes?'

'How do you keep your shirts so nice?'

I have no house, no car, no job and I am not getting married.

I am riding pillion, heading to an unknown destination with someone I have only just met.

I think this is what happiness feels like.

If my life were a film this would be:

THE BEGINNING